I0556036

When Angels Speak

An Historical Fiction Account of Mary, the Mother of Jesus

Angela W. Buff

Word of His Mouth Publishers
Mooresboro, NC

All Scripture quotations are taken from the **King James Version** of the Bible.

ISBN: 978-1-941039-92-2
Printed in the United States of America
© 2015 Angela W. Buff

Word of His Mouth Publishers
Mooresboro, NC
www.wordofhismouth.com

All rights reserved. No part of this publication may be reproduced in any form without the prior written permission of the publisher except for quotations in printed reviews.

Dedication

How could I not dedicate a book on the mother of our Lord, to my own parents, Larry and Eva Walker.

Parents who worked all of their lives to teach me right from wrong and that every decision made should be done so by first seeking the will of God.

Parents who have encouraged me to pursue my dreams, yet gently reminded me that "working" for the Lord should never take the place of "worshiping" the Lord.

Parents who have stood, not only by their children, but by one another as well, through both good times and bad, allowing my sister and me to see firsthand what God expects from a married couple.

For all their love, their prayers, their support, and their example, I dedicate this book to my parents.

Special thanks to my Pastor, Dr. Bo Wagner, for his endless wealth of both patience and knowledge during the writing of *When Angels Speak*. It would not have been possible without him! Thank you, Preacher!

Angels: Heavenly beings created by God

Chapter 1

Anna stepped from behind the curtain which separated the small, two-room house she shared with her husband, her daughter, and her husband's aging father. The news she would share with her husband this day was a cause for celebration, but it also brought a bit of sadness to Anna's heart. She had sent Mary out with instructions to deliver two loaves of bread she had baked extra during her preparations for the day. One was to go to Debra, the recently widowed seamstress in the center of town, the other to her friend Lydia, who had just given birth to a strong baby boy.

She knew the home of Lydia, just outside the gates of the city, was a bit far for Mary to venture on her own, but she needed time to speak with her husband and the distance Mary would travel would assure her the time she needed. Grandfather was snoring quietly on his mat by the window, granting Anna exactly the privacy she desired to speak with her husband.

Seated at the small table in the center of the largest room, Heli worked diligently to repair a piece of leather he used in the stables. Anna approached him with apprehension, knowing he, as was she, would be

1

both happy and saddened by the news she was about to deliver.

Heli glanced at his wife as she neared him. Seeing her face, he knew immediately that something weighed heavily on her mind. His wife was simple, plain, and absolutely beautiful. The life they shared had not been an easy one, but Jehovah had blessed them and for this Heli was ever thankful. Never had they passed the night with empty stomachs. They had a small portion of property including their earthen-brick home, a small stable to house their one donkey, a goat for milking, and a few chickens. A wonderful daughter and Heli's father completed their immediate family, with extended family and good friends surrounding them. Most importantly, they all shared a belief in the God of Israel that could not be shaken.

Even with Herod on the throne, imposing more and more taxes upon the people of Nazareth in order to increase his own worldly gain, Heli never failed to end his day by thanking his God for His many blessings. Jehovah would send the promised Messiah in His time, and His people would be delivered. Of this Heli was sure. The time in which the blessed event would take place, he was not sure. Over four-hundred years they had been waiting for a sign from the heavens. A sign yet to come, however, he had never ceased to trust in the God of his father, nor his father before him, and he was not about to do so now.

Heli took in the strained features which crossed his wife's face.

"Are you well, Anna?" Heli asked of her as he gently laid the piece of leather on the table in front of him.

"I am well," Anna confirmed, attempting a smile. Her upturned lips wobbled as she choked back her tears. "The time has come, Heli," she began to explain as she slowly took the seat beside her husband. "Our daughter," a lone tear slid down her face, "is no longer a child." Anna paused and swallowed the lump in her throat which threatened to cause her voice to break. After a deep breath she continued. "She has entered into the ways of womanhood," she finished absolutely.

Heli sat silently for a moment, then let out a small laugh as understanding dawned. "I always thought this day would be one of celebration," he began, "but I must confess, I feel an ache in my heart of which I cannot explain."

"It is there because you know, as I do, that because of this, our Mary will not be with us much longer. She will be asked to leave us to begin her own family," Anna could hold back the tears no longer. As they began their course down her cheeks in a torrent, she attempted to go on. "Our sweet Mary is now a woman. Whatever shall we do when she is gone?"

Heli pulled his wife to rest her head on his shoulder. He allowed her to cry for a moment, then spoke softly to her.

"Hush, now Anna," he comforted her. "Mary will be with us a bit longer yet, and you can be assured that she will be a fine wife and as good of a mother as you. You have and will continue to teach her well. Yes, we shall miss her laughter and presence in our own home, but she will most likely remain close." Heli rubbed his wife's head now securely against his chest. "I will find her a good husband. One who will care for and love her as I do you."

Anna raised her head and looked deeply into her husband's eyes. "Promise me, Heli," she pleaded with him. "I know things have been strained since Herod began demanding more and more of our people, but please promise me that you will not rush this. Think of poor Shira. She is so unhappy. Uriah gave her away to a man who seemingly earns much, but He seems so cruel to her. Please, promise me that you will be patient in your search for a husband for Mary. We have managed thus far!"

Heli brushed his rough fingers over his wife's tear stained face. "We will pray and seek Jehovah's will in this matter, as we do in all matters that concern our lives, Anna. We have stated before that we wonder of Uriah's relationship with Jehovah. Other decisions he has made has proven he acts in haste and unwisely, without seeking God's perfect will. I will find a good man for our Mary. I will give Him time to show us the man He has planned for her," he promised, pointing to the heavens. "You must trust me with this."

"Oh, I do trust you, Heli," Anna hurried to reassure him. She never meant to imply she did not believe her husband capable of the task. "Mary is just so special. I do not know who will ever be worthy of her."

Heli chuckled at his wife's words. "Those same words were uttered by your own mother to your father, many years ago," he stated as he turned her face to look into his. "I think your father did well in his choice for your husband." Heli smiled broadly, shrugging his shoulders and knowing he had just paid himself a huge compliment. It was exactly the light banter that Anna needed.

Laughing quietly, so as not to disturb Grandfather, she allowed her husband to embrace her in a warm hug. "It is Jehovah's way and Jehovah's time, Anna. Go now," he dismissed her gently. "Wash your beautiful face and worry no more. This is a happy time! We shall gain a son, not lose a daughter!"

4

Anna stood and turned to go, but stopped as she approached the wash basin. Turning again to look at her husband, she silently thanked Jehovah for the man who had requested her hand from her father and prayed for the husband He would send for her Mary.

"Heli," she spoke softly. He looked again to his wife and noticed how her eyes had softened and the smile that played on her lips was again genuine. "I love you," she whispered.

"And I you, my Anna." he smiled in return. It was only after Anna had turned her head from him and bent over the basin that he allowed his own smile to fall. His little girl was grown and would soon be running her own home. Whatever would he do without her?

Chapter 2

Mary quickened her pace along the road back to town, a loaf of bread wrapped neatly and tucked securely in her arm. She had not meant to dwell so long with her mother's friend, Lydia. It was just so difficult to hand the tiny, squirming infant back to his mother. He smelled fresh and his skin was soft. Mary smiled as she remembered the feel of his tiny body nestled snuggly in her arms. She could have easily rocked him all day were it not for the sun beginning to drop in the sky. Now she must hurry in order to complete the task her mother expected of her and return home before darkness fell upon the city. She would not be caught outside the security of her family's courtyard once night had descended upon Nazareth. One never knew when Herod's soldiers, drunk with wine, would forage through the streets. Women and children were expected to be very close to their homes, if not locked inside, before the sun had fully set.

At last the city gates were in view, and she slowed her pace, allowing herself to catch her breath. Wisely she had ventured to the destination farthest away from their home first. Now with her town in sight, she had time to slow her pace in route to the seamstress' home, deliver her bread with all the niceties expected of her, and still be home before dark.

As she approached the gates, Mary paused a moment to enjoy the serenity of the evening. It was so amazing to her that one gate could make such a difference. Looking through the gates into the city, she could see the familiar bustle of merchants in the marketplace who were beginning to busy themselves collecting their wares to store through the night. Come morning, those same merchants would again display their blankets, linens, and wools along the city streets, looking for those who would pass their way and were willing to barter over some coveted item or those with silver of which they were willing to part. Children played among the alleys, their laughter reaching her ears, as mothers completed final trips to the well in the center of town to gather enough water to see them through the night.

She knew that at her own home, around the bend at the opposite edge of town, her mother would be making preparations for their evening meal. She would no doubt be stirring her stew pot, wondering what was keeping her daughter. Father would be finishing up in the stable, and aged Grandfather was probably just beginning to wake from his afternoon nap due to the rumbling in his stomach.

She still loved her town, but she missed the simplicity it used to offer. There was an unwelcome tension lately that seemed to seep from the seals of each home. Merchants had lost their tender hearts for the people and were not as willing to work with the villagers on the price of their wares since Herod began to demand more and more of the people. Mary closed her eyes to the memory that poured into her thoughts as the wicked king came to mind.

The last time his soldiers had stormed the town, a child had stumbled in his defeated efforts to clear the street. Due to his fall, he had been trampled by one of the horses as the soldiers quickly made their way through. Without even so much as a glance over his shoulder, the murderous soldier had jumped from his horse to inspect the animal's hooves to make sure they had not been damaged by "whatever it was" he had run across. Mary flinched as she remembered hearing the mother's screams once she realized it was her child who had been the victim of the soldier's carelessness.

Another soldier had made his way to each of the merchants, demanding "Herod's rightful share" of their earnings. They then turned to the villagers, promising their return within the month, at which time they must be prepared to pay their taxes. There would be no debate. Either they would pay whatever amount the soldiers deemed necessary, or they would *lose* whatever the soldiers deemed necessary–regardless if that amount was their property, their child, or their lives. The same soldier then turned to the grieving mother, telling her she should be happy that she now had one less mouth to feed.

Mary shook her head to dispel the images from her mind. Her mother had often told her that her smile was as precious as a box of gold in times such as these. Though her heart ached for her people, she would not visit the widow nor return home burdened by past images which she could not change.

Redirecting her thoughts, she turned to focus on the oliveyards which lay peacefully outside the city gate. Mt. Carmel stood tall and proud in the distance behind them, creating the perfect backdrop for the evening. The setting sun was beginning to cast beautiful colors of reds and blues across the sky as the wind softly whispered through the oliveyard causing the trees to rustle as it gently swept across their branches. Mary decided to make an excuse to escape there soon. She felt safe among the tangled limbs and loved the serenity of being alone and away from the troubles and worries which life in Nazareth now provided. It allowed time for her mind to wander to what life might be like once Jehovah delivered His people and sent the promised Messiah.

Deliverance. Deliverance which Jehovah promised would be theirs once the Messiah had come. Would she see that day? No one knew when the blessed event was to take place or if they would live to see it happen, but Mary prayed that it would be soon. Her people struggled under Herod's evil rule, yet, she knew that God Himself was in control of even this, and that nothing happened without His consent.

Four hundred years her people had gone without a word or a sign from God. Some had begun to doubt. Mary had heard people speaking of "the forgotten promise" and knew that it was God's promise of the Messiah of which they were speaking. She tried not to think harshly of them, after all, they were weary, but Mary knew God had not forgotten them. She knew that in His time, He would again make Himself known. After all, all one had to do was to look around them to hear and see His presence everywhere, from the birds which sang and worked overhead, to the budding of the trees in the spring.

"I will bless the Lord at all times; his praise shall continually be in my mouth," Mary reminded herself, quoting aloud one of the Psalms of David. With a song in her heart and her smile back in place, Mary turned from her view of solitude and entered the gates of the city.

The bustle of the evening did much for her spirits and the children's laughter caused her own to come forth. Seeing her approach brought them bounding to her side, tugging on her tunic and begging for a story. She hugged each of them with the promise that she would visit again very soon and meet them "in their special place" to share another tale, but this evening she must hurry to the seamstress' home to share her bread. The children took her promise to heart and bounded back to their games and their mother's sides. Mary smiled her greetings to the other women who returned her gesture with genuine smiles of their own. Yes, even in the present times of trouble she loved her town and the people who called it home. She could not imagine being anywhere else.

Finally approaching her destination, she was glad to see the seamstress still at her tables, beginning to gather what would not remain accessible through the night. "Greetings, Debra!" she called to her as she stepped out of the street and under the tarp which covered the table.

"Mary! How pleasant to see you this evening!" Debra reached to give Mary a warm hug, which Mary returned graciously. "What brings you into town this late in the day?"

"Mother asked me to deliver this loaf of bread to you," Mary answered with a smile as she handed the bread over to the middle-aged woman.

"How thoughtful! Please thank her for me and thank you, Mary, for bringing it out to me. Come, sit inside for a minute and rest your legs."

"Allow me to help you gather your things," Mary offered. "It will cut your work in half, and we can carry them in before our visit."

With a smile and an appreciative nod from the woman, Mary began to turn and gather fabrics and materials of every size and color. She was glad that Debra would still be able to provide for herself although her husband was gone. Like her own parents, Debra and Benjamin had only one child, a daughter, who had married and moved away to a city in Juda several years ago. Because of complications while carrying her first child, she had not been able to make the journey to Bethlehem to be with her mother during the burial of her father. It was a hard time for Debra, but Mary's family had supported and encouraged her. Mary made a mental note to visit with Debra more often than she already did to make sure her needs were being met socially as well as physically.

As Mary continued to gather fine linens and wools, a particular piece caught her attention. Allowing her curiosity to get the best of her, she reached to pick up the single article. Running the soft fabric between her fingers, she realized she had not seen a veil such as this before. It was smooth and soft, almost like wool. The color was unique, a pale blue like the sky after a rain, but that was not what fascinated her so. It was the ivory trim that sparked her interest, which ran elegantly along the border of the piece. A lovely scroll design was embroidered along the ivory, in the same color blue as the background of the veil. It was such a drastic contrast to the drab, tan one she wore. Immediately Mary scolded herself and repented for being unthankful. She had never been one to long for things she could not have. She had been taught to be content with her lot. Still, had she been born the daughter of a wealthy man, she would have purchased this piece to save for a special occasion. An occasion such as her wedding, which now that she was of age, would happen soon enough.

"Ah," Debra spoke upon seeing Mary's close examination of the veil. "That is a very special piece."

Mary continued to run her fingers along the trim, being extra careful not to allow her rough, work-worn fingers to pick the fine threads of the embroidery. "I purchased that material from a band of travelers who came from the East several years ago," Debra continued as she gathered the final pieces. She paused, but only for a moment, when she noticed the young carpenter across the street. Upon seeing Mary examining the veil, his hammer seemed to have frozen in mid-air. Realizing that Mary was not aware of her audience, Debra continued about her business, smiling to herself. She had noticed the way the carpenter had seemed taken with Mary in the past. "Ah, young love," she thought to herself. She remembered that feeling. The thought caused tears to flood her eyes as she thought of her recently departed husband. Blinking quickly to hide her sorrow, she again turned her attention to her visitor who was speaking to her.

"It is lovely." Mary agreed. Gently she folded the fabric and added it to the top of the pile Debra had in her arms. Then, she reached and took the pile from Debra, who sincerely appreciated the help. Debra did miss her husband and the help he had never failed to offer. "How is business?" Mary asked as they made their way into Debra's small home.

"A bit slow," Debra admitted. That was not the answer which Mary was hoping to hear. "Herod's constant increase in taxes leaves little room for the pleasantries I have to offer," she continued. "And I admit, I do not charge enough to cover my expenses to those I know who are in need. Still, Jehovah will provide. He has yet to allow me to go to bed hungry." Debra sliced a piece of the bread Mary had brought and offered it to her friend.

"I cannot," Mary gently declined. "Mother will have supper as soon as I return."

"Well, in that case, no, you may not." Debra laughed as she withdrew her offer. Both ladies laughed and Mary glanced out the one window in the room to notice the sun falling farther in the sky.

"I must go. Father will begin to worry if I am not home soon." She hugged her friend and promised to return soon for a long visit.

Debra watched Mary as she hurried down the street and around the corner toward her home.

"What a special girl," she thought aloud to herself. "Always willing to be of aid to those in need." She then gave thanks and focused upon her meal of bread, olives, and cheese, refusing to allow her tears of loneliness to fall.

Chapter 3

Mary pulled the youngest of the nine children gathered about her feet into her lap. They were settled under a lone tree which had been allowed to grow along the side of the road at the corner of their small town. Here they were out of the way, yet still in sight of cautious mothers and other villagers. No one worried about the children being with Mary. It was, again, Herod's soldiers which concerned the people. Never knowing when they might storm the village, families were meant to be kept close and under watchful eyes.

Nili settled herself in Mary's lap, her eyes wide with anticipation as Mary continued her story. "Then David took five smooth stones from the brook, and his sling which he kept in his hand, and drew near to Goliath. When the giant saw the small shepherd boy, he laughed and laughed because the boy was so small, and he, Goliath, was SO BIG. But David did not fear the giant. He was confident that the Lord was on his side. He looked into the giant's face, and told him *this day will the Lord deliver thee into mine hand; and all the assembly shall know that the Lord saveth not with sword and spear: for the battle is the Lord's, and he will give you into our hands.* And then do you know what happened?" Mary looked into the faces of her captive audience.

"I know! I know!" Mary looked to Daniel who was on his feet with excitement.

"Tell us, Daniel!" she encouraged him.

The small boy pretended to load his sling and take aim at the top of the tree. "David used a stone he had taken from the brook and placed it in his sling! Then, he shot the giant right in the forehead! Down Goliath fell, and as soon as he hit the ground, David ran and stood right on top of him!" Mary laughed as Daniel ran nearby and climbed to the top of a large stone. "Then he reached and took the giant's own sword…pulled it from the sheath and cut off the giant's head!" Daniel ended his demonstration by scraping a stick soundly across the stone, then standing tall and proud over his "conquered giant."

"Very good, Daniel!" Mary and the other children applauded him. Daniel reclaimed his spot under the tree, his face beaming with the praise Mary had given him. "Never be afraid to do what God asks of you, children. With God, nothing is impossible," Mary reminded them. "Now, that is all the time we have for today. You must run along to your mothers! I have water to collect from the well and much more to do before the day is done!"

Mary gently lifted Nili and stood to her own feet. She was very pleased to have no protests from the children, only hugs of gratitude and thanks before they hurried back to their mother's sides. Mary smiled and waved goodbye, making sure each of them were once again in the care of their mother. She loved her time with the children and the stories that she shared with them.

Smiling to herself she sighed in contentment and turned to collect her water jug. To her surprise, her jug was gone. With a quizzical look on her face, Mary brought her hand to her forehead in contemplation. "I know I set that jug at the base of the tree," she said to herself. She turned again to look toward the children. Perhaps one of them had picked up the jug as they left. Mary could still see all of them except for Nili, and she was too small to have carried the heavy clay jug. Her jug was nowhere to be seen.

Turning back to the tree, she laughed out loud at what she saw there. Standing where her jug had originally been was Joseph, the carpenter, and in his hand, her water jug.

"Looking for something?" he asked innocently.

"Hello, Joseph," she laughed at him, ignoring the way her heart pounded at the realization that he was teasing her. "Searching out things which do not belong to you?" she asked in jest.

"Hopefully not for long," he answered her seriously, though a smile played about his lips. Mary blushed to the roots of her hair and dropped her face to the ground. He did not mean to cause her embarrassment, but he loved to see the color in her face. "I enjoyed your story," he tried, changing the subject. "I never tire of hearing about our ancestors." Mary again raised her head to look at him.

"Especially when that ancestor happens to be a man after God's own heart," she smiled at him. "How long have you been hiding behind that tree?" she asked accusingly.

"Oh, I do not know," Joseph pretended to be concentrating on the question, "since Goliath began to taunt the Philistines, I guess. You are wonderful with the children, Mary. You captivate them." His eyes

17

were soft and his smile genuine. "I know how they feel."

Mary shook her head and laughed again. "Joseph, you are a piece of work," she smiled. "Now, speaking of work, may I have my jug back please? Mother will not be pleased if I return from the well empty handed." Mary held out her hand for the jug. Joseph stayed firmly in place, clearly with no intent of returning the jug to its rightful owner.

"Allow me to keep the jug, and I," he paused and held up his hand as she began to protest, "I shall fill it with water and accompany you home." He slightly bowed as if he were paying homage to a princess of Rome. Mary looked at him shaking her head. "It is an awfully heavy jug once filled with water," he continued attempting to persuade her. "And I am not terrible company," he stated matter-of-factly emphasizing the word terrible as he rose from his bent position to stand tall before her once again.

Mary rolled her eyes and laughed at the way he playfully batted his eyes before her. "Very well, Joseph," she agreed. "I appreciate your kindness."

Anna heard Mary's laughter approaching before she saw her daughter. One of the children must be following her home again. Nazareth was filled with so much sadness these days; the sound of Mary's laughter did her soul good. *A merry heart maketh a cheerful countenance* she thought to herself. She loved that her daughter was so good with the children of the village. Anna was certain she would make a fine mother someday.

She was just about to call out a greeting to her daughter when another sound came to her ears. This time a much deeper sound. The sound of a man's voice. A twinge of fear struck Anna's heart. Was a stranger following Mary? Anna left the milk she had been churning and walked to the open door of their home.

Heli, also hearing the voice, had come from the stable. The two dwellings were close enough together that she could see her husband's shoulders square and the hammer which he clenched firmly in his hand. The voice that met her ears was low yet firm. "Is Nathan not in the fields? Were you expecting him this evening?" Heli asked of his wife, speaking of their eldest nephew. He stood tall outside the stable door. She knew he would fight for his family. Neither Herod's soldiers nor anyone else would harm them as long as Heli was living.

"No," she answered solidly. "I know not who approaches with our daughter."

She had barely finished her sentence when they saw Mary round the corner in a fit of laughter. Behind her, Joseph worked to balance the heavy jug in one hand, an almost impossible feat, which had water sloshing over the sides in a torrent. Still unnoticed by the couple, Heli let out the breath he was holding and smiled to his wife. "It is only Joseph, the son of Jacob," he mouthed to her with a shrug of his shoulders. A thought occurred to each of them at the same time and the married couple looked to one another, eyes wide. Heli stepped back into the stable and Anna stepped back inside the house before they were seen watching the approaching couple. She folded her hands in front of her indicating prayer as Heli gave a satisfactory nod in her direction. The words passed between them unspoken. Joseph was a good, Godly man. He would be a welcome addition to their family were Jehovah to allow it.

"Hello, Mother!" Mary called as they neared the house, completely oblivious that she had already been spotted by both of her parents and over the concern she had caused them. "Joseph was kind enough to carry the water home for me, but I fear most of it ended up on his garments!" Joseph looked embarrassed at being called out, but his smile was soft and pleasant.

Anna looked to her daughter and stood shaking her head. "That I can see," she laughed with them.

"I apologize for my carelessness with the water," he blushed. "I can return to the well and fetch more for you if you desire," he spoke to Anna.

"There is no need, we shall have plenty," she assured him. "Joseph, thank you for assisting Mary. I am sorry the jug was not more cooperative. Will you not stay with us for our evening meal? I am sure Heli has a dry cloak you may wear."

"I do not wish to impose," he stated as he filled the wash basin for Anna and then settled the jug in the corner of the room. Taking a nearby cloth, he began to dry the water from the sides of the jug.

"It is not an imposition, Joseph. We would be honored to have you join our meal. I fear it is not much this evening, but the bread is fresh and the olives ripe. We also have lentils and cheese," she added, clearly trying to tempt their guest.

Joseph looked to Mary who smiled sweetly in his direction as she began to ready the mat where they would sit as a family and dine.

"I would be honored to join you," Joseph replied to Anna, though it was quite apparent his eyes were for Mary alone.

Chapter 4

Planting season was upon them, and the young women of the village were gathered in the west field sowing seeds of grain. Mary had been paired with Rebecca walking up and down the long rows, scattering their seeds until the bags swinging from their shoulders were empty. They would then return to a large basket, which was too big to carry, located at the top of the field where an older woman would fill their bags with more seeds. Mary would have much rather been working beside her best friend, Myah, but Myah's mother had needed her in the marketplace for a few hours this morning. Myah had promised to join Mary once she was finished there.

The girls had been working in broken conversation for some time, but Mary sensed all of that was about to change when Rebecca spoke her next words.

"I saw Joseph walking you home the other day," Rebecca chided as they worked. Mary looked away, knowing the conversation was headed in a direction she did not wish to go with Rebecca. Her relationship with Joseph was not something she wanted to talk about. Rebecca did not hide the accusing tone in her voice when Mary ceased to comment. "AGAIN!" she added for emphasis. "I did not realize you had ever had such a hard time carrying a water jug before, Mary," she stated sarcastically as she cast a side glance at her companion. She did not really wish to anger Mary, but she did want to know if something was going on between her and Joseph. After all, she had been hoping to gain his attentions for herself.

"Hush, Rebecca! Joseph is simply being helpful. I do not wish to be rude by declining his offer of help," Mary commented matter-of-factly. *Nor did I want to*, she thought silently.

"Oh, no. Why would you decline his offer?" Rebecca's question dripped with sarcasm as she placed her hand over her heart for emphasis. "After all, Joseph is quite handsome," she admitted, looking to Mary for a reaction.

"And he's single!" Tamar danced by the two girls singing the words so that anyone in close proximity would be able to hear. Tamar then began to run toward the basket at the top of the field, clearly in a race with another young girl to fill her seed bag.

"Both of you stop it!" Mary exclaimed. "Joseph is a very kind man, and I am honored to be in his company."

"And," Rebecca continued, completely ignoring Mary's plea to close the subject, "he has been very busy building a house in town not far from your father's!" Mary did not care for the way Rebecca emphasized her words nor the attitude in which she spoke them.

Mary stopped abruptly to gain Rebecca's attention, her stance indicating she had had enough. "Rebecca, he is a carpenter." Mary spoke slowly hoping to kindly make known that she would not continue the conversation. "Building things is what he does. You do not know who he may, or may not, be working for."

"Mother says he is working for the blacksmith on a new stable. The house I am speaking of, he builds *after h*e is finished with his work for the day." Rebecca's words were heavily emphasized and quick, both hands now planted firmly on her hips. Mary recognized the gleam in her eye. She was looking for confirmation to her suspicions that Mary and Joseph were a couple. Mary did not want to be rude, but she knew she must be very careful with her words–words which would be taken back to Rebecca's mother, Dinah, who was known to speak freely as to what was on her mind to any, and all, who would listen. Her daughter was growing to be just like her.

Mary had no need to defend her actions nor those of Joseph. Neither of them had done anything wrong in any way. Yet the mood Rebecca had created was one of defense, and Mary did not wish to be the "talk" at the well where the women gathered. Her mother had taught her to protect her reputation at all cost.

Tamar had made a circle and caught back up with the two girls. She had lost her race and was now pouting because of it. "He is old," she stated rudely as she stopped between them to catch her breath.

"He is not old!" Mary defended him. "What he is, is more mature than most of the other young men in our village. Those of whose company the two of you seem to keep." Mary straightened her spine to stand tall. "I refuse to speak any more on this subject. My relationship with Joseph, or the lack thereof, is no concern of yours." Mary turned to continue spreading her grain.

"Well, I never!" Rebecca pretended to be appalled, but Mary knew she was just angry that she had not gotten the information she was after. "Come, Tamar. We shall work together on the opposite side of the field." Mary watched as the two girls began to stomp away. It only lasted for a moment before they were each chasing one of the immature boys Mary had just spoken about and throwing handfuls of grain as they ran. Mary shook her head at the scene. It was always fun and games to some. They did not know when to play and when to work nor when it was necessary that they should act their age.

"Well done," Myah spoke approaching Mary, slowly clapping her hands. "I did not know anyone could stop Rebecca once she begins a quest to secure gossip for her mother." Myah situated her seed bag around her neck preparing to work. Mary rolled her eyes while shaking her head and the girls began to walk and scatter their seeds. "Do not let Rebecca and Tamar bother you. They are simply jealous because you have the prospect of a good husband, and they only gain the attention of boys who occasionally pretend to be men."

"Myah, what are you speaking of?" Who else was contemplating a relationship between her and Joseph? Mary again stopped her work and looked at her friend. She was not angry at Myah; she was just puzzled.

Myah laughed sarcastically. "Mary, you cannot be so naïve that you do not see what is clear to everyone else. Joseph has accompanied you home from the well for weeks. Despite how Rebecca gained her information, it is true he is working on both the blacksmith's stable and another house. He has no wife. You are of age," she studied the expression crossing Mary's features. Was her friend really so oblivious or was she simply not admitting what everyone could see. "You cannot tell me the thought has not crossed your mind."

Mary looked at her friend for a moment and then walked to a nearby tree and slumped in the shade, Myah close behind her. The sun had been beaming on their heads, and a brief rest in the shade was perfectly acceptable in the heat of the day. "Well, no. To tell you that it has *never* crossed my mind would be a lie. But I do not believe that Joseph would seriously consider me for a wife. We do have a wonderful time together, but in all the times we have kept each other's company, he has never spoken of marriage. He is honestly a kind and friendly person. I do not know that he does not show as much kindness to any other girl in our village when we are not together."

Myah looked at her friend and shook her head. Mary honestly had no idea of the beauty she possessed. Not only was she physically pretty in her appearance but her sweet spirit and willing attitude to help those around her made her one of the most beautiful people in all of Nazareth. Mary could make anyone smile in any circumstance just by walking into a room. She was a genuine treasure to all who knew her, yet she was humble enough that the fact completely eluded her. Myah also noticed the trace of fear that crossed Mary's features and chuckled.

"No, he does *not* show that kindness to the other girls in our village," she smiled to Mary repeating her friend's words. "It is you whom he looks for at the well each day. Many other girls come and go before you. He is not rushing to their aid, Mary. He waits for you." Myah laughed at Mary's expression. "What do you look so afraid of? Joseph would be a wonderful husband."

"It is not that I fear having Joseph for a husband, Myah," Mary spoke honestly, lowering her voice because she did not want to risk being overheard. "I would be honored to marry him, but vows of commitment have not been mentioned. What if his thoughts are different than my own? He may have no intentions of marrying me. My family does not have a lot to offer; we barely get by as it is. Perhaps he really is just being kind."

"Mary," Myah scooted closer and looked into the face of her dearest friend, her curiosity really getting the best of her. She would never ask this question to anyone other Mary. "What do you mean, if his thoughts are different from your own? Do you love him?" At Mary's pause, a smile split Myah's pretty face, her eyes wide with anticipation. "You do love him!" she exclaimed in an exaggerated whisper so as not to gain the attention of the others.

"I believe love is a bit strong of a word, but I do appreciate him." Mary glanced over her shoulder to make sure they were still alone. "I enjoy his company very much, and mother and father have talked to me about the fact that I am of age and will be married soon enough. As will you," she pointed out. "I would rather marry a man like Joseph, than someone I barely know like Shira was forced to do."

Mary paused as their thoughts turned momentarily to their friend. Shira was a beautiful girl who had inadvertently caught the eye of Elias, a man new to their town. He was a wealthy man and seemed to be on good terms with Herod's soldiers, always giving, and always having, exactly what they asked without question. Many of their village feared he was a spy from within the palace, placed within their city to alert Herod's men in case the people of Nazareth were suspected of planning a revolt.

26

Shira had always been friendly and outgoing. She never met a stranger and approached everyone with a smile on her face and laughter in her voice. That was before her father had fallen short of the money Herod's soldiers demanded of him. At his first opportunity, he struck a deal with Elias–his daughters hand in marriage in exchange for the money he owed to Herod.

The ill-fated couple had wed in less than the year which was customary for betrothal. Now, Shira was quiet and withdrawn, only seen outside when gathering water from the well or doing other household chores, and very seldom away from the watchful eyes of her overbearing husband. It hurt the girls that their friend had been caught in such a circumstance. They each prayed their own fathers would make better decisions when seeking out a husband for them.

"But again," Mary continued, "Joseph has never spoken of marriage. I would be horrified if he heard that I was voicing such thoughts when he has not," Mary finished.

"But you would be alright with it, with marrying him?" Myah was focused in on the fact that her friend was actually interested in someone.

"Like I have said, Joseph is a good man," Mary confirmed, picking up the conversation again. "He is very strong in his faith, and he is extremely kind. He makes me laugh, and…" Mary thought about her last statement before she finished. She was afraid she had said too much already, even to Myah, with whom she shared so much.

"And…he is handsome!" Myah finished for her. Both girls giggled out loud.

"But again," Mary continued more seriously, "I do not think Joseph's intentions are to marry me.

There are many other girls in our village who would be well suited for him." Mary looked at several of the other young girls about her age who were working with them today. All of them were not as immature as Rebecca and Tamar. Several of them were considered friends and many of them had families much better off than Mary's.

"Also, I do not know that he does not have an interest in a girl back at his home in Bethlehem." Mary looked to her hands, the thought bothering her more than a little.

"Do not give up, Mary! From what you have said, Joseph is not the type of man to mislead anyone." Myah smiled. "And again, it is not another girl whom Joseph accompanies home each day. Plus, you know not what Jehovah has planned! You have said time and again that it is HE who controls every situation. You and Joseph would make a fine match."

"That may be," Mary admitted, "but he nor any other man will wish for a wife who sits around talking all day. We must get back to work!"

The girls rose to begin spreading their seed again. They continued to speak in hushed tones of Joseph, who they would consider a "proper husband" for Myah (she secretly admitting that Mary's cousin, Nathan, would suit her quite well), and of the house they each hoped to run one day.

As they approached the end of a row, Mary glanced up and saw her mother coming toward the field. It was not like Anna to seek Mary out when she was working. Immediately her grandfather sprang to mind and both Mary and Myah ran to meet Anna.

"Mother, what is it?" Mary asked, the alarm in her voice obvious. "Is it Grandfather?"

Anna looked to her daughter with a small smile on her lips. Her palms on each side of Mary's face she spoke seriously. "Grandfather is well," she assured her, "but you are needed at home. Immediately," she added, her face serious.

"Of course." Mary removed the seed bag from her neck and handed it to Myah.

"I hope all is well, Mary," Myah called to her friend as she rushed away with her mother. Myah watched them until they were out of sight and then returned to her work, a silent prayer in her heart for her friend.

Anna and Mary walked quickly through the village. Anna had not spoken again, and Mary was afraid to question her mother. Her heart was racing, and it was not due to the pace her mother was keeping. Mary glanced toward the stable Joseph had been building and was surprised not to see him at his work. She did not give his absence much thought, however, since she was so focused on how her mother kept her face down and continued her hurried pace. It was clear she did not wish to be summoned into a conversation with anyone.

Soon enough, the two women approached their small courtyard. Anna paused outside the threshhold of their door and turned to look at her daughter. Mary's cheeks were flushed from the brisk pace they had kept from the field. The color brought beauty to her face. Anna reached out to straighten her daughter's veil and to tuck a lock of hair back into place. Anna knew it was of no use to caution her daughter as to what was about to happen. Kissing Mary quickly on the cheek, she turned before she could be questioned and opened the door, beckoning Mary inside without a word.

Mary walked into the room and took in the scene before her. Her grandfather was in his place on his mat by the window, a smile making his weathered face bright. Her father was in the center of the room, standing between Joseph and his father, Jacob. Heli's face was warm, yet very serious.

Mary looked from her father to Joseph and then back again. "Father?" she spoke softly. The simple word was enough to voice the question in her head.

Her father spoke to her directly. "Joseph and his father have come with the ketubah," he began, speaking of the contract needed for betrothal. "Mary, Joseph wishes to make you his wife, and I have agreed to the terms of the arrangement."

Mary, looking as if she had been slapped, caught the breath which threatened to leave her. Realizing the surprise had to be evident on her face, she quickly dropped her head. Had she and Myah not just been speaking on this very subject? Is this not what she had subconsciously hoped would eventually happen? Why then did the house suddenly seem so very small? Mary knew her first impulse, which was to flee, would show disrespect to both her parents and to Joseph. Her mother sensed her uneasiness and placed her hand on her shoulder to support and steady her daughter.

"You will make Joseph a fine wife, Mary," she whispered for Mary alone to hear.

Attempting to look up at Joseph, Mary realized that he looked as nervous as she was. The carefree attitude she had grown attached to over the past weeks had been replaced by a serious man, who was seeking something far more from her than a friendly companion. Quickly she again lowered her gaze from locking with his and tried to wrap her mind around what was taking place.

Joseph stepped forward slowly. "I will make a good husband for you, Mary," he spoke gently. "We get along very well. We share many of the same interests and thoughts, and most importantly, we share a strong faith in Jehovah. There is not a woman in all of Nazareth whom I hold in higher regard than you. I have already begun to build a home for us to call our own. We will not be rich, but I promise with the help of Jehovah, I will provide a good life for you." Mary again glanced at him and attempted a small smile. For the third time today, she could not understand the emotions whirling in her head. For weeks they had talked and laughed together, yet never had she felt the queasiness in her stomach which she was experiencing now. Joseph extended his hand and held out a small bundle. "A gift," he smiled to her, "for my bride."

Mary swallowed the lump of fear in her throat and slowly accepted his offering. Her hands were trembling as she took the plain cloth from him. She could not help but notice, however, that the nervousness she had detected in Joseph when she first arrived, seemed to be gone. His hand was steady and his gaze gentle. *Get a hold of yourself, Mary*, she thought harshly to herself. *He does not wish for a woman who quakes in fear.*

Mary begin to pull the simple cloth away from the bundle. Suddenly, the fear welling up inside of her was replaced by disbelief. She rubbed her hand gently across the smooth, pale blue material, a smile lighting her face. In her hands, she held the veil from Debra's that she had secretly longed for. How had he known? Mary, forgetting her nerves, looked into his face. "I do not know what to say. Thank you, Joseph."

31

"I hope it is to your liking. I saw you admiring it in the village when you visited the seamstress. The beauty it possesses cannot compare to your own, but I knew it would look lovely on you. I hope you will honor me by wearing it during our marriage ceremony." Mary was sure the tears which flooded her eyes were due to her nerves being so unsettled and she blinked rapidly to keep them from falling.

"It is beautiful, Joseph. I will cherish it always." The smile Mary gave him in affirmation was genuine and enough to promise Joseph that she would honor their marriage. Looking to Heli, he gave the nod her father had been waiting for.

"It is settled then," Heli spoke from behind them. "Mary will remain with us for one year, as is customary, before going into your home, Joseph. The two of you will consider yourselves husband and wife in all manners, except for that which is reserved for the bridal chamber."

Joseph shook his head agreeing to her father's words. "I understand," he spoke absolutely.

"I understand," Mary also agreed. Discreetly she leaned her shoulder against the wall, attempting to control the spinning in her head. She was scared, she was happy, she was excited, and nothing could have taken her more by surprise than what had just happened. Well, almost nothing.

Chapter 5

Mary and her mother walked slowly toward the marketplace. Her mother carrying the extra loaves of bread, Mary with their jug in which to return filled with water. While in town, they planned to visit with the seamstress, Debra, in order to make selections needed for Mary's marriage attire.

"Are you happy, Mary?" her mother questioned, seeking only the truth from her daughter.

"I am happy, Mother, but I confess, when I think of becoming a wife, I am also fearful. You make marriage to father look so easy, yet I know things cannot always come so simply. I worry about the wife I will be, and I worry about the mother I will become. I confess the tasks seem somewhat overwhelming." Mary loved that she could talk so openly and honestly. Many of her friends did not have that kind of relationship with their mother.

Anna looked at her daughter with loving eyes. "You will do well, Daughter," she assured her. "And you will do so because you will seek to please your husband in all things. Remember that he must always be top priority in your life, second only to God. When children come, you must remember that you are a wife first and a mother second. Keep his happiness and comfort at the forefront of your mind. Joseph is a hard worker and he will want a pleasant wife, a good meal, and a clean home to return to each night. Provide these things for him, and he will rush home to be with you. Joseph is a good man, and he will honor you and your marriage. Your father would not have agreed to the marriage if he did not believe so."

"Thank you, Mother. I know that you and father always have my best interest at heart. I do not know if I could live as Shira is living." Mary quieted as they approached town. She would not be accused of gossip, even though what she said was said in truth. Mary did not, however, miss the shudder which passed through her mother's frame when Shira's name was mentioned.

"Uriah was hasty in his decision for Shira to wed; it is true. Yet, all we can do now is pray for Jehovah to have mercy upon her and to provide her husband with a more gentle spirit toward her–at least he does provide well for her."

Mary loved these conversations with her mother. She was never without encouragement and made Mary feel like she could handle anything that came her way. She was also quick to point out the good in any circumstance, a trait Mary expected herself to put into practice more.

Debra's home was in view, and Mary could not stop the smile that came to her face as she thought of the purpose for their visit. She also glanced in the direction of the blacksmith's stable, hoping to catch a glimpse of Joseph as he worked. Anna caught her daughter's excitement and loved that although Mary was naturally fearful; she was also happily anticipating her marriage.

Anna paused and handed Mary a loaf of bread. "Run ahead to your husband and make sure he is not hungry," she instructed her daughter. "My visit with Debra is long overdue. I will talk with her for a little while, then you can return, and we will pick the material for your garments." Mary quickly hugged her mother and accepted the bread.

"I promise I will not be long!" she called over her shoulder as she ran. Nearing the structure, she slowed her pace and caught her breath. Joseph had not looked up to see her approach but was working intently on placing a board in exactly the right way. She did not wish to interrupt him, but she was anxious to talk to him. As soon as the board was in position, Mary called out a greeting to him. She loved the smile she received when he saw her.

"Mary! What do I owe the pleasure of seeing you this time of day!" he beamed at her.

"Mother and I came into town to purchase material for our marriage ceremony," she said shyly. "I wanted to make sure you had taken time to eat," she finished handing him the loaf of bread. Joseph quickly wiped his hands on his tunic and accepted the bread she offered.

"A break will do me good," he grinned to her as he broke a piece of bread from the loaf. Mary paused with him as he gave thanks and then took a seat on a nearby bench. He held the loaf out to her, which she declined with a nod.

"Are you almost finished with the stable?" she asked, as she took in the sturdy structure.

Joseph loved that his future wife was interested in his work. "I am," he said around a bite of his bread. "It will not be much longer before it is finished. Actually, if you have time, I would love to walk you down the street to show you the progress I have made on our home." Mary accepted his offer with a nod, and the couple walked together down the street. She saw admiration and acceptance on the faces of most of the villagers who greeted them, and envy and regret on the faces of some of the young ladies who passed them by. Yes, Mary was proud she would soon become the wife of the carpenter. He was well respected and would be a good husband; however, she was not haughty in that respect and sent up a quick and silent prayer for God to provide good husbands for the other maidens of their village.

Their conversation was easy, and they did not have to go far before they came to the home they would call their own. Joseph was already far enough along on the structure that he had moved into the dwelling. Most of the work left to be done was on the inside.

"I plan to build our courtyard out of these bricks here," he told her pointing to a mound of hardened clay bricks stacked at the side of the house. "And inside, you will have an area for cooking which is completely separate from the main room." Joseph was animated in his description, and Mary loved seeing this side of him. The two dared not go inside alone together, but instead peered through the windows Joseph had so strategically placed along the outside walls of the house. She had never seen a home with so many windows! There were at least four! How beautiful and bright it would make their home!

"To the back," he pointed, "will be the room we share when retiring for the evening, and there will be a separate one for children as they come along." Mary noticed Joseph's cheeks burned when he mentioned children, and she turned her face from his. "Over here," he continued leading her to the back side of the dwelling, "will be a wonderful place for you to grow a small plat of vegetables if you would like, and I plan to build a stable for a donkey, cow, and goat at some point, which will stand there." Joseph finished his tour and looked to Mary for her thoughts. "I welcome any suggestions you may have. This will be your home too."

Mary would not have offered a suggestion if she had one. So much thought and consideration for her own comfort had been put into this home–this home he was building for her. A home bigger than she could have ever dreamed of having.

"Joseph, it will be perfect," she answered honestly. "I would not change a thing." His face beamed with her praise and for a moment, Mary hated she had to wait at least nine months more before coming to live with him here. The gaze they shared was tender, and Mary appreciated the fact that she got to see him so often. Many girls were separated from their betrothed during the year leading to their marriage. Just another of Jehovah's blessings upon her. She felt her face heat at his close inspection of her.

"Hello, Joseph, Mary." The couple was interrupted by a deep voice that Mary did not immediately recognize. It came from behind her but before she turned to see who had spoken, she noticed the tender gaze she was sharing with Joseph had hardened and was now stern. Daring to look over her shoulder, she saw Elias with Shira behind him, her gaze on the ground before her.

Mary swallowed hard as Joseph stepped around her to put himself between her and Elias. "Elias," he spoke in greeting. Joseph's tone was not angry, but neither was it particularly friendly.

"Home looks nice. You have spared little expense in the building." Elias's tone was filled with malice. "Your future wife must be a pretty special lady to deserve so much." Elias crossed his arms across his chest as he examined the structure from where he stood.

"It helps when you are a carpenter. You do not have to pay for someone else to provide your labor," Joseph began. "However, Mary is worth every cent and more of the cost it took to build this house. I will cherish my wife, Elias. Just as the scriptures instruct me to." Joseph was firm in his words, and Mary knew he hoped somehow the man would take to heart what he was implying.

"I miss talking with you, Shira. Are you well?" Mary spoke from behind her betrothed's shoulder. Her words were light in an attempt to dissolve the tension which hung in the air. Shira raised her head for an instant to look at Mary. Her words were stone, but her face was humble behind her husband.

"I am well," she spoke curtly. "Once you begin fulfilling your duties as a wife, Mary, you will find time is not something to be squandered with mindless chatter."

"Well spoken, Woman!" Elias laughed cruelly. He threw his arm around Shira's neck so forcefully that she almost dropped the heavy jug she was carrying. "My woman knows her place, Joseph, with or without fancy dwellings and *tender* moments." His voice dripped with sarcasm. "Come now, Shira. You have water to draw before you begin my mid-day meal."

Mary held her place behind Joseph as Shira was led away by Elias. Once the couple was out of sight, Joseph turned to look at his future bride. He saw the sorrow for her friend reflected in her eyes.

"I am sorry, Mary. I know you were close to Shira before her marriage to Elias."

"I feel so bad for her. It almost makes me feel guilty to be so happy," she confessed.

"Do not feel guilty for the blessings Jehovah has bestowed upon you. I meant what I said, Mary. Marriage is not something to be taken lightly. I have looked throughout the village. There is not another woman I would choose for my wife. You are meant to be cherished, and with Jehovah's help, I will always do my best to do just that."

Mary smiled into the face of her future husband, thanking Jehovah again for such a good man. "Walk me back to Debra's?" she asked sincerely.

"I would be delighted," he replied with a nod.

The couple made their way back down the street and approached the seamstress' home quickly. Mary thanked Joseph for escorting her and then watched as he returned to the stable that he had told her would be finished within the week. He would then be able to focus on adding the finishing touches to their home. Mary could not contain the excitement beginning to build inside of her.

"Mary!" Myah yelled, running toward her from across the street! "I am sorry I am late! I had to assist father before I could come." Myah's father was the only potter in the village. Their family worked hard to provide beautiful, as well as practical, pieces for the villagers. From large clay jugs, to small cups and bowls, there was nothing Myah's father could not fashion. Her mother and brothers also assisted with the business, seeing to customer's needs and making sure there was plenty of supply for the demand.

"I just got here myself," Mary assured her friend as she reached her side. "Mother is already inside with Debra."

The girls were welcomed into Debra's quarters and immediately began holding up to Mary's face select materials that were kept in the back for special occasions. Pieces were soon selected that would be used to complete Mary's wedding attire.

"You will be a beautiful bride, Mary," Debra assured her with a hug. "I only regret that I will not be here to see you."

Mary broke the embrace and looked sharply at the woman whose visits had become so special to her. "Whatever do you mean, Debra?" she questioned her.

"A visit to her daughter is long overdue," Anna spoke for the seamstress. "Debra is going to visit her daughter for a while in Jerusalem. She is anxious to meet her grandchild!" Anna smiled at Debra who returned a small smile of her own.

"Yes, I am anxious to meet the child who bears my name," she agreed. Mary could not help but feel a secret was passing between the two older women, yet she knew better than to question them further.

"I will miss you, Debra," she said sincerely, "but I wish you a safe journey. When you return, Joseph and I will have you to our home for a meal." Mary promised with a hug.

"I plan to travel with one of the merchant's families who will be passing by that way as they seek out goods to purchase and bring back here to sell, but I will not leave until your final fittings are done. I want you to be pleased, Mary. Your family has been good to me, and I will never forget that."

"And we shall never forget the friend you have been to us," Anna stated, closing the topic. "Now, Myah, hold that ivory back up to Mary's face. I want to see how it compliments her complexion once more."

Myah held the fabric to Mary's face. "That is lovely," Myah agreed. "And it will be beautiful alongside the veil Joseph gave her!" The ladies agreed and final items were selected. The day was beginning to grow late, so they all decided it would be best to return another day for measurements and specific fittings.

Myah returned to her father's to help begin storing items for the night, and Anna and Mary hurried to the well to draw their water. Joseph was working late on the stable in order to get it finished quickly, so he would stay in town this night and not accompany Mary home. As Anna and Mary finished gathering the water, Anna saw Shira rushing by them.

"Shira! Shira! Wait!" Anna called. Shira stopped abruptly and looked their way. Anna and Mary met her and saw the panic on her face.

"I am sorry to be so rude, but I must hurry. Elias will be furious if I have not returned soon. He sent me to one of the hunters for mutton, but he had none. I had to take venison instead, and he will be angry already. Please, I beg of you, forgive me but I must return!" Shira gathered her skirts and ran through the village. Mary and Anna watched her flee with sadness in their hearts. She had changed so drastically in such a short amount of time.

"She is little more than a slave to him." Mary commented, speaking her mother's own thoughts.

"Come, Mary," Anna instructed turning her daughter in the opposite direction. "It is time we were getting home as well."

Chapter 6

Mary walked slowly toward the city gate. She could not get away from the overwhelming desire for a moment alone. She had been working non-stop with her mother, making sure she knew all "the little things" that were important in running a home. Plans for her marriage were coming along quickly. Just that morning she, her mother, and Myah had again returned to Debra's for more fabrics and more fittings. They had also included a trip to see the progress Joseph had made on the house, which would be ready in plenty of time for the marriage ceremonies.

Mary could feel the tension rise in her neck when she thought of the actual ceremony. Though she was excited, her nerves were about to get the best of her. Some time in the oliveyard would do her good. Time did not allow her to go often, but she loved to hide herself in the tangled branches and reflect on the blessings of Jehovah and to think on whatever happened to be on her mind. Today, her thoughts were centered on the change that would take place in her life in less than six months.

Mary settled herself at the base of one of the largest olive trees in the oliveyard. Though she had passed other villagers on her way, here she was alone and could enjoy a moment of solitude, only the wind to keep her company.

One of her favorite Psalms came to mind, and it certainly fit the situation, bringing her peace almost instantly. *The Lord will perfect that which concerneth me: thy mercy, O Lord, endureth for ever: forsake not the works of thine own hands.* Mary had no doubt that Jehovah would bless the union of her and Joseph and that they would build their marriage with God alone at the center of it. It was no coincidence that Joseph and his father had settled in Nazareth after the death of his mother. They had come for a new beginning years ago and hearing that the only carpenter in the village had recently passed, it was the perfect place to begin again. Although Mary was sad that she had never had the opportunity to meet her mother-in-law, she was thankful Jehovah had found a way to bring them to her village. He had blessed her with a fine man who would treat her with respect and appreciation all the days of their lives together. Mary smiled to herself. She had no doubt that she and Joseph would find love just as her parents and his parents had. Actually, Mary felt she was already learning to love this man who would be her husband. How much easier this would make things when Joseph came for her. He would be gentle with her, and she would be willingly receptive of him. She pushed away the thoughts of Shira and of the fear she must continue to endure. This was a time of peaceful reflection for Mary, and she did not want anything to interrupt her comforting thoughts.

Mary closed her eyes and listened to the wind whisper through the trees. It had such a calming effect on her nerves. "Mary," her name came to her ears in a gentle whisper. What was that? Mary opened her eyes and looked around her. Who had called to her?

"Mary," she heard again, a bit louder this time, though still a soft whisper. She sat up straight and looked around, seeing no one. The wind softly stirred the tangled branches of the orchard. Surely she had dozed off and had been dreaming, but she was certain she had not slept.

"*Hail, thou that art highly favored, the Lord is with thee: blessed are thou among women,*" she heard plainly.

Mary grabbed her basket and stood so quickly that she almost lost her balance. Before her stood a man dressed in white with a glow about him which she had never seen. He was tall and beautiful, and definitely not human. Her heart threatened to leave her chest as she realized this vision before her was an angel who was speaking directly to her. Terrified, her first instinct was to flee but as she was about to bolt from the oliveyard, his next words stopped her instantly.

"*Fear not Mary: for thou hast found favour with God.*" His voice was no longer a whisper, though still low, while loud enough for Mary to hear him clearly. Turning to face him, she was suddenly filled with peace and knew that no harm from him would come to her. She looked into his face and then fell to her knees, remembering she was in the presence of a heavenly being.

"*And behold, thou shalt conceive in thy womb, and bring forth a son, and shalt call his name Jesus. He shall be great, and shall be called the Son of the Highest: and the Lord God shall give unto him the throne of his father David: and he shall reign over the house of Jacob for ever, and of his kingdom there shall be no end.*"

Mary could not believe how much control she had over her emotions at this moment. She did not quake in fear, but was able to think and contemplate what the angel had said. She was to conceive and bear a son? When? After her marriage to Joseph of course. But the angel was speaking as though this would happen very soon. Before her marriage? Impossible.

"*How shall this be, seeing I know not a man?*" she asked him innocently.

"*The Holy Ghost shall come upon thee,*" he answered her, "*and the power of the Highest shall overshadow thee: therefore also that holy thing which shall be born of thee shall be called the Son of God. And, behold, thy cousin Elisabeth, she hath also conceived a son in her old age: and this is the sixth month with her, who was called barren. For with God, nothing shall be impossible.*"

Elisabeth was expecting! Mary bowed her head in reverence to this angel who had delivered this news to her. "*Behold, the handmaid of the Lord: be it unto me according to thy word.*" Mary felt the pressure of the angel's hand upon her head. Then, as quickly as he had come, he was gone.

Mary did not know how long she remained on her knees. Her life had again been drastically and quickly altered. "A child?" she said aloud. "I am to have a baby? The Son of God?" Looking around her from her place on the ground she was hoping the angel would reappear to answer the questions now flooding her mind. Mary looked at her stomach. Placing her hands over it she sank gently back to the base of the olive tree. How would she tell her parents? It had been over four hundred years since they had received a sign from God, and now He had chosen to deliver that sign through her. They would never believe her. They would never believe she had miraculously conceived.

And Joseph. Mary sat upright quickly. How ever would she tell Joseph? He would think she had been unfaithful. Sudden fear began to overtake her heart. He could have her stoned for a crime she had not even committed! She closed her eyes and prayed quickly and fervently. "Oh Lord, give me direction!" she pleaded as tears begin to burn her eyes.

Be of good courage, and he shall strengthen your heart, all ye that hope in the Lord. The Psalm flooded her mind and brought peace to her troubled soul. A thought suddenly came to Mary. "Elisabeth," she stated out loud to herself. "The angel said Elisabeth is expecting!" She too had experienced a miracle. Surely she would believe Mary and in her wisdom be able to offer guidance.

Mary grabbed her basket and ran from the oliveyard. "Dear God," she prayed under her breath as she pushed her way through the tangled branches, "will you not grant me another miracle this day? Help me convince father to let me go."

Mary's prayer had been answered, and only three weeks later she was packing a few belongings that she could easily carry. The next morning she would begin her journey. Her mother had baked enough bread so that neither Mary nor her fellow travelers would hunger while on the road, with an extra loaf for Elisabeth and Zacharias once she arrived in Juda.

The timing had worked out well. She would travel with the merchants and Debra as they went and then return with the merchants as they passed back through the hill country to return home. She would only be gone for a couple of months and be back in plenty of time for her marriage to Joseph. That he was not very excited about her departure was an understatement.

"Mary I do not understand why you do not wait until after we are married to make the journey. I shall accompany you then. Why this sudden desire to go?" he had asked her.

"Once we are wed, Joseph, there will be no time," she had answered honestly. "I will be busy with our home, and you will be working. There may not be an opportunity in the near future for me to see my cousin again. The merchants are going soon and will return months before our marriage is to take place, plus Debra will enjoy my company on the journey. It is the perfect time for me to go. Please give me your blessing Joseph," she pleaded with him. "I will not go if you ask me not to," she finished and she made the statement truthfully.

Joseph could not refuse her. "You will come back to me?" he asked and Mary felt her heart break at the sadness in his eyes.

"I promise," she assured him. Joseph took her hand in both of his own and brought it to his lips. It was the first physical contact they had allowed. A shiver ran along her arm and down her back as he gently kissed it.

"You have my blessing," he smiled to her, "but that does not mean I have to like it," he said, mockingly stern. "Return to me soon, sweet Mary."

Mary now rubbed across her hand remembering where he had kissed it. She would miss him. That was a good sign their relationship would be a good one.

Suddenly her stomach rocked. Mary sat down on her mat attempting to calm the uneasiness. It was not working. Again her stomach clenched, and she knew she was about to lose her breakfast. Hearing her discomfort, her mother came to her side with a wet cloth as she finished.

"Are you ill, Mary?" her mother asked. Other than being a bit peaked, she did not feel warm or seem to be unwell.

"I am not sure, Mother. That happened rather suddenly." As Mary spoke the words, realization dawned on her. She did not know when, but the aches she had been experiencing the past couple of days and the sudden queasiness in her stomach was proof to Mary that she had been "overcome by the Holy Spirit" just as the angel had said.

Her heart raced at the thought. She had to see Elisabeth. If her mother thought she was ill, she would not allow her to make the journey. "I am sure I am fine mother. Perhaps something I ate did not agree with me."

Her mother looked at her skeptically. "Perhaps that and a combination of nerves," she said. "You know you can change your mind. Joseph would be glad to hear if you did so," her mother continued looking at her.

"I wish to see Elisabeth and Zacharias before I am wed and I will have no other opportunity." Mary's face was solemn, and she wished she knew what was going through her mother's head as she continued to study her daughter. Finally the older woman turned from her. Mary watched her mother return to her work and then continued to secure her belongings. The next morning could not come soon enough.

Chapter 7

Joseph was among her family the next morning as they bid her, the merchant's family, and Debra farewell. Debra hugged them all, promising to remember them. It had finally been revealed that she did not plan to return to Nazareth but would stay with her daughter's family in Jerusalem. She would work as a seamstress there and had sold her trade in Nazareth to one of the local women who would continue to supply the villagers and meet their needs. Joseph again kissed Mary's hand quietly reminding her of her promise to return to him.

"I will return soon," she assured him once more as the caravan began to pull away. The merchants had a wagon which they hoped to fill with goods before returning, but Mary chose to begin by walking. It would take about three days for them to arrive in Jerusalem, but thankfully, their route would pass right through the town which Elisabeth and Zacharias called home. Debra's family would meet them there, and together they would take her the rest of her way.

The journey was a good one, but it was long for Mary, though she did enjoy sights which she did not normally get to see. The conversation was light, and the times when Mary did not feel she could take another step, she would ride in the wagon. Once the jostling of riding began to get to her stomach, she would again walk. Nightfall was a blessing, and she had never enjoyed sleeping by a fire so much. Debra commented once as to her surprise that Mary was so spent, but quickly blamed it on her being unaccustomed to travel, which was probably the reason her stomach was remaining upset as well.

Finally, the town she had been longing for came into view. She bid Debra a tearful farewell and then almost ran the rest of the way to Elisabeth's. She paused right before she entered the courtyard, caught her breath, and chased a fearful thought from her mind. What if Elisabeth was not expecting? What if the news the angel bore was not true? Mary shook her head to clear her doubts.

As she approached the house she could hear Elisabeth singing to herself. Was she singing a lullaby? Mary could not stop the pounding of her heart, nor remain quiet any longer. "Elisabeth!" Mary called from the doorway. "It is I, Mary! I have come to see you!"

Elisabeth's song abruptly stopped and Mary could hear the older woman rushing to the door. The door opened quickly, and Mary was wrapped in a warm embrace. She could feel Elisabeth's extended stomach pressing into her own still flat one and could not stop the tears which began to fall.

Pulling away, Elisabeth wiped the tears from the young girl's face. "*Blessed art thou among women, and blessed is the fruit of thy womb. And whence is this to me, that the mother of my Lord should come to me? For, lo, as soon as the voice of thy salutation sounded in mine ears, the babe leaped in my womb for joy. And blessed is she that believed: for there shall be a performance of those things which were told her from the Lord."*

Mary pulled her into a tight embrace once more. Pulling away she could not stop the emotion which burst forth from her soul. Tears streamed down her face as she began to praise her Savior and rejoice at the sight of her expectant cousin.

"My soul doth magnify the Lord, and my spirit hath rejoiced in God my Saviour. For he hath regarded the low estate of his handmaiden: for, behold, from henceforth all generations shall call me blessed. For he that is mighty hath done to me great things; and holy is his name. And his mercy is on them that fear him from generation to generation. He hath shewed strength with his arm; he hath scattered the proud in the imagination of their hearts. He hath put down the mighty from their seats, and exalted them of low degree. He hath filled the hungry with good things; and the rich he hath sent empty away. He hath holpen his servant Israel, in remembrance of his mercy; As he spake to our fathers, to Abraham, and to his seed for ever."

Elisabeth embraced this precious young soul before her. Ushering Mary inside her home, the ladies wiped their tear streaked faces and took a seat in the main room of the house. Mary could not stop looking at Elisabeth's stomach, and fresh tears continued to fall. Though she had believed everything the angel had told her, she had still had to fight the nagging fear that she would arrive to find Elisabeth had remained barren.

"How did you know to come to me, Mary?" Elisabeth questioned her.

"An angel came to me and told me that I was to bear a child and that you were also expecting a baby. I had to come and see you Elisabeth. How did you know I too am expecting?" Mary asked, suddenly realizing Elisabeth knew immediately of her pregnancy although she had not yet begun to grow.

"The angel who appeared to Zacharias told him that our son would make ready a people prepared for the Lord. When the babe within me lept at the sound of your greeting, the Holy Ghost filled me, and I knew it was He whom you carried within you."

"An angel appeared to Zacharias?" Mary asked, suddenly finding herself at Elisabeth's feet. "Please tell me, Elisabeth. Tell me of the angel's visit," she begged her cousin.

The smile faded slowly from Elisabeth's face. "Zacharias has written of the account to me time and time again," she began directing her view from Mary's face to the floor.

"Written to you?" Mary asked looking around the room from where she sat. "Where is Zacharias? I do not understand."

Looking again to the young woman before her, Elisabeth began her story. "Zacharias was chosen to offer the incense on the altar at the temple during our morning worship several months ago," she explained. "I was so proud that he had finally been chosen. I will never forget the look on his face, though solemn and reverent, beaming with pride as he entered the temple. It seemed like an eternity passed before he emerged, and I was beginning to fear something terrible had happened. Once he emerged from within the walls, I knew that something had happened indeed, but it was not something terrible. It was something wonderful!" Elisabeth's smile returned as she relayed the events to Mary. "Zacharias has written to me since, that while inside the temple an angel appeared to him on the right side of the alter of incense which he was burning. He was terribly afraid, but the angel told him to fear not, for his prayer had been heard and that I would bear a son whose name was to be called John."

Mary hung intently on Elisabeth's every word, hundreds of questions filling her mind. Patiently she held her tongue and continued listening intently.

"The angel told him," Elisabeth continued, "that our *son shall be great in the sight of the Lord, that he shall drink neither wine nor strong drink, and that he shall be filled with the Holy Ghost, even from him mother's womb.*" Elisabeth laid her hand upon her stomach, laughing at the activity her son was producing inside. "*Many of the children of Israel shall he turn to the Lord their God. And he shall go before them in the spirit and power of Elias, to turn the hearts of the fathers to the children, and the disobedient to the wisdom of the just; to make ready a people prepared for the Lord.*"

At Elisabeth's pause, Mary voiced one of the many questions filling her head.

"But you keep saying Zacharias writes these things to you. Why is he writing them and not speaking of them?"

Elisabeth again looked away from Mary, the smile lingering yet small across her withered face. "Zacharias questioned the angel," she spoke matter-of-factly. "He said, *Whereby shall I know this? For I am an old man, and my wife well stricken in years. And the angel answering said unto him, I am Gabriel, that stand in the presence of God; and am sent to speak unto thee, and to shew thee these glad tidings. And behold, thou shalt be dumb, and not able to speak, until the day that these things shall be performed, because though believest not my words, which shall be fulfilled in their season.*"

"Will he speak again?" Mary asked, sincerely afraid for the man.

"We are not sure. I pray daily that Jehovah will loosen his tongue and allow speech to come forth from his mouth once again. However," Elisabeth swallowed the lump which had formed in her throat, blinked the tears from her eyes and smiled again, "even so, he is happy. The joy and gladness over our coming son shows in his face every day."

As if he had known he was being spoken of, Zacharias entered the door in a flourish! Holding out his arms, Mary ran into them, accepting an embrace from this man she so loved and admired. Pulling away from him she noticed a single tear sliding a course down his weathered cheek. Elisabeth joined them at the door, and the three of them spent a moment wrapped in an embrace right in the middle of the open doorway, silently thanking Jehovah for bringing them together and allowing them to share this special bond.

"Come now," Elisabeth spoke eventually, "the day grows long. Let us prepare for our evening meal and get Mary settled for her stay."

They dined on venison Zacharias had brought from the market and the bread Mary had brought from her mother. It was the most delicious meal she had ever eaten.

"Zacharias insists on some type of meat at least once a week. He says our son needs it to be strong," she laughed. Zacharias nodded his head firmly. Mary laughed at the expression Elisabeth gave him. How she hoped she and Joseph would be this close in their old age. The thought of her future husband pained her heart. Elisabeth noticed the expression cross her features.

"Mary, are you well? Is the meal disagreeing with you?" Elisabeth asked, fully aware of how quickly that could happen early in a pregnancy.

"No, the meal is perfect," Mary rushed to assure them. She saw the concern in both of their faces and was thankful for the opportunity to seek guidance from them.

"I have not yet told anyone at home of my pregnancy or the visit I received from the angel. You see, father has chosen a husband for me, and we are to marry within the next six months. I do not know how to tell them, how to convince them that I have done no wrong. They will never believe I have not sinned against Joseph or against Jehovah."

"I know this Joseph must be a Godly man, else your father would not have chosen him," Zacharias wrote on his tablet.

"Oh, very much so," Mary quickly responded, "but you can imagine how hard my story will be to believe. If the two of you had not experienced the same type of miracle, would you have believed me?" Mary looked to both of them and took note of the serious look on their faces.

Elisabeth spoke first, "You can stay here, Mary. For as long as you wish. We will pray together and seek God's will in the matter."

Zacharias picked up his tablet and penned a familiar Psalm. "*Trust in him at all times; ye people, pour out your heart before him: God is a refuge for us.*"

"Zacharias is right, of course," Elisabeth said, taking Mary's hand. "We must trust God to guide us in this matter. It is His plan, Mary. He will make a way for it to come to pass."

"I have no doubt, and as I said, I am a willing vessel. I just do not wish to bring pain to Joseph or my family." Mary could not stop the tear which ran along her cheek. Her emotions were so out of control these days.

Elisabeth reached to gently wipe the tear from her face. "Trust Him, Mary. Seek His face and He will again make Himself known."

Of course He would. She knew He would. Mary just hoped it would be soon.

Chapter 8

The days quickly turned to months, and time and again Elisabeth was glad for Mary's presence in her home. She had been such a help to her as her stomach continued to grow and her days began to wax long. Many were the times she found herself dozing off in the middle of the day while working her loom or as she churned milk into butter.

Mary was a constant companion, always at her side and doing the physical chores of the house so Elisabeth did not have to. Her own stomach was beginning to expand, and each of the ladies knew she must return home soon. Mary so hoped Elisabeth's baby would come before the merchants returned to see her home to Nazareth.

Finally the time was upon them. It was late one afternoon when Elisabeth experienced her first pain. She grabbed her stomach and dropped the bowl of dough she was shaping into small buns for baking. Mary was immediately at her side. "Elisabeth! What is it! Has your time been fulfilled?"

Beads of sweat began to cover Elisabeth's brow. "Get Zacharias!" she managed to get out between breaths. Another pain hit, and Elisabeth gripped Mary's hand. Once the pain had passed and Elisabeth released her hold, Mary sprang to the door and screamed the man's name at the top of her lungs. She was afraid to leave the house for Elisabeth's pains were coming too close together.

"Zacharias!" she screamed. "Zacharias!" Quickly she ran back to Elisabeth's side who had managed to make her way to her feet. As another pain hit, she grabbed the table and sank again to the floor. Mary's heart and mind were racing. She had never assisted in the delivery of a baby before! What was she to do?

Fortunately, Zacharias had been watching his wife closely in recent days. He had taken notice of the way her brows would knit together occasionally for no apparent reason. He chose to remain close to the house at all times and had a mid-wife nearby and ready as well. The two of them sprinted to the house upon hearing Mary's cry, and neighbors began to gather in the courtyard.

Bursting through the door, the mid-wife began sounding off a list of instructions as she rushed to Elisabeth and began to assess the situation. She commanded for water to be heated and rags to be submerged into the warm water. Firmly, she instructed Elisabeth to sit on a stool she had brought with her–a birthing stool Mary heard her call it. Slowly, Elisabeth lowered herself onto the small stool, assisted by Mary and another lady, as the midwife knelt in front of her.

Zacharias exited the room, pulling the door shut behind him, his face ashen and pale at the pain he had witnessed his wife experiencing. A prayer for her safety was heavy on his heart as he thought over what the angel had told him. Gabriel had promised him a son, who would be sent to pave the way for the Christ, but he had said nothing of Elisabeth's safety in bringing that son into the world. Though not common, Zacharias had heard of women losing their life while birthing another and Elisabeth's age was against her. Zacharias closed his eyes and knelt on his knees in the middle of the outer room.

Less than an hour had passed before the room quieted, causing all who had gathered outside the door with him, to turn and gaze at the unopened portal. Those in attendance held their breath until suddenly a baby's cry filled the air. Neighbors outside the house rejoiced as the women assisting with the delivery filled the home with song and praise. Zacharias closed his eyes in thanksgiving as he heard the midwife speaking to Elisabeth.

"You have given Zacharias a son, Elisabeth!" the midwife cried. She held the baby high in the air as Elisabeth was laid upon a mat nearby where her aging body could rest after being racked with the pain of childbirth.

"I knew it would be a son," she crooned, as the wriggling baby was laid in her arms and directed to her bosom for nourishment.

"The angel," one of the ladies whispered to the other, and Mary did not miss the skepticism in her voice, nor the, "Oh," of unbelief in the response of the other.

Mary could not comprehend that after witnessing this miracle anyone could still be in disbelief. It also reminded her that she had her own story to tell. One much harder to believe than a barren woman giving birth to a son in her old age. Zacharias was brought back into the room and quietly approached his wife's side.

She was worn and she was tired, but she was beautiful. She had used all that was within her but had safely delivered his son. He gently stroked her worn cheek and tears wet his own face as the tiny baby wrapped his small fingers around his father's larger one.

Mary felt as if she were intruding on a very personal scene. She left Elisabeth's side, knowing she was not needed at the moment, and began to assist the ladies with cleaning the room where Elisabeth had given birth. Jehovah had allowed her to be present at the birth of the child who would grow and prepare the way for her own son. At that thought, her own stomach felt as if one hundred tiny butterflies flitted across it. Her child had moved. For the first time, she had felt him stir within her.

She hurried around the door into another room where she would be granted a moment's privacy and laid her hands on her own extending stomach. Yes, she was beginning to grow, as well as the child inside of her. "Help me, Father," she whispered in prayer. "Show me how to tell my family and Joseph of the coming of your Son through me. God, please let them believe me."

Looking around the door frame at the new parents, she was surprised when Elisabeth looked up to meet her gaze. They locked eyes only for a moment before Elisabeth smiled softly to her and then closed her tired eyes in sleep, Zacharias nestled beside his wife and their baby snuggled securely between them.

Eight days had passed and the day of circumcision had arrived. Mary felt for the child, knowing what was about to take place from hearing of it within her own village. The cut was made and the child comforted by his mother.

"His name shall be Zacharias!" the priest proclaimed in a loud voice, and was shocked speechless at Elisabeth's instant protest.

"Not so," she said firmly, *"but he shall be called John,"* she smiled into the face of her son.

"But, Elisabeth," the priest argued, "there is none of thy kindred that is called by this name. His name shall be that of his father."

"No," Elisabeth held her stand, matter-of-factly though never taking her eyes from her son. "His name is John," she smiled at the infant once again.

The priest and others who had gathered to witness the event stared at one another in disbelief. "Let us ask his father. What does his father say?" he asked turning to Zacharias.

Zacharias took his tablet and wrote in large letters, "His name is John."

Murmurs sounded throughout the room. "What is the meaning of this?" "Why the name John?" were some of those which Mary picked out. The murmurs continued for a moment before another voice echoed throughout the room.

"HIS NAME IS JOHN!" Zacharias spoke out loud and plain.

Elisabeth was to her feet immediately, handing the baby over to Mary. She rushed to her husband's side wrapping her arms about his waist. "Oh Zacharias!" she beamed at him. "Your tongue has been loosed!"

"His name is John," he spoke again, laughter filling his voice. "Praise be to God in the Heavens, for the son He has given me. We will follow the commandment brought forth by the angel Gabriel. Our son shall be called John!"

Everyone in the room held their breath at the sound of Zacharias' deep voice which had not been heard in nearly a year.

"What manner of child shall this be?" one of them stated in awe.

Zacharias walked to the front of the room, his old face beaming with what youth was left inside of him.

"Blessed be the Lord God of Israel: for he hath visited and redeemed his people, and hath raised up an horn of salvation for us in the house of his servant David; As he spake by the mouth of his holy prophets, which have been since the world began: That we should be saved from our enemies, and from the hand of all that hate us; To perform the mercy promised to our fathers, and to remember his holy covenant; the oath which he sware to our father Abraham, That he would grant unto us, that we being delivered out of the hand of our enemies might serve him without fear, In holiness and righteousness before him, all the days of our life." Zacharias motioned for Mary to bring him his son. Taking him in his arms, he looked into his face, tiny eyes wide with wonder glaring back up at his father. *"And thou, child,"* Zacharias continued watching his baby, *"shalt be called the prophet of the Highest: for thou shalt go before the face of the Lord to prepare his ways; To give knowledge of salvation unto his people by the remission of their sins, Through the tender mercy of our God; whereby the dayspring from on high hath visited us, To give light to them that sit in darkness and in the shadow of death, to guide our feet into the way of peace."*

Zacharias looked to Mary, and the two of them shared a simple smile. At that moment, Mary heard a knock at the outside door. The merchants had returned. It was time to go home.

Chapter 9

The wagon was laden with goods, but Mary was still able to find a spot where she could sit comfortably. She was glad the older women in the group were not chatterboxes, for she had little to say on her return home. Instead, she spent the journey in silent prayer for wisdom and guidance from Jehovah.

The story she had heard many times of Queen Esther played in her mind. She, too, was used by God, yet in a far different way. Esther had been married to King Ahasuerus of Persia. He had not known of her Jewish heritage at the beginning of their marriage but had learned of it only after a decree had been signed to destroy all the Jews, Esther included.

Knowing not whether she would live or die, Esther risked her life to save her people and went before the king unannounced. Circumstances which could only be credited to Jehovah had taken place and the Jews were spared. Her pleas for her own life as well as those of the Jews were met. God had used Esther to redeem her people, much as He was indirectly using Mary now. She would bear the Messiah who would save His people from their sins, and she did not yet know what price she would have to pay in order to carry out His plan.

She knew she could not hide her pregnancy for much longer. She would have to tell her family and Joseph soon. Yet, how did one even begin to profess that you have been chosen by God in a miraculous way to bear His son. Not only that, but while you are betrothed to another, and though you have not sinned, you currently carry that child? Mary sighed as the city gates came into view. The journey home had ended all too quickly. She would trust Jehovah to open the door of opportunity and continue to seek His guidance until then.

The sun had begun to drop low in the sky as the wagon rambled through the city gates. She saw the children begin to run ahead announcing that the travelers had returned to Nazareth.

"Please, Father," she silently prayed, "give me the words and the opportunity. Please give them hearts to believe me when that time comes and I must reveal my secret." A thought suddenly flitted across her mind. Would they know as soon as they saw her? Her stomach was not large yet, but if her tunic were pulled tightly, there was definitely an indication there.

"I will do all I can to keep you safe, my son," she spoke to her unborn child. Mary forced a shaky smile across her face, though her heart ached with fear. The wagon lurched to a stop, and Mary prepared to dismount. What she was not prepared for were the strong hands which reached up to lift her down. Joseph was standing there with a smile stretched across his handsome face, arms uplifted, anxious to help his bride from her perch upon the wagon.

Smiling back at him she took his hands in each of hers, attempting to direct his grip more under her arms than about her waist. It was a useless attempt. She saw the look of confusion cross his face as his hands settled about her waist to lift her down. The smile quickly faded and was replaced by a look of shock. Still, he lowered her gently, but did not immediately remove his hands once she was on the ground. Instead, he discreetly pulled her tunic more tightly about her waist and stared at the small mound where her flat stomach should be. He knew. She could tell in his eyes that he knew she was different. That her frame had changed. That she carried a child.

"Mary?" Her name was a question, painfully soft, and said for her ears alone.

"Joseph, it is not as you think," she began to quietly defend herself, but she knew her breath was wasted.

Being the man he was, he did not make a scene. Instead, he released his hold on her, dropped his face toward the ground, then slowly turned and began to walk away.

"Daughter! You are home at last!" her mother ran to her excitedly, pulling her into a tight embrace. Mary felt her mother tense as soon as she felt the bulge at her waist. Pushing Mary away, her eyes fell to the same place Joseph's had.

"Mary!' she exclaimed her voice expressing shock and fear and pain.

"Mother, please. Let me explain!" Mary pleaded. "It is not as you think!" Anna shook her head quickly, instructing her daughter to keep silent. On-lookers gasped, and murmurs began to sound, speculating as to what exactly was taking place.

"Come, child," Anna ordered, in a voice Mary had not heard since she was a young girl. Anna grasped tightly to Mary's hand as the two women began their hurried walk through town. Mary saw Myah attempting to question Joseph, though he held up a hand to stop her as he went into the home they would call their own, shutting the door forcefully behind himself.

Anna did not speak a word until she called for Heli as they entered their courtyard. Quickly he came from the stable, sensing the urgency in his wife's voice. Entering their home, Anna pointed to a chair, too broken to speak. Mary took her place, her own tears coming now. "Jehovah, please," she silently, yet urgently, prayed. "Give me the words to speak and give them hearts willing to listen." Grandfather looked to Mary, his eyes full of questions, clearly having no idea as to what all the tears were about.

"Anna, whatever is the matter?" Heli asked, seeing only Anna, as he entered the room.

"Your daughter," Anna managed to speak and then paused, the words refusing to come from her mouth.

Heli turned to where Anna was pointing. "Mary!" he exclaimed in joy, realizing his daughter had returned. He held his arms open to his only daughter. Though he was expecting a joyful reunion at the fact that she had returned home, he was not expecting the torrent of tears and was still wondering at Anna's emotion.

Mary rushed into her father's hold, her tears continuing to fall, desperately needing his strength and comfort. His embrace was genuine, though Mary felt his body tense as soon as he realized the reason for his wife's despair. He continued to hold his daughter for a moment and then gently pushed her away from himself, looking carefully at this girl he had raised. Heli had always been a very patient man. He did not typically rush into anger, realizing that once words were spoken, they could not be taken back.

He swallowed deeply before he spoke. "Mary," he asked gently, though his voice shook at the words, "is this the reason you rushed from Nazareth?" he asked slowly while looking sternly at his daughter. He attempted to hold himself in check, though it was apparent he was struggling to keep his emotions in check. "Have you something to share with us?"

Mary wiped the tears from her face. She had nothing to be ashamed of, other than the fact she had not told her parents of the visit from the angel immediately following the encounter. A thought suddenly occurred to her. She should share her story with all of her family together. Putting this off had already caused enough shock and pain to those she loved.

"I will give the explanation you seek and that which you deserve once my husband has come." It had to be Jehovah's timing, but at that moment, as if he knew he were being spoken of, Joseph appeared in the doorway. He entered slowly, then turned and pushed the door closed behind him. Mary could tell tears had recently been wiped from his face, which was still red from emotion. The thought of causing him such pain brought fresh tears from her eyes which spilled down her cheeks.

"Joseph, did you know about this?" her father asked as he turned to face the man he had been so sure about.

"Not until Mary returned, and I was assisting her down from the wagon," Joseph answered.

"Is the child she carries yours?" her father asked pointedly.

"I have broken no vow, Heli. The ceremony has not been performed. The child is not mine," he spoke softly yet plainly, his eyes never leaving Heli's face.

"Mary, did one of Herod's soldiers…" Anna's voice trailed off, being unable to say more.

"No. No one has wronged me," Mary began.

"But you have wronged everyone," Anna cried out.

Heli moved slowly to his wife's side, comforting her. "Let her speak, Anna," he spoke, his arm firmly and supportively around his wife. "Mary. What is the meaning of this?" His voice was hard, and Mary knew he would have a hard time accepting what she was about to tell them. He was struggling with his frustrations as it was. Heli's eyes held fear for his daughter, anger at the reasoning, confusion at it all.

"Before I left to visit Cousin Elisabeth," Mary began slowly, "I was visited by an angel in the oliveyard. He told me that I had been chosen by God," Mary paused and took a needed breath, "to bear His son. The angel said the Holy Ghost would come upon me, and the power of the Highest would overshadow me." She noticed the looks of unbelief on the faces of her parents and the unreadable expression on Joseph's face. It broke her heart anew. "He also told me that Elisabeth, who was considered barren and is well past child bearing years, was expecting a son in her old age. Her child, John, will be the forerunner of God's son. Of this child," Mary spoke placing her hands on her abdomen. "I went to see Elisabeth, Father, to see proof of the miracle which had taken place within her."

"Was Elisabeth with child?" Heli asked pointedly, never looking at Mary directly but more at her feet.

"Yes. She knew immediately of my pregnancy. Her own child leapt within her at my arrival, for he knew he was in the presence of our Lord," she explained. Mary stood to her feet unable to keep her seat any longer. "I know this is hard to believe," she cried, her voice agonizingly pleading with her parents to believe her. "But I have done no wrong. I know not why God has chosen me to carry His son, but every word I have spoken is absolute truth."

"Mary," her mother was the first to break the silence. She had regained control of her emotions and was speaking to her daughter very matter-of-factly. "We have not heard from God in over four hundred years, and you expect us to believe an angel appeared to a young, unmarried woman, whom God Himself has chosen, to deliver His son? Daughter, have you taken a complete leave of your senses? Do you not realize the danger in what you have done?" Anna had left Heli's side and stood directly in front of Mary. Her voice was extremely firm, but had never risen in pitch. "You could be stoned for this," Anna whispered through quiet tears and clenched teeth. "And what of Joseph?" she asked sternly. As if suddenly remembering the man in their presence, they all turned to look at him.

He had remained in his place, arms crossed; leaning against the door as if he needed the support it could offer him. He had spoken not a word during her explanation, but continued looking at the floor. Mary could now see anger replacing his pain, yet his voice remained even as he spoke. Looking at her, and only her, he began. "Mary, do you remember what I told you when we were confronted by Elias in front of what was to be our home? I told you that I had looked throughout Nazareth and could not find another woman whom I would choose for my wife. I saw something in you that I had sought for, yet never found in another. I saw a woman I wanted to spend my life with. You were kind, you were good, and you were pure. You came from a strong and God-fearing family, a family I would have been honored to be a part of."

Mary cringed at the continued use of his words in past tense. He had moved closer to her, though distance still separated them, and his voice remained low and even. She was not physically threatened in the least, but she was shaking in fear over the words she knew she was about to hear. "The months we were betrothed before you left I felt so honored for the privilege of getting to know you more. I felt as if I was indeed becoming a part of your family and that you would be a beacon in mine. You could brighten my father's day with but a word and he was looking so forward to our wedding day. Not to mention the way I felt each time you were near me. I had no doubt that the decision I had made, the decision I had prayed and sought God's will over, was the right one. I had no doubt that you were the woman, whom God had created just for me, but now..." Joseph stopped speaking, his voice catching.

"But now you do not know that," Mary finished for him. "You do not believe me," she stated looking into his face, tears dripping from her chin.

"I want to, Mary." His expression was blank, but Mary knew she saw tears glistening in his eyes. "But I fear, the story you tell is too much for me to comprehend." Joseph turned from Mary and walked to the door. She did not go after him. What could she possibly say? Placing his hand upon the handle of the door, he did not turn to look at them, but instead spoke to the solid wood. "I will not make a public example of Mary. I cannot do that to her or to you. I will not press charges, so there will be no trial. However, I cannot claim to have fathered a child which is not mine. I will issue a writing of divorcement privately." Mary heard, rather than saw, through her tears, the door open and close as Joseph left. Her father continued to hold his wife, who had begun to sob into his chest. After a moment of silence, the two of them left as well, exiting the room for some much needed time alone. Mary held her place in the center of the room, her heart broken into pieces. What would she do?

The voice which broke the silence was one which she had forgotten was even present. "*Behold a virgin shall conceive, and bear a son, and shall call his name Immanuel.*" Mary slowly turned to look at her grandfather and saw the tears running along his weathered face. "*For unto us a child is born, unto us a son is given: and the government shall be upon his shoulder: and his name shall be called Wonderful, Counsellor, The mighty God, The everlasting Father, The Prince of Peace.*"

Mary ran and sank to her knees by her Grandfather's side, embracing the aging man. "You believe me, Grandfather?" she asked astonished.

"I have no reason not to believe you, child." He said honestly as he held her head to his bosom. "The virgin birth of a Messiah is spoken of by both the prophets Isaiah and Micah. Why would I not believe He could come through you? Am I frightened for you? Yes," he answered honestly. "But I do not claim to know the thoughts of the Most High."

"Oh, Grandfather," Mary cried against his chest, his withered hand stroking her head. "Please remind them of these things. Help them to believe me."

"They are only afraid for you, Mary. Your story is a most unusual one. Just give them time." Grandfather continued to comfort his granddaughter inside the house while Heli and Anna sought comfort from one another outside in the stable.

"I cannot believe this has happened Heli," Anna admitted to her husband, her head resting on his shoulder. "Her future was before her. She was betrothed to a good, righteous man. How can this have happened?" Anna no longer cried, for now she had no tears left to shed. She looked into her husband's face. "Is it possible? Could she be telling the truth?"

Heli removed his arm from around his wife and walked to the open doorway of the stable. He gazed at the millions of stars now twinkling overhead. How could he believe that his daughter had been visited by an angel and had conceived a child, God's Son, by the Holy Spirit? But, it was his Mary. How could he not believe her?

Anna walked to her husband's side once again, giving words to his thoughts. "She has never been one to conjure up stories or fancy embellishments. We have never once caught her in the telling of lies or exaggerations. We have never doubted her being a believer of the Most High. She is good, Heli. She has a good head on her shoulders and an even better heart within her." Fresh tears began to form as she struggled with her thoughts.

"I want to believe her Anna, so help me I do," he finally said, breaking his silence. "But like Joseph, I am just not sure that I can," he spoke honestly. Heli paused as he sensed someone approaching. The night was bright and the moon full overhead as grandfather stepped from the shadows.

"Father, what are you doing outside?" Heli asked of his father. The old man shuffled through the doorway of the stable, leaning heavily on his cane. Heli assisted him to a nearby workbench and helped him settle himself.

"I am wondering the same of the two of you," he spoke clearly. "Your daughter is facing a very difficult situation and is, at this moment, inside the house weeping. Alone."

"I do not know how to face her right now," Heli spoke honestly.

"Grandfather, how can we believe such a story?" Anna asked of the man she so admired.

"Why would you not?" he asked them matter-of-factly. It was clear he had fully gained both of their attentions. Grandfather smiled at their confused faces. "You do not typically act so quickly. Why start now just because something seems unlikely. Did Jehovah not promise a Messiah who would descend from the lineage of King David? I have taught you since you were a boy, Heli, that a Messiah has been promised." For the second time this night he quoted the familiar scripture. "Did Isaiah not tell us, *Behold, a virgin shall conceive, and bear a son, and shall call his name Immanuel.* Do you question the scriptures, Son?"

"Of course not, Father!" Heli quickly defended himself.

"Then why is this so impossible for you to accept?" he asked, looking at both Anna and Heli.

They were silent for a moment before Anna's voice cut the silence. "But grandfather," Anna began, "our family descended from David's son, Nathan. The scriptures prophesied the coming Messiah to be a descendent from David's son, Solomon."

"And it appears all hope ended with the curse of Jeconias because his line is not allowed to take the throne due to his wickedness," Heli finished for her.

"Son," Grandfather looked at the couple in front of him, shaking his head at their lack of faith. Slowly, he folded his hands over top of the cane stretched in front of him. It was so clear to the old man. How he wanted them to see! "First, the two of you need to remember that with God, nothing is impossible. Disregard your fears and your anger, and

77

think through this for a moment. Yes, Solomon's son Jeconias was a wicked man, and because of that wickedness, his line was cursed from ever taking the throne. However, because God has promised a Messiah who would descend from David, through Solomon, it will happen. God will make a way. He will not back Himself into a corner. The blood line of David runs through Mary's veins. As you said, our ancestor, Nathan, too is a son of David, therefore having legal rights to the throne."

"But the line must come through Solomon, Father, not Nathan," Heli interrupted, thinking his aging father confused.

Grandfather held up a hand to silence his thick-headed son. "As it shall," he continued slowly. "Heli, do not forget from where *Joseph's* family descends."

"Joseph *is* a descendent of Solomon," Anna spoke, slowly trying to comprehend what Grandfather was trying to make them see, "but according to both he and Mary, he did not father the child."

"The Messiah would have to be born without man's sin nature, Anna," Grandfather patiently explained, "and no mortal *man* can father a sinless child. Mary said the child within her was conceived of the Holy Spirit," Grandfather continued. "If what she says is true, and I believe her, then this virgin birth which has been prophesied, bypasses the curse of Jeconias. Jehovah himself placed the child inside of the womb of Mary who is a descendent of Nathan. Once Joseph, who is a descendent of Solomon, believes and sees the truth, in doing so he will accept the child, therefore legally adopting Him. Being in David's physical bloodline through Mary, and in the adoptive bloodline through Joseph, the child would qualify to be not only *a* true King of the Jews, but the *only* true King of the Jews."

Heli looked to his wife who was still contemplating all her father-in-law had revealed to them. "Could it be?" Anna asked, looking to her husband.

"I do not know," Heli admitted, "I need more time to think on these things, but at least I can go inside and look at my daughter without malice for the moment," he promised his wife. Anna lifted her skirts and began to run out the stable doors. She could not get to her daughter fast enough. What she did not expect was to almost run straight into Myah.

"I heard voices and hoped to find Mary with you. Please tell me the rumors circling throughout the village are not true." Myah's face was streaked with tears, and Heli knew the way he phrased the answer to her question would forever mark this girl's opinion of his daughter.

"Myah, why are you outside the safety of your own home since darkness has fallen?" Anna asked, as she wrapped this girl who was like another daughter to her, in a warm embrace. "Do your parents know where you are?"

"Please, answer me," Myah continued, ignoring Anna's questions. "I cannot believe what they are saying in the village is true. Mary is not capable of such as I have heard." Myah could not stop the tears which continued their course along her cheeks.

Anna embraced her and let her cry, looking to Heli over the young girl's shoulders. Words passed unspoken between them. They did not know what to say, so each chose to say nothing. Anna allowed Myah a moment to grieve while Heli kept watch over the two of them. After a moment, he broke the silence.

He had decided he would not tell Mary's story. He would allow his daughter to do so. Myah could draw her own conclusion as to the truth of it. He had to consider the possibility that she may indeed be telling the truth and he would not intentionally cause another to doubt her. Why God would choose her, he did not know. Their family was nothing special, yet all grandfather had brought to their attention was, in fact, truth.

"Come, Myah," he spoke placing his hand on the girls shoulder. "You may pass the night with us and hear Mary's story from her own mouth." Anna began to lead Myah toward the house as Heli stayed behind to assist his father.

"There is one more thing we have not considered," Heli mentioned, as he helped the old man to his feet. "There is still the possibility that Joseph will not accept Mary's words. It is asking a lot to expect a man to believe his betrothed has been faithful though she is expecting a child."

Grandfather looked up at the son of whom he was so proud. Heli was a good man, though at the moment he was struggling, and understandably so. He knew that it would take time for Jehovah to reveal His plan, and though he chose not to mention it, the same thought too had crossed his mind. He decided to trust in his granddaughter and in the God whom they served. "Oh, ye of little faith," he said simply as the two of them quietly made their way back inside.

Chapter 10

Joseph sat in the darkness of the room in complete and utter silence. No one stirred about the village streets this night. All of the animals had quieted and stilled, the world outside completely silent. Joseph was not sure how long he had been staring at the one dark spot on the floor where he had knocked his oil lamp from the table. His pain and anger had finally gotten the best of him once he was in the privacy of his home. He had lashed out at the flame which danced so elegantly inside the glass, causing the oil to spill and stain the floor. Luckily the flame had gone out immediately and had not caused a fire. Not that it would have mattered.

This home which he had put so much time and effort into, this home that he had built with his own hands, was for a woman he could no longer call his own. She was no longer pure. The proof–another man's child growing inside of her–and her story was that the child she carried was the Son of God.

Joseph leaned forward, placing his head in his hands. How could he believe her? Why would he choose to? It was a completely fabricated story, impossible to believe. Yet, how severely he wanted to!

Mary was nothing special in the eyes of the world, but she had become everything to him. Her smile, her grace, her presence alone had filled him with such joy. When she was beside of him, he felt a strength he did not know he could possess, though his limbs weakened at her touch. As long as she was near him, he felt he could conquer anything. How terribly he had missed her while she was away. He had worked well into the night, many nights straight, to get their home ready. She was supposed to have been joining him in this house in less than three months' time. They would have built a good life together. Grown old together, but now?

Why part of him continued to play her story through his head again and again, looking for something he could believe, he did not know. He tried to put her words from his mind. Even if he convinced himself that what she spoke was truth, no one else would ever believe them. If he allowed her to get to him, even if she convinced him to be a father to her child, he would always be looked at as a man who was naïve and weak, allowing his love for a woman to overshadow his good judgment. Or as a man who could not control his passions until the betrothal period was over.

To say the child was his, would be an outright lie. As he thought of another man using her in that way, a fire kindled in his stomach that no amount of water could quench. Joseph struggled to control the anger rising within him once again. He thought of men like Elias, wooing her, tempting her, whispering their lies to her. Joseph clenched his hands tightly, attempting to control the anger building in the pit of his soul once again. How had Mary fallen prey to one of them? She was so much smarter than that, and then to fabricate such a story to protect the man, whoever he was!

Joseph took a deep breath and walked quickly to one of the windows in his home, fighting to again regain control of his emotions. He had chosen to add many windows because he wanted his home to be filled with light. He wanted a bright and happy marriage, filling a bright and happy home. The marriage he had planned to have with Mary. The stars seemed to mock him as they twinkled in the clear skies above him. How foolish a man he had become.

For a moment, he had thought Mary was beginning to love him. Her smile would light her eyes when he approached, and there was almost no limit as to what he would do to see that smile stretch across her face. He had thought her so genuine. She did not tease and taunt as many of the other girls did but had always been open and honest, and…pure.

Then there was the prophecy…Joseph shook his head to dispel the unpleasant images he was remembering. He could not let himself forget the small mound resting beneath her rib cage. There was a child there. A child which did not belong to him. Joseph made his way back to the chair in the center of the room. He was defeated. He would keep his word to her parents; he would not press charges. To do so would result in a trial. A trial which would result in a stoning. He may have to live with the pain of betrayal, but he would not live feeling like a murderer. No matter how hurt, no matter how torn his heart, he could not allow physical harm to come to Mary by his hands. He could not have her, but he would always love her.

With another deep breath, Joseph realized he had experienced enough turmoil this night. He would go in the morning to draw the necessary papers for divorcement and begin his life alone. Years from now he would die old and alone, for he was certain that no woman could ever stir the emotions within him as Mary had. Happiness, excitement, and now... brokenness.

Joseph was not sure when he had finally fallen into a fitful sleep, but he had slept, his tears finally flowing and then catching up with him, pushing him past exhaustion. Now, however, he was sitting upright in his bed, sweat streaming along his brow and down his back, his heart pounding in his chest as if he had been running. It was a dream, he was sure, but so much more than a dream. It was a sign, a sign sent directly from Jehovah. Joseph remembered every detail so vividly that he could have argued that it had taken place while he was awake. The angel had been standing in front of him. Right before he was about to sign the decree of divorcement, quill in hand, ink dripping on the parchment, blotting the smooth ivory surface. Just before he touched the tip of the quill to the line, the angel had reached out and touched his arm, stopping him from continuing the act.

"Joseph, thou son of David," the angel had spoken softly, yet so clearly that Joseph would never forget the sound of his voice, *"fear not to take unto thee Mary thy wife: for that which is conceived in her is of the Holy Ghost. And she shall bring forth a son, and thou shalt call his name JESUS: for he shall save his people from their sins. Now all this was done, that it might be fulfilled which was spoken of the Lord by the prophet, saying, BEHOLD, A VIRGIN SHALL BE WITH CHILD, AND SHALL BRING FORTH A SON,*

*AND THEY SHALL CALL HIS NAME EMMANUEL,
which being interpreted is, God with us."*

Then Joseph had jolted awake, or the angel
had disappeared, he was not sure which had happened
first. He wiped the sweat from his face, his breath
beginning to slow, his heart resuming a normal pace.
Questions continued to swirl about his brain, but there
was one thing he knew now without reservation. Mary
was to be his wife. Her story held true. The angel had
told him not to be afraid. She had been chosen by God
to carry and deliver the Messiah, and he had been
chosen to aid her in that course. Joseph did not know
how things would turn out. He did not know what they
would be asked to endure, but whatever came their
way, they would face it together. He would do
everything in his power to protect Mary and the
unborn child, and he would start with the rising of the
sun.

Mary awoke early as she did every morning,
yet this morning her heart was heavy with sadness.
She was honored to have been chosen by God, but
saddened by the fact that, unless God intervened, she
would be raising His Son without the influence of an
earthly father. Perhaps that was Jehovah's plan, she
thought, as she kept her place and lay staring at the
ceiling of her home. A lifetime of loneliness seemed a
small price to pay if that was what God asked of her.
Still, her heart broke when she thought of Joseph.
Turning to her side with a heavy sigh, she spotted the
veil which had been a gift from him at their betrothal.

Slowly she forced herself from her bed,
keeping her eyes focused on the beautiful garment.
Gently she took it from the shelf where she had so

carefully kept and cared for it and held it to her face. Tears began to fall as she thought of Joseph and the life they would have shared. She allowed herself a moment of sorrow as she prayed for Joseph and asked for God to shelter him from the gossip he was sure to endure once her pregnancy was known throughout the village. She also prayed that God would direct her in the path He would have her take since currently she had no idea what to do next. After pleading with Him for several minutes, she finished her prayer with a heart of peace that could have only been sent from Jehovah.

Deciding to attempt a normal day, she began to dress for her morning chores. As she removed her bed clothes, she took a moment to look at the small mound protruding from her body. Slowly she laid her hand on her bare stomach, feeling the child within her move at her touch. She could not stop the smile that spread across her face, or the tears which followed. "I will never be alone," she realized in the stillness of the moment. Looking to the window and the rising sun, one of her mother's favorite verses from the scriptures came to her mind. "*Wait on the Lord: be of good courage, and he shall strengthen thine heart: wait, I say, on the Lord*," she quoted quietly from the Psalms. How many times had she heard her mother quote that verse to her father when he was discouraged.

Mary again closed her eyes and prayed for continued strength from Jehovah. She then quickly dressed and went to see what all needed to be done. Myah had already returned to her parents in order to help them prepare for their day at the market. Grandfather was still snoring quietly on his mat in the back room, and her father and mother were no doubt already busy in the stable. Mary saw that the wash basin remained partially full, so she washed her face, then picked up the basin to pour out the old water and refill it with fresh. Opening the door and tossing the water in one fluid movement, she did not notice Joseph rounding the corner until it was too late. Now he stood before her, face frozen in shock, dripping from head to toe, drenched in the water she was discarding.

Mary stood there, her mouth gaping open, her breath leaving her as quickly as Joseph's had, having no idea as to what to say or do. Joseph faced her, blinking rapidly as the shock of the water continued to seep through his clothes and into his body sending chills throughout him. Before either of them could speak, Heli and Anna came from the stable where Anna had been collecting eggs from the chickens as her husband milked the goat. The older couple stopped short as they took in the scene before them.

No one spoke, each of them waiting on the other to go first. Joseph surprisingly found his voice before the others. "Perhaps I should have come later in the day when the sun was at its highest, instead of during the chill of early morning. I must admit, I was not sure at the greeting I would receive from you, Mary, but this was not one which I had anticipated."

"Joseph, I am so sorry," Mary began, "I had no idea you were approaching." Mary looked to her parents who stood gawking at her in disbelief. "I was emptying the basin and did not see Joseph coming around the corner," she defended herself quickly. The awkward moment seemed to stretch out forever. Finally, Heli cleared his throat to snap himself and Anna from their trance of confusion.

Heli was not only embarrassed for his daughter, he was also frightened. Joseph could not yet have acquired the documents needed for divorce. Why then, was he here at this early hour? Had he changed his mind about pressing charges or in his anger developed a plan of revenge against her? He decided on the direct approach.

"Joseph," he began, "is there something we can do for you this morning?" he asked hesitantly. "Besides perhaps offering you a dry cloak?"

"I have one for you," Anna spoke, pushing Mary aside and entering the house. In but a moment she returned with a dry cloak in hand. "It is Heli's, the same one you wore the last time you and Mary had an incident with water." She attempted a smile as she handed him the cloak.

Joseph accepted the garment, but did not move to put it on. Mary continued to stand in the doorway, the basin in her hand, her face flaming in embarrassment.

"Actually, I came for my wife," he answered matter-of-factly, looking to Heli. The basin fell from Mary's hand with a thud to the ground beneath her.

"What?" she questioned taking a step closer to him. Joseph knew he was dripping wet and looked horrible, but he also knew Mary was scared and no doubt in fear of being alone. He knew that Heli and Anna were attempting to come to terms with their daughter's story and were afraid for her life. It was time for him to end at least a portion of their fears. Gently, he reached out and took her small hands in his own.

"And she shall bring forth a son, and thou shalt call His name JESUS: for He shall save His people from their sins," he quoted looking into her face.

"You believe me?" she asked as her eyes filled with tears. Joseph nodded his head without taking his eyes from hers.

"Yes, Mary. I believe you," he stated. "And I am here to take you home. To my house, to OUR house," he corrected himself. "Today. I will not allow my wife to go through this alone. God has chosen you, and in doing so, He has chosen me to help you face this task. What kind of man would I be, to reject the Son of God?"

Mary looked to her parents, "Praise be," Anna said her own tears streaming down her face.

"Joseph, I do not understand," Heli admitted, still a bit fearful for his daughter. It would be uncharacteristic of Joseph, but anger could do strange things to a man's heart.

Joseph turned to him, understanding his hesitancy. "Jehovah has shown me, in a dream, Heli, that all that which Mary has spoken is true. An angel appeared to me and told me to take Mary as my wife. That this which is conceived in her is of the Holy Spirit and that her child will save His people from their sins."

"You have seen the angel, as Mary did?" Heli asked skeptically.

"In a dream, Heli," Joseph repeated himself. "Not in the oliveyard as Mary did. But he was real, just the same." Joseph looked back to Mary. Heli looked to Anna, who could sense the uncertainty in her husband's eyes. Placing a hand on his arm, a gentle nod was just the assurance he needed.

"Very well," he agreed. "Joseph, please come inside and dry yourself. We will make the necessary preparations for Mary to accompany you. Anna, please help Mary with any belongings she may need and ready her. It appears the time has come. Our daughter will join her husband in his home. Today."

Chapter 11

Mary walked through the street, arm in arm with her husband. She was nervous, but not so much that it hindered her joyous spirit. Anna had sent for Myah, who had come quickly to assist Mary with her wedding attire. It had taken Myah a while to understand all that Mary had told her about her miraculous conception, but loving Mary as she did, Myah did not doubt her friend. The fact that Joseph now believed as well gave Myah even more confidence that her friend was telling the truth.

The procession to Joseph's home was small, consisting only of the bride and groom, Myah, Anna, Heli, Nathan, and Joseph's father, Jacob. Grandfather had wished the couple well before they left her parents' home and remained there in prayer for their future. It was not a normal procession, filled with crowds and dancing as the couple had planned, but it was proper and it was enough. Mary looked radiant in the gown Debra had fashioned for her, thankful that she had not yet grown so that she could not wear the garments. The veil Joseph had given her at their betrothal was draped across her head and hung elegantly around her face. He had never seen her more radiant.

The small party managed to continue the wedding festivities with a banquet for all who would attend. Few did, as many had drawn their own speculations as to what had happened during Mary's absence and would not believe the truth whether Joseph did or not. Rumors had circulated quickly throughout the small village from those who had witnessed the reactions to Mary's return. They now wondered at Joseph's sudden change of heart, those who had seen him convinced there was turmoil in their betrothal. Today was not the day to question him, however, and even Elias kept his peace, though he was ever watchful of the events taking place.

The celebration finally ended with the wedding party leaving the newly married couple in peace at their new home. It was not until this had transpired that Mary realized just how nervous she really was. What would Joseph expect of her now that they were legally married? The prophecy demanded a virgin birth, and if she were to give herself to her husband, as was expected, would that not go against what God demanded of her?

Fortunately for Mary, Joseph sensed her discomfort.

"I will not touch you in the way a man is allowed to touch his wife until after the child has come, Mary," he assured her. "I will not go against God or against you in that way."

Mary looked to her husband and smiled, a new respect of him budding within her. "I was not sure how to handle that," she admitted shyly.

"Do not be afraid to talk to me, Mary. Our situation is very different from other married couples, at least at the present time. Besides that, I wish for our union to be one of mutual trust and understanding." He picked up the small bag her mother had provided for her and carried it to the room she would use for cooking. Placing it on the table, he turned and again looked at his wife, a smile on his gentle face.

"I will be outside for a few moments as you settle yourself. Do not be afraid to move things around to your liking and to make this home yours, for it is." He turned to go but was stopped by her next words.

"Not mine–ours." She stepped closer to her husband. "Thank you, Joseph. For believing me." Joseph looked at this woman who was his, though not yet completely. Gathering her hands he brought them slowly to his lips. The gentle kiss he placed upon them sent chills throughout her body. He then released his hold and walked away.

Mary watched him go, closing her eyes as the door gently shut behind him. Sinking into a nearby chair, she took a moment to thank God for His many blessings. She thanked Him for his intervention in her life, for the miracle He was allowing her to be a part of, and for the husband He had provided to help her carry out His will. She then asked Him to help her to be the wife Joseph deserved and the mother Jehovah Himself expected of her. She then allowed herself a moment of "quiet" time before she rose and began to do as Joseph had asked. To make their home her own.

The weeks passed quickly as Mary settled into her new life as the wife of a carpenter. Joseph had found work close by, and Mary worked hard to keep their home running and his meals prepared. Her parents had shared some of their chickens with them so Mary had fresh eggs for cooking. Joseph had also obtained a goat recently and the milking of it had become another morning chore for her. Most of her days were spent preparing meals and making cheese which she was able to sell to the neighbors for extra income–at least to those who would purchase from her.

She preferred gathering water in the middle of the day so she could take Joseph his mid-day meal. By doing so, she was also able to avoid most of the other women who gathered at the well later in the day, knowing it was she who was usually the topic of the gossip taking place. Myah was really the only friend that Mary had left, though Mary had noticed her parents were keeping her busier than before. Apparently they were not as willing to believe Mary as Myah had been.

Joseph did not speak to her of the words she knew he must have had to endure, but she had seen the way men who were supposed to be his friends had begun to shun and even avoid him after their marriage. By taking her as his wife, it looked to the village as if he claimed to have fathered her child and that the child had been conceived before the legal obligations had taken place; otherwise he would have had Mary stoned for adultery. She was now growing much too fast for the babe to have been conceived after she had come into his home, though neither of them would have claimed that had they been questioned.

Thinking of her husband and the strange relationship they shared made her sigh. Though not as much as before their marriage, she still felt nervous around him. They had wonderful conversations, conversations she would often play over and over in her head as she spent her days at home alone. She missed him when he was gone, the way he made her laugh, and the ideas that he shared with her. He was quickly becoming her dearest friend. She loved that he was close by even when he was working.

He had kept his word by keeping his physical distance from her. Yet, on the rare occasion he would reach out to touch her arm or her back, she experienced a feeling she could not describe. His touch caused her heart to race and a shiver to run throughout her body. And even though it was slightly uncomfortable, she had caught herself almost wishing he would take her hand or embrace her at times. Was it normal for a wife to long for her husband's touch? Of course, nothing else about her life was normal anymore, she thought as she placed her hand on her well-rounded stomach. She realized she was almost feeling sorry for herself. That was something she would not tolerate.

The growing baby was active today and a few of His kicks had become slightly uncomfortable. Perhaps a walk would do her good, she thought, pushing the milk she was churning for butter aside. Standing to her feet and stretching her back, she thought it was close enough to midday to warrant her daily trip to see Joseph. A hunk of bread and cheese which had already been prepared, and a few olives, completed a nice meal for her husband. She never tired of seeing the smile on his handsome face, and his presence alone would uplift her spirits. Grabbing her water pitcher and the basket containing her goods, her heart had grown lighter just in anticipation of seeing him.

Joseph was only a short distance away, and Mary reached him quickly.

"Mid-day already?" he asked looking, at the sky as she approached.

"I am a bit early today," she admitted.

95

"Could not wait to see me, eh?" he asked, smiling as he reached into her basket for a bite. Mary laughed as her face slightly flushed at his playful words. Joseph noticed that her blush was not as deep as before their marriage, but still, it was present.

Rolling her eyes at her husband, Mary summoned enough courage to voice the words in her head, though she was not sure from where the courage had come. "Do you never tire of teasing me, Joseph?"

"Not as long as I continue to get the reaction from you which I am hoping for," he admitted to her. He moved closer to his wife. "And a word of warning," he lowered his voice for her ears alone, "it is becoming harder and harder to cause your face to flush with only words." He smiled a devilish smile as her face shot red, exactly the reaction he was hoping for. Reaching out to her, he placed a finger on her chin to lift her face back to his. "Now that is exactly the reaction I am looking for," he grinned smugly, running his finger across her cheek. Mary noticed those shivers again, though she did not pull away.

"Well, well. It looks as if the man is still at practice *wooing* his new bride." The voice interrupting them dripped with sarcasm.

Joseph dropped his hand and shot an icy glare at Elias. "Can I help you?" he asked firmly. Mary noticed Shira, again in her familiar stance behind her husband, face averted, expression solemn.

"Just passing by on my way to the market. However, I could not help but wonder," Elias began and then stopped, slowly crossing his arms and placing his hand under his chin in fake contemplation. Mary noticed he seemed to be glaring straight at her and instinctively she stepped closer to Joseph. Joseph noticed her movement behind him, and appreciated the fact that she had good instincts about her. In turn, he blocked her from view with his own body stepping closer to the man who was clearly making her uncomfortable.

"Elias, please," Shira began, clearly hoping her husband would not continue his thought.

"Was I speaking to you, woman?" he asked her gruffly. He did not bother to turn and look at her; he barely even glanced at her over his shoulder, but his voice was sharp and menacing. Mary's heart pained within her at the way her friend flinched at his words. Quickly Shira lowered her head again and pressed her lips together tightly. Mary was afraid of what was about to come forth from Elias' mouth. Joseph continued to stare at the burly man in front of him and Mary noticed her husband's hands clench at his sides.

"I could not help but wonder what made me choose this woman for my wife," he said pointing back at Shira, "instead of yours. You had no claim on her at the time." Joseph's face hardened and his breath became deep and slow. "Shira and I have been married over a year now," Elias continued in a low, wicked tone, "and she has yet to produce a son for me, or even a daughter. Yet, your wife looks as if she is almost ready to deliver, and your marriage took place what, two, three months ago?"

Mary dropped her head, her eyes widening at the audacity of the man before them. She felt Joseph tense and reached to lay her hand upon his arm reminding him to keep his composure. His arm flexed at her touch, and she knew he was struggling to control his anger.

"Elias, if you have nothing more to say, I suggest you continue on your way to the market." Joseph's voice was low and firm. Wisely, the offender backed away, his hands raised mockingly, almost knocking Shira over in the process.

"Just thought you might want to share your secret. No harm intended." He grinned smugly before he and Shira continued down the street, his cruel laugh making its way back to their ears. Joseph calmed his emotions then turned to his wife.

"Mary, I am sorry you have to endure…," without thinking, she reached up and placed her finger over his lips. Whatever in the world could he be sorry for? She could not believe he was apologizing to her.

"You owe me nothing, Joseph," she began, "especially an apology. God chose *me* to be His servant and *I* accepted that without a thought to anyone else who would be involved. I was so honored to have been chosen by Him for this task that I did not even consider the consequences of what He expected of me when the angel appeared. You have come into this marriage willingly, yet you have to endure as much, or even more, than I do. It is I who should be apologizing."

"For humbly doing the will of God?" he questioned her. "For graciously accepting what He asks of you?" Joseph placed his hands on her shoulders and pulled her to him in a gentle embrace. It was the first time he had held her so close, and it was enough to make her knees weak. Mary rested her head on his chest and allowed her arms to encircle him as well. His chest was broad and firm from the physical labor he endured daily. She felt his voice rumble beneath her ear resting there as he began to speak.

"Do not ever apologize for being a willing vessel of Jehovah, Mary. He will not allow us to endure more than we can handle. It will not always be easy, but the path He has asked of us will be better tread than what we would have faced were we not to graciously accept His will."

Mary pulled back and looked into her husband's eyes. She had never thought about it that way. He never ceased to amaze her with his wisdom, his self-control, his strength. Never could she have asked God for a better man to be the earthly father to her unborn child. Again without thinking, she allowed herself to reach up and touch his face allowing her palm to rest against his cheek.

"Thank you, Joseph," she said sincerely, looking deeply into his eyes.

"Thank you, Mary," he said as he reached up to his face and took her hand in his. "Thank you for allowing me to be a part of this miracle with you." Gently, he kissed her palm, then turned and went back to work.

Chapter 12

The next day Mary had just come inside from gathering eggs when she heard a knock at the back door of their home. Joseph had already left for work, and at first she hesitated. Why would someone come to the back of their home to request entry and not to the front which was facing the street? The knock came again, more urgently this time, and Mary reluctantly cracked open the seal just enough to see who was on the other side.

"Shira!" she exclaimed opening the door wide for her friend to enter. "Please, come inside!"

Shira looked around and then darted inside the open door. She gently pushed Mary aside and quickly closed the portal to the outside world. Mary noticed her take note of where the windows were placed in her home and that she hid herself between them so she could not be seen from anyone on the outside.

"I should not be here, Mary, but I had to tell you," Shira began, her voice little more than a whisper.

"Please, sit…," Mary began, but Shira quickly shook her head and held up her hand to request Mary's silence.

"Mary, I cannot stay. If Elias knew I had come to you…," she paused letting her sentence hang in the silence.

"Of course, what is it?" Mary asked her friend as alarm coursed through her body where she remained standing as well.

"So often throughout our marriage, Elias has disappeared without reason," Shira began quickly. "He thinks I am too naïve to notice or to care, but I am not, and I know he has been up to something. Yesterday, my curiosity finally got the best of me, and I became determined to know what is going on. Because I am afraid to question him directly, I decided to secretly follow him and find out for myself."

Mary stared at her friend in confusion, trying to listen as fast as Shira was talking.

"Mary, the rumors which have circulated throughout our village are true. Elias *is* a spy for Herod's men. He reports to them at least once a month, giving them tips on anyone he feels may be encouraging a rebellion or showing signs of leadership among the people. In return they pay him based on the information he brings. That is where all the money has been coming from. I knew he could not be earning so much simply from the trades he occasionally makes. I could not hear their voices well because of the low tones in which they were speaking. At first I heard nothing I felt was really of any interest." Shira rubbed her head, seeming to attempt to recount the conversation in her mind. "There was mention of the old prophecy, which Antipas believes to be nothing more than tales, yet Herod is afraid there is some bit of truth in them, something about a king who would overcome and rule all of Judea…something about a census coming from Caesar in an attempt to find the man who will try to overcome him…" Shira continued to ramble somewhat to herself.

Out of instinct, Mary protectively placed a hand to her abdomen. Her companion did not appear to realize how important that information alone was to Mary. "I was afraid to move closer in fear of being found out, and it was hard to hear everything." Shira seemed to be frustrated with herself in an effort to get to her point. "Anyway, I am not sure what else or who else they discussed at this meeting, but what alarmed me was the one name which I was able to hear specifically." Shira looked closely at her friend. "Joseph. Mary, I fear what Elias may have planned and what they may demand of your husband. Will you be able to pay the taxes when Herod's men return to collect them again?"

Mary suddenly realized Shira had directly asked a question of her.

"I, I do not know," she stammered, trying to catch up to the conversation and the turn it had taken. "Joseph and I have not discussed finances…I…"

Shira pulled a small pouch from her cloak and pressed it firmly into Mary's hands. "Take this just in case. Mary, you must understand, the tax collectors could not care any less of what they take or from whom they take it. They target a man within the village, name a price higher than they think he is able to pay, and then take something precious from him in place of that payment, just to strike fear and demand obedience among the others."

She approached Mary and laid her hands gently on Mary's stomach. "You must protect your child, Mary. Whatever you do, do not give them an opportunity to harm Him." Shira quickly hugged her friend. "I am so sorry for my demeanor as of late. I just cannot begin to tell you how horrid…" her voice broke and Mary pulled her into an embrace and cried with her.

"We will pray, Shira," she promised her friend, "even more so than we have been, for God to ease your burden. Nothing is impossible for Him, even the heart of Elias is capable of change."

Shira pulled herself away from Mary and wiped the tears from her face. "I am not so sure of that, yet I hope you are right. I do not know how much more of his cruelty I can endure." With that she turned and was gone even more quickly than what she had come.

Mary stood behind the closed door for a moment, trying to comprehend all that she had heard. She looked at the forgotten pouch she had been gripping tightly in her hand. She did not open it, but the weight proved that there was an enormous amount of silver within. Mary had no doubt that Shira had taken it from her home. This alone frightened her for her friend. What would Elias do if he realized the money was gone? Was it possible he had earned enough through his betrayal to the people of their village that he would not even miss it? Mary suddenly remembered her promise and instantly bowed her head. She prayed for her friend and for the man to whom she was married.

As she finished her prayer, she thought more on the beginning of Shira's conversation, the part Shira did not realize so important. She did not wish danger to have come upon her friend, but how she wished she would have heard more concerning the prophecy! Mary glanced out the window. If she went to Joseph this early, he would worry something was wrong and indeed it may be. It could also cause speculation, and attention was one thing she did not need to draw, yet she knew she could not contain herself until time for Joseph to arrive home.

"Think, Mary!" she demanded of herself.

A thought finally occurred to her, and she jolted from the stool where she sat as soon as it crossed her mind. Hurriedly, she packed his meal and set out to her father's house. It had been too long since she had enjoyed a nice visit with her parents. Additionally, she would pass by her husband on her way and have a good reason to be doing so.

As Mary approached Joseph a few moments later, a look of concern crossed his face just as she had expected.

"I am well, Joseph," she assured him to ease his worry.

"Well, I know you are not *that* anxious to see me, I have been gone only a couple of hours," he grinned.

Mary laughed softly, handing him her basket. "I am going to visit my parents and to take them a block of my cheese. I was afraid the time would catch up with me. I wanted to bring this to you as I passed."

"That's a wonderful idea," he encouraged her. "I know your parents miss having you with them every day."

"What's to miss?" her cousin Nathan teased her. He had been working closely with Joseph on this project and the two had formed a solid relationship. "One less woman in the house to keep up with," he chided. Mary made a face at him in jest. She was glad Nathan and Joseph had bonded so well. It was good for the both of them.

Nathan had always preferred to be at his Aunt Anna and Uncle Heli's more often than at his own home while growing up and had often spent more time with them than with his own father. Nathan was more like an older brother to Mary than a cousin, being only three years older than herself, and the two of them had always shared a special bond.

Nathan's mother, Anna's sister, had died years before when Nathan was a young boy, misery driving his father to indulge in strong drink at every opportunity. Mary prayed for Nathan daily, knowing that he had never quite gotten over losing his mother. Many times she had heard him ask the same question to her father when Heli had tried to speak with him about his bitterness toward Jehovah.

"What kind of God would take my mother, knowing it would turn my father to strong drink and outbursts of rage?" he would ask. "I do not want anything to do with a God such as that!" he would yell before running off to hide in the oliveyard. Mary would follow him often and sit with him as he cried. Finally, her father had decided it was better to simply live for Jehovah before Nathan than to speak directly to him and cause him to run away.

Nathan had softened over the years, taking part in religious ceremonies and prayers with her father, but even through his pleasant disposition Mary knew there was not true peace within him where his relationship with Jehovah was concerned. She knew Joseph would be a wonderful influence on him in this regard. Perhaps he would continue to soften as he grew closer to Joseph and continue to learn to embrace Jehovah's tender mercies as well.

"Mary!" her father hailed her as he neared. Mary turned and almost ran into his embrace. She was still able to see them often, but although she was enjoying her new life with Joseph, how she missed not being under their roof! "I was just coming to invite the two of you to dine with us this evening."

"And I was heading for a visit with mother," she exclaimed.

"We would be honored to dine with you," Joseph accepted while greeting his father-in-law. "Mary, enjoy your visit," he turned to his wife, "and I will join you later. We will return home together this evening."

"That sounds wonderful!" she exclaimed, pleased at the turn of events. Suddenly, she remembered the reason she had sought out Joseph in the first place. Heli had turned his attention to the building Joseph and Nathan were working on and had begun to talk with Nathan about the quick progress.

"Joseph, may I speak with you for a moment? Alone?" Mary asked him discreetly.

"Of course," he quickly assured her. Leading her by the arm to the back of the structure he pretended to be showing off his work. "What is it, Mary?" he asked quietly once away from the others.

Mary glanced around to make sure no one else was within ear shot. "Joseph, Shira came to visit me this morning in secret," she began and quickly recounted the conversation to her husband. She then pulled the pouch of silver from her tunic and handed it to him. "I have not opened the bag, but the contents are sure to be plenteous. I know we cannot accept this, Joseph, but I do not know what to do. If Elias finds out she came to me there is no telling what his actions would be; yet, what are we to do if indeed he is plotting evil against us?"

Joseph gently lifted his hand to quiet her. "Let me think on all you have told me," he instructed her sweetly. "Go enjoy your visit with your mother and I will be along soon. Nathan has promised Levi he will watch the sheep this evening so he will be leaving me shortly after noon today anyway. I will not be late." His next action took Mary by complete surprise as he lowered his head and softly brushed her cheek with his lips.

As if he knew he had caused a shock to her system, he turned with a smile to rejoin the others, Mary coming behind him in a stupor. She lagged behind a bit, attempting to have her composure in check before approaching her father and Nathan. Once she was sure her face had regained its natural color, she waved goodbye to the men and was about to continue on her way.

The commotion which ensued next, however, stopped her in her tracks. It began so quickly that no one saw it coming. The sound of hooves were heard just before they were able to see the soldiers storming into the village streets knocking down anyone or anything in their way as they came. Mary stood in shock as they raced toward her, Joseph reaching her just in time to pull her from harm's way. He quickly ushered her inside the dwelling he was working on and instructed her to stay inside until he returned for her. She did as she was told, hiding behind the thick wall. Listening, she could hear the voices of the soldiers as they shouted their commands.

"By order of royal command, your rulers King Herod and the mighty Caesar Augustus, a decree has been issued which shall be heard throughout the land!" the soldier yelled. "All men are hereby ordered to participate in a world-wide census. Every man is to return to the city of his birth, along with the members of his family, to be counted!"

Murmuring began to float throughout the gathered crowd. "This is madness!" someone yelled.

"We cannot leave our business!" came a second. Shouts of rage began to come forth from the villagers but quickly quieted as one of the soldiers dismounted his steed, his hand on his sword ready to draw as he neared the crowd from where the protest had begun.

"What was that?" he questioned them all threateningly. "Does anyone else have something to say?"

"There will be no exemptions," the messenger continued once order was regained. "You have one month to report to your home cities and register for the census. If you do not comply," he finished slowly as an evil smile began to spread across his face, "necessary force will be taken."

Mary closed her eyes and sank along the wall where she was hiding. The census Shira had inadvertently spoken of had been ordered much faster than she had expected. Closing her eyes, she slowly exhaled the breath she had been holding as she looked at her enlarged stomach. The baby kicked within her. She heard the horses as the soldiers stormed from the village the same way in which they had entered. She could hear the protesting loudly once again now that the soldiers had left and taken their swords with them.

Joseph walked slowly into the room where Mary was crouched against the wall, sinking down beside her. Reaching for her hand, they simply sat, staring at nothing for a moment before Joseph spoke.

"Did you hear?" he asked without looking at her, tenderly cradling her hand in his own.

"I did," she affirmed. "Shira did not realize the importance of what she was saying, or mention how quickly a census would be ordered. How long will it take us to travel to Bethlehem?" she asked now looking to her husband.

"Close to four days usually," he answered quietly. "But I fear, in your condition…" he began.

Mary reached to turn his face to hers. "God will be with us," she assured him placing her free hand on her stomach.

Joseph let out a small laugh as he looked to where her hand rested. "Yes, I suppose He will," he agreed. "I suppose He will."

Chapter 13

Mary and her mother finished preparations of the meal and joined her father, Joseph, and grandfather in the main room. Each of them took a seat on the mat as her father broke the bread and blessed it.

"Joseph and I have been discussing his return to Bethlehem," Heli began around a bite. "Mary you will rejoin us here until he returns, at which time…"

"No." Mary interrupted him, looking first to her husband and then to her father.

"Daughter, I do not feel it will be safe for you to remain home alone," her father began again. "Your mother and I can care for you here and for the child who is likely to arrive before Joseph returns."

"I do not intend to stay home alone," Mary began. "The soldiers orders were clear, Father. Men, along with the members of their family, are to return to their homeland for the census."

"Mary, you cannot travel," her mother began, cooing as though speaking to a child. "Your time of travail is very near." She patted her daughter on the hand as if the matter were closed.

"I must," Mary began again. Looking to her husband for his view on the subject, she saw the uncertain look cross his features. He did not wish for her to stay behind in Nazareth, but she knew he did fear for her to travel with him. She also knew her place was with her husband and that he would protect her and her child with every part of his being. "I will go with my husband," she stated sternly.

"You cannot be serious," her mother protested, growing angry. "Mary you cannot give birth on the side of the road! There are wild animals and thieves! You know not what you may face!"

"I know not what I face each day that I breathe," Mary argued. "This child inside of me is a miracle in Himself. Do you think not that Jehovah will protect us? Will He not protect His own son?" The silence which followed weighed heavily inside the small room.

Mary looked from her mother to her husband once again. "I do wish to accompany you," she spoke looking only to him, "but I will not go against your wishes. What say you, Joseph?" she asked her husband.

"Did not Micah prophesy the Messiah would be born in Bethlehem?" Grandfather reminded them from his place on the mat.

Looking to his father and mother-in-law before he spoke, Joseph turned his attention to his wife. He knew that she was right. God was with them wherever they were. He had placed them in this together, and together they would stay. He reached for her hand.

"We shall leave in the morning," he spoke firmly yet respectfully to her parents with Mary's hand held tightly in his, "together. We will be in Bethlehem before the week's end and there we shall remain until after the child is born."

"Joseph, no!" Anna began to protest.

"Enough," Heli stopped her with a raise of his hand. "We will honor their wishes, Anna. And we will not go against the prophecies." Though he too was frightened for his daughter, he appreciated the man to whom she was wed. He was not afraid to stand up for what he felt was right for his family, even if Heli did not exactly agree. "Joseph, please take our donkey so that Mary may ride when she tires?" It was a question, not a command. Joseph nodded his head in thanks. "Anna, bake more bread to send with them and anything else we have that you think they may need." Anna nodded though the tears in her eyes threatened to spill over.

"I will protect your daughter, Anna," Joseph assured her. "I will protect her and the child with my very life," he promised her. His look was respectful yet determined.

"We have no doubt of that Joseph," Heli affirmed placing his hand on his son-in-law's broad shoulder.

"We should pray," Grandfather spoke plainly from his place by the window, "for Jehovah's protection and guidance as they travel."

The family bowed their heads and joined hands as Grandfather led them in fervent prayer. Anna cried quietly, Mary's heart breaking at the sound. She knew her mother only feared for her safety and for that of her child. Her family had dealt with so much of late because of her. She said her own prayer asking for peace for the parents she loved so much as Grandfather prayed for their safety on their journey.

When the prayer was completed, they finished their meal while Joseph and Heli decided the path they should take. It would be faster to cut through Samaria and then Ephraim to reach their destination but much safer to stay close to the Jordan River as they traveled.

More travelers would choose that path, therefore providing safety in numbers. It was more likely women would be in that vicinity as well, should Mary require the aid of a mid-wife before they reached Bethlehem.

Once their path was decided upon, Joseph relayed the conversation which had taken place earlier in the day between Mary and Shira to the family. He pulled the pouch of silver from his robe and poured the pieces upon the mat.

"How did she come across so much silver?" Heli questioned, counting out an unbelievable sum.

"I assume it is payment Elias has received for his treachery," Mary answered. "I only hope he does not realize it is missing. How will we ever get it back to Shira without him realizing it has been taken?" Mary asked her husband.

"Leave that to me," Anna spoke, more at peace after the prayer. "As I bake bread for the two of you, I will bake enough to also share with them. That is not unusual. I will hide the pouch inside the wrappings and take it to Shira tomorrow, after the two of you are safely out of the village."

"She was so worried about us," Mary shook her head emphasizing her words. "She was concerned about us not being able to pay the taxes, but she did not realize the importance of the prophecy the soldiers were speaking of, nor of the part that we play in that prophecy."

"No doubt Herod is looking for an established king to overtake his throne. I do not believe he will be searching for a babe." Joseph continued, "It would be to our advantage were he to continue to do so."

"You are right, still, you must always be attentive, Joseph," Heli reiterated. "If he looks deep enough into the prophecies he may realize it is a babe he should be seeking."

"Of course," Joseph nodded in agreement.

"Will your father accompany you as you travel?" Anna asked of Joseph, somewhat changing the subject.

"I do not believe so," Joseph answered her honestly. "He will prefer to get his affairs in order here before he leaves Nazareth. I am afraid to wait any longer for fear of making things harder on Mary." Joseph looked to his wife who thanked him with a loving smile.

"We must be on our way," Joseph announced soon after. "I want to leave at sun-up, and the night will not be long enough as it is."

"We will be at your home before first light with the beast and more bread for your journey," Heli promised.

Mary bent and kissed her grandfather on his forehead. He wrapped his frail arms around her and pulled her close to him. He knew this could be the last time he saw his precious granddaughter, chosen by God to give birth to the Messiah they had long awaited for. How honored was he to hold the mother of his Lord in an embrace. "God be with you, my child," he smiled into her eyes. "I love you, Mary."

"And I love you, Grandfather," she answered through tears.

The couple exited and walked slowly through the streets of Nazareth toward their own home. The sun had not yet set, and beautiful shades of blues and reds lit the sky. Joseph stopped at the entrance to their courtyard and took in the view before him.

"When we left Bethlehem and came to Nazareth, I never once dreamed of returning there," he began. "We established our carpentry trade quickly, and I acquired this land as soon as I could in hopes of one day building a home for my own family here. Jehovah allowed all of that to take place, yet now I must leave it behind. I confess I do not understand why we left Bethlehem in the first place since His obvious plan was to direct me back there."

Mary stepped in front of her husband, blocking the view which he was so focused on. "Because you had to find me," she answered him honestly. "I was here. In Nazareth. Just as Jehovah has chosen me to be the mother of His Son, Joseph, He has chosen you as His earthly father. Besides, our leaving here is only temporary. Once the child is born, we can return to Nazareth."

Without allowing himself time to think, Joseph pulled Mary close to him in a tight embrace. He loved to hold her and did not allow himself to do so often enough. Surprised, he felt a light punch to his mid-section.

Mary laughed as she pulled herself away from him. "It seems you were a bit close for comfort," she laughed as the babe within her kicked again. Joseph looked at her rounded stomach.

"May I," he asked holding his hands out to her. Mary nodded her absolute approval as Joseph gently placed his hands on her abdomen. The baby moved inside and Mary laughed again as a wide grin split Joseph's face. "I feel Him moving," he exclaimed. Mary could do little more than nod as she blinked back tears of happiness. Joseph slowly lowered himself to his knees and spoke directly to Mary's stomach.

"I promise to protect and love You as my son," he said, his hands unmoving, "yet while doing so, I will do my best to always respect and honor You as my Lord."

In the stillness of the moment, the scene was a precious one, even to the spectator who was hidden from view. Slowly, so as not to bring attention to his presence, Elias pulled himself further into the shadows now being cast by the coming night. So it is true, he thought to himself. Joseph and Mary honestly believe her child to be the Son of God. He had heard mention of such a thing, but had cast it off as an unreliable rumor. What imbeciles! Yet, Mary's story had to hold enough merit that Joseph believed what she had told him, otherwise, he would have had her stoned.

Stories told to him by his grandmother when he was a small boy stirred within his head. Stories of a "coming King" who would be "born of a virgin and would save their people." He had always written them off as fancy tales for spiritual people who had nothing better to do than squander their time searching for a hope that did not exist. He thought for a moment but could remember little of the details she had so often told him. Elias had decided as a young man to make his own destiny rather than to search or await the guidance of another to do so for him. In doing so he had lost most of the details of what she had so often said.

A smile split his wicked face as another thought occurred to him. Patience Elias, he thought to himself as the idea continued to manifest itself inside his twisted mind. No doubt Herod knew less about the details of the prophecies than he himself, focusing more on keeping his throne than on the details of pointless promises carried through the generations. Herod was concerned about a powerful king who would suddenly arise from the midst to overtake him. He only thought he had problems. He had given no thought to the possibility that the king was yet to be born.

A bit of his grandmother's stories suddenly sprang to mind, and it was a bit Elias planned to reflect more upon. Risking another peek at the couple, he saw they were now making their way safely inside the confines of their home. Yes, to provide information on a child such as this would bring a hefty amount of silver to his already-lined pockets, but how much more would it benefit him to hand over that very child himself to Herod? The child who some believed not only to be the ruler of the Jews but the ruler of all the world.

Chapter 14

Mary glanced behind her and once again the scriptures of Lot's wife came immediately to her mind. Quickly she turned her head and faced the direction they were heading instead of the direction from where they had come. The city gates had faded from view long hours ago and though Mary would never admit it to Joseph, she was already weary from the miles they had come this day. He had said Bethlehem was a four day journey at a normal pace, which she was sure she could handle, but she had not factored in the rough and hilly terrain. Mary had determined not to slow him, but was not sure she would be able to keep that promise which she had made to herself.

Her goodbyes to her family early that morning had been bittersweet. At first, she was a little excited about the journey she and Joseph were about to embark upon. She was nervous too, but it was a nervous excitement. Now, however, as her legs and back had begun to protest against the miles, she realized that her excitement had been short lived. More than excitement, wariness grated at her nerves and she began looking to the sun to see where they were in the day. They had eaten their mid-day meal of bread and olives as they walked, Joseph promising they would make camp before nightfall, but Mary longed for a rest before that if possible. She was sure there was a certain milestone he was aiming for, someplace safe to bed down, and she prayed he would find it soon.

"Are you well, Mary?" he asked, cutting into her thoughts. She had not even realized he had slowed his pace to come along beside her.

"I am," she answered with a smile, "though I confess, I am growing a bit tired."

Joseph stopped so abruptly that Mary almost stumbled. Without a word, he began dragging bundles and provisions from off their donkey's back.

"Joseph, whatever are you doing?" she asked though it was quite clear. He turned to her and she noticed a look of anger on his face. For a moment, she was almost frightened it was she who had angered him.

"I cannot believe I have been so thoughtless and careless as to your well-being, Mary. We have been traveling all day. I apologize that I did not sense your weariness before." He moved quickly to unloose their packs from the animals back.

"Joseph you cannot carry all of this! I can continue a while longer and rest when we make camp. Please, I will be fine."

"Mary, no. I am the one who will be fine," he assured her as he began to situate their belongings on his own back and across his shoulders. "There," he smiled as he threw a blanket across the back of the donkey and patted it firmly. "Not the most stylish ride, but one that will help you rest your legs for a while." He led the animal to a large rock nearby and helped Mary climb onto it before she began to settle herself across its strong back. Relief to her legs was instant though her back still ached.

"Thank you, husband," she said sincerely as she wound her fingers into the animal's mane. A brief nod and smile was his reply as he began to lead the animal carefully across the rocky terrain.

"We will make camp tonight at the base of Mt. Gilboa," he began pointing to a mountain in the near distance. "We should be approaching that base within the next hour," Joseph predicted looking to the sky. "Yes, we shall make it easily before nightfall. I have no doubt we will find others there as well and be able to join their campfire. There will be clear streams for water for ourselves and the animal, and perhaps I shall even catch some fish for our empty stomachs." Mary noticed the excitement creeping into his voice.

"It sounds wonderful," she managed, already smelling the fish cooking on the campfire. The gentle swaying of the animal under her tired body was almost more than she could bear. Joseph continued to speak but his voice had become little more than a mumble. She was so tired. Rocking slowly back and forth. So…so…tired. Imagining the smell of the cooking food and the warmth of the blanket under her body. So…extremely…tired. Suddenly, her head nodded and she felt her body begin to slide. In the same instant she felt Joseph's strong arms reaching to catch her right before she collapsed to the ground.

"Mary!" he almost yelled. Quickly she grabbed for his shoulders as he steadied her on her feet. "You must stay awake, Mary. You cannot risk a fall like that!"

"I am so sorry, Joseph. I had no idea I had fallen asleep."

"It is my fault," he said as he looked over her. "I have pushed you too hard this day. Are you well? Is the baby well?" His hands rubbed across her shoulders as his eyes fell to her stomach.

"Yes, yes," she assured him somewhat embarrassed, "we are fine." Mary continued to steady herself and smooth her garments. "Yet, I think it may be best if I walk instead. I do not trust myself to try to ride again right now. I will be fine," she promised as she saw the questions in his eyes. "You said we were near, did you not."

Joseph took in the landscape around them. "We are and I do feel it would be in our best interest to continue there. We would be much safer there overnight."

"I can make it, Joseph. I know I can," she insisted looking into his eyes.

Slowly he turned from her and took her hand as they continued their path. Mary was surprised at how much those few moments on the donkey's back had helped her tired legs. It was just enough time to rejuvenate her limbs and though she still lacked a spring in her step, her body did not feel quite as heavy.

It ended up taking a little less than an hour before they saw the base of the mountain where others had begun making camp for the night. Joseph spoke pleasantries as they approached at least half a dozen other couples already there, and they were welcomed into the small community of strangers. Mary was surprised to find she was not the only expectant mother traveling; however, she was much more advanced in her pregnancy than the others.

Joseph helped her spread their blankets and unpack what few things they would need for the night. He then assured himself that she was settled before going with a couple the other men to attempt catching fish for their supper. Mary grinned at his back until he turned and gave a quick wink in her direction. Shivers tickled along her spine once again and this time he was not even within touching distance.

"Your Joseph is very attentive to his young bride," an older lady who was called Bayla laughed. "Have you been married very long?" she asked curious.

Mary thought about her answer. She rubbed her stomach. "Not VERY long," she answered honestly. "He is very watchful," she smiled hoping that would end the question as to the amount of time they had been together. Bayla seemed content with her answer.

"I remember when Reuben and I were expecting our first child. It was such a joyful time. That was before all this taxing began. Before Cyrenius was governor of Syria. Times were somewhat better then," she sighed.

"But every era has its own share of problems to deal with, I would think?" Mary commented with a smile.

"I suppose you are right, dear. Yet, I keep hoping for a sign from Jehovah that the Messiah has come or is at least about to make His presence known. I would like to see that come to pass before my days on this earth are over."

Mary looked away from Bayla's face. She was not sure if she should say more or just let the conversation lag.

"Bayla! Do not discourage the young one!" another lady called to her. "She has enough on her mind than to be burdened with your goings on!"

"Ah! Listen to me whine like a newborn calf!" Bayla chastised herself. "You are right Aliza and in front of such a sweet young mother as this one. Tell me dear," she began turning her attention back to

Mary as Aliza came over to join them. "You are near are you not? To your time?" she pointed to Mary's stomach. Mary welcomed the turn in conversation.

"I am. My best calculations are that I will deliver near the end of the month. That is why my husband and I are trying to get to Bethlehem quickly, just in case the time comes earlier than what we have figured."

"You have a good way to go to reach Bethlehem, but have no fear! You will make it! You are strong, and you have a good husband who will protect you. He would not ask more of you than what he thinks you can handle." Mary enjoyed Bayla's enthusiasm. The older lady patted Mary's hand and looked into her eyes. "There is something special about you, dear. Though I cannot quite put my finger on it." Bayla wagged her finger in Mary's direction. Mary could not help but laugh as other ladies from the group began to ramble over to join their conversation. "Your son, He will be strong. Like His mother and His father," she assured her. Mary welcomed the female conversation. Talk ranged from her own pregnancy to that of two of the other ladies in the group.

She noticed from the corner of her eye, a figure who emerged discreetly from the woods. She assumed from the build it was a man, though he kept a hood drawn about his head and a careful distance from the others. Instead of approaching the fire already built, he began to gather wood for his own, and set up his camp behind the rocks near the backside of the mountain. Mary shrugged her shoulders to herself. Must be a loner, she thought, though she could not stop the nagging feeling that something was not quite right where this visitor was concerned.

It was not long before the husbands returned and the smell of fish filled the camp. What a joyful time they had sharing stories and getting to know a little about one another. Joseph had moved behind Mary allowing her to lean her body against his own. Resting in the cushion of his arm, she was surprised how warm and comfortable she felt against him, though they were out in the open wilderness and in the company of people they barely even knew.

God had sent Joseph to protect her and His Son, and Mary could ask for no greater comfort, but what of the man behind the mountain? Should she mention him to Joseph? Maybe someone else had seen him as well and checked on his well-being? Mary tried to summon enough strength to mention him, but her eyes were so heavy and she was so tired. As soon as the conversation the men were engaged in lagged, she would mention him. It would be rude to interrupt.

Joseph held Mary close as he continued to talk with the others, pretending it was a natural occurrence between the two of them, though he was very aware of her closer-than-normal presence. He was also aware when her body became limp and realized that she had fallen into a deep and peaceful sleep. Carefully, he moved to lay her down and could not help but notice how serene she looked. Gently he bent down and kissed her cheek. She did not even stir.

"God, help me," he prayed silently. "Help me to be what You have asked of me and to be the husband she needs."

The fire had dwindled to embers, and the other campers had made their way to their own blankets. Joseph gently pulled another blanket over his sleeping wife, carefully situating the veil he had given her months before close about her face and over her shoulders. Once he was assured of her warmth and comfort, he moved to lie down close beside her on his own blanket. Now that he was satisfied of her safety, he too would close his eyes for some much needed rest. She was between him and the base of the mountain. No one would get near her this night or any other without him knowing. Especially the man he had seen watching them so carefully from the other side of the mountain.

Chapter 15

Shira glanced out the small window of her two room house. There was still no sign of Elias. He had told her he would be gone for a while when he left so quickly, but she did not realize how long of "a while" he had meant. The items he had thrown so carelessly into his satchel had indicated the urgency he felt to be on his way, so she had not questioned him. However, two days had now passed and there had been no sign of her husband's return.

Thoughts had begun creeping into her mind. Had he abandoned her? What kind of trade could he possibly be making that kept him from his home for so long? Had something gone wrong when he was reporting to the soldiers and they had taken his life because of it? Shira shrugged her shoulders as she allowed the cloth to fall back in place over the window. What saddened her the most about the whole situation was that she really did not care.

Her marriage had turned out far differently than she had ever imagined. Though she had not known him well, she was not completely distraught at the thought of marrying Elias when her father had demanded it. After all, it was what was expected of a girl of her age and until then, she had not been spoken for. Most marriages were arranged far in advance, but it was not uncustomary for maidens to be unspoken for until a year or so before the wedding. However, suitable husbands were becoming hard to find and it was extremely rare for love to come before a marriage. In addition, Elias was strong, he proved he could provide for her and, though not overly so, he was handsome enough. His sour disposition had not shown until after the wedding had taken place.

The circumstances in their village were very grim. Money was hard to come by making stomachs hard to fill. The soldiers were relentless in their demand for more and more tax money in an effort to make Herod the richest king to have ever lived. Elias had appeared at a time when her family was struggling and the offer to take her off her father's hands, with no more dowry than what he could provide, was an opportunity Uriah could not pass up. What made the deal even sweeter was that Elias had secretly promised Uriah that he would be able to ease the burden which the soldiers demanded of him each time they stormed the village. He had seemed desperate for her hand and was willing to obtain it at any cost.

"How then," she wondered aloud, "did I lose his interest so quickly after our marriage vows?"

Elias often spoke cruelly of her inability to produce an heir for him, but truthfully he did not seem overly excited about having children. The only thing he seemed overly excited about was lining his pockets. He had no idea she had discovered his secret occupation of earning that income or that she had found where he was keeping the silver he obtained. Evidently he thought her beautiful…but stupid. Perhaps that was the reason for his desire to have her– he wanted a comely, yet ignorant, wife.

Shira closed her eyes as thoughts of a happier time flooded her memory. Times when she would assist her mother in daily chores, then run about the village in the afternoon talking with Mary, Myah, and countless other friends. They, like all teenage girls, dreamed of the future and which of the village boys they may someday call husband.

When Elias arrived in the village, Shira had somehow caught his attention. Her friends had joked about the "strange" new man but Shira had thought there was more to him than what he allowed others to see. How little did she know the "hidden" Elias was not pleasant at all. Still, she had not intentionally captured his attention. She was simply as pleasant to him as she was to everyone else. If only she had known then what she knew now.

Shaking her head to clear her mind, she refused to allow the tears to fall again. She had cried until her eyes were raw, prayed until her heart felt as if it would burst, and agonized with Jehovah over her present state until she was sure He was tired of hearing her empty pleas. Nothing was going to change the man she was married to, and unless He or someone else prohibited Elias' return, she had more to do than sit around feeling sorry for herself. She better have her chores completed and his supper waiting.

Joseph glanced over his shoulder once again, keeping a close eye on Mary. Her laughter was a balm to his weary body. She was happy, content, and still very pregnant. She had not mentioned pain or discomfort, but Joseph knew their time was limited. He had noticed her hands clenching her stomach more often, especially when she did not realize he was watching her. He did not think her pains serious as of yet, but he knew she was beginning to experience more discomfort.

"God please," he silently prayed, "please, let us make it to Bethlehem before she delivers."

Mary was still close to him, as she had promised to stay, but continued walking and talking with one of the young expectant women they had met at the base of Mt. Gilboa. He was glad for female conversation for his wife, which took her mind from the miles they had yet to go. At his best calculations, and barring no unexpected delays, they should arrive in Bethlehem within the next two days. Perhaps this night would be the last they had to camp in the wilderness.

However, he was fearful that tonight would be the most dangerous of nights they had spent while on their journey. There was safety in numbers, but most of the caravan they had met and now traveled with would be breaking away from them around noon, continuing their own journey to Emmaus. The others would be stopping in Jericho a short while after. Not only would this leave Mary and Joseph alone in the desert, but the land they were passing through now was barren and void of the mountains which had provided shelter for them the past two nights. There were no mountains between where they currently passed and the Holy City of Jerusalem, which was still too far away to even attempt reaching today. Yes, they would spend this night with little shelter from the elements.

They continued their travel alongside the Jordan River and Joseph's new found friends had taught him the skills of fishing with a spear, which he had mastered quite well. Because fish was not something they had at home often, neither Mary nor

Joseph had minded partaking of it numerous times over the past few days. At least they would not go hungry, and the food was actually pleasant.

The only traveler which no one seemed to know anything about was the man continuing to follow them while showing care to keep his distance from the caravan. Joseph had inquired of the others, but no one knew where he had come from or where he was headed. There was something very familiar about the stranger in the way he walked and held himself, but Joseph had yet to see his face because of the way he always kept it hidden under the hood of his cloak. In the heat of the day, it protected his head from the sun, and in the night it provided shelter from the cold. He had not posed a threat to anyone in their company, but something about the whole situation did not settle well with Joseph. He had not mentioned it to Mary, but his wife was wise, and he had noticed her watching the man as well.

As they approached Ephraim, their pleasant company bid them farewell. Mary's separation from her friend was a tearful one. The ladies had become attached in their short time together, their unborn children being the main topic of their conversation. The woman felt certain she carried a son, and his name would be Simon, like his grandfather. Their journey was far from over and as soon as they had registered per the demands of Caesar, they would continue their path and settle in the somewhat newly formed country of Cyrene. Mary hugged her new friend and wished her well, each of them praying their paths would cross again at some other time and place.

Again, Mary and Joseph were alone, save for the lone traveler who continued to follow them from some distance back. Joseph noticed the stranger's actions seemed uncomfortable once he realized the others had gone their separate ways, which made him more suspicious, and he had stopped early in the evening making his camp in a small clump of trees by the river. Another sign to Joseph that something about him was not quite right. Joseph used the time to his advantage, pressing on in an attempt to put more distance between his small family and the man who seemed to be following them.

As the sun began to drop low in the sky, he realized they too should make camp. Mary had grown quiet and he recognized that as a sign that she was exhausted. They had made good time today, so resting a bit longer than usual would do them good. Joseph led the animal and his wife to the banks of the river.

"We will make camp here tonight," he smiled to her as though nothing was out of the ordinary.

Mary looked around. On one side of them was the river, on the other, miles and miles of open land. A lone tree, drawing just enough water to make an attempt at growing, popped up here and there, and a few large rocks scattered about were their only companions. Otherwise, they were completely out in the open and completely alone. Mary managed a small smile in the direction of her husband. He could tell she was uncomfortable, but she trusted his judgment enough to try not to show it.

"I am afraid there will be nothing more between us and Jerusalem but open land, Mary. The Holy City is too far to attempt before nightfall. I will keep you safe," he promised her.

The smile she gave him was genuine. "In that I have no doubt, husband." Her smile did wonders for his soul. "I will gather some wood for a fire," she said, pointing to one of the straggly trees nearby.

"And I will catch our supper," he returned, taking his spear and turning toward the river.

In a short amount of time, the aroma of frying fish filled the air. Mary took what was left of the bread her mother had sent and laid it near the hot coals. The meal was quite a delicacy for travelers. They ate in comfortable silence, and once they had finished, the animal had been fed and cared for, and their remnants cleared away, Joseph settled himself against a nearby rock. Mary pulled the veil he had given her close about her shoulders, wrapping the warm material around her body.

"I had no idea when I gave that to you just how useful it would prove," he said as he whittled at a piece of wood. Mary recognized that as one of his favorite past times.

"It is still beautiful, though I fear it is beginning to show some wear," she frowned as she inspected the seams.

"That shows it was not only beautiful but, indeed, a practical gift. Though not nearly as beautiful as the one who wears it," he smiled to her. "Are you warm enough? I can get more wood for the fire." He moved to get up.

"No, Joseph, I am quite well," she assured him. He settled back into his position at her insistence and began to whittle again; Mary watched him as he worked.

"Are you afraid, Mary?" he asked her gently, catching her watching him. She knew he was not talking about their current surroundings.

"A little," she admitted to her husband. "I fear the unknown. Not so much the birth, as I have witnessed the experience and know what to expect where that is concerned. I am more fearful of being the mother expected of me to the child whom I carry." Mary looked out over the river beside them, enjoying the serenity it provided.

"I have never a known a woman more capable of this task," Joseph answered, laying his wood aside and looking across the fire and into her face. "Jehovah would not have asked this of you if He were not certain you were capable of it."

"And you, Joseph?" she asked in return. "Are you fearful? Of being the earthly father to the Son of God?"

Joseph contemplated his answer carefully. "I," he began slowly, thinking carefully about his next words, "I…I am scared to death," he admitted truthfully causing Mary's laughter to sound throughout their lonely camp. Joseph laughed with her and went back to his whittling.

"Joseph, you are such a good husband," she smiled to him once her laughter had subsided. "Constantly attentive to my care and needs and to that of my child. Thank you for being the man Jehovah desires you to be."

Quickly moving closer to her husband, before she could change her mind, Mary picked up one of his sandaled feet.

"Mary! What are you doing?" Joseph asked jumping to pull his foot from her reach.

"I am going to wash your feet, Joseph. They are soiled and tired," she answered him matter-of-factly.

"I cannot allow the mother of my Lord to wash my feet," he protested in shock.

Mary looked at him somewhat surprised. "Then allow your wife to do so," she rebuked him gently. "Jehovah blessed our betrothal before He told me I would carry His child. I do not believe He expects me to be a slothful wife."

Slowly she took his foot back into her hand and began to release the straps which held the sandals there. She could tell Joseph was uncomfortable, but it was the least she could do for him for the care and love he was constantly bestowing upon her. She had not fulfilled her wifely duties in every way, and she would not until after the child was born, but there was much more to being a wife than simply the physical aspect. She was ashamed of herself for not being more attentive to him before now, especially as the straps loosed and his bare foot was in view.

She stifled a gasp as the raw skin, where the straps had been, stared up at her. Dirt and dried blood from hours of walking across the dry, dusty ground, as well as puss-filled blisters, were scattered across his toes, heels and ankles. How had she missed this? For days, she had ridden the donkey off and on, and if she rested, Joseph had continued about the camp, preparing for the next day's journey or gathering wood, food, and water. He had been on his feet continuously. Without a word, she stood and ripped a piece of cloth which they used for covering the donkey's back. Joseph had used it to protect the animal's haunches from the load he carried, whether it had been herself or their goods. That donkey was currently in better condition than her own husband.

Taking the cloth and a small pot she had brought with them, she gathered water from the river and returned to her task of caring for him. Gently she began to pour water over his wounds and pat them with the water soaked cloth. She felt him wince only once before finally relaxing enough to allow her to complete her mission. First one foot and then the other, she carefully and lovingly cleaned his tired feet as best she could.

Only after she had finished her task did she allow herself to look up at Joseph's face. She did not think she could bear seeing the pain she must have been causing, yet she knew it had to be done. While working she had to blink back her tears over the discomfort she knew he must be in, yet she allowed them to fall when she finally looked up at him and saw his head resting on the rock he was against, his eyes closed in peaceful sleep. Her motions must have had more of a relaxing effect than she realized. She took his sandals to the river cleaned them, then set them by the fire to dry. She then washed her own feet, which was a bit of a task in her current condition, then stoked the fire to keep it burning a bit longer.

Mary did not think Joseph had truly slept in days. She was glad he did so now and moved quietly so as not to disturb him. Looking around, however, she did not feel safe on the other side of the fire from her sleeping husband. He stirred, but only to lift his arm enough to allow her beneath it, as she settled herself beside him, sharing the large rock he leaned against. Pulling a blanket across them both, Mary allowed her head to fall against her husband's chest before allowing sleep to overcome her as well.

Chapter 16

Elias stood and kicked dirt across the remaining embers of his fire. He was astounded Mary had not yet delivered her child! They had been walking for three days, with little rest. What more must it take for the child to come! When he left Nazareth less than two hours behind Joseph and Mary, his plan was to follow them until the child was born, overcome them, take the baby, then deliver the child to Herod before the week's end. He had no idea she would make it so far without delivering. His provisions were running low, but he would not return to Nazareth without that baby! If the child some proclaimed King was not enough to promote him to a position within the palace, nothing would be.

Gathering his meager supplies, Elias set out to catch up to them. He would have to be more careful now that the group they were traveling with had dispersed. He was not sure he had been spotted, but more than once he had seen that meddling carpenter looking his way. Elias was sure he would have to kill him to get to Mary and the baby. Luckily for Elias, that would not be an issue.

Joseph and Mary rose early, had a breakfast of beans and rice, and then set out on their way. Joseph assured Mary they would approach Jerusalem shortly after noon and should be in Bethlehem by nightfall.

"There are several inns located within the city walls of Bethlehem," he told her. "I was quite close to one of the owners before we moved to Nazareth. We will find lodging there."

"And, perhaps a mid-wife?" she asked hopefully. She did not want to alarm her husband, but the baby seemed to be pressing more this day than in recent others.

"Mary," Joseph stopped suddenly and looked her over. "Is it time? Are you ready?"

"The time is not yet come, Joseph, but I fear it will be very soon," she answered him honestly.

"Should you ride?" he asked her.

"Perhaps if I am off my feet, it will calm Him some?" It was more of a question than a comment. Mary was not sure what to do. All she knew was that the baby must not come on the side of the road. She must do anything she could to prevent that from happening.

Mary was soon situated on the donkey's back, with what was left of their provisions upon Joseph's, and they were again on their way. She noticed he moved them cautiously, yet quickly. Very little was said in the way of conversation. Other than Joseph occasionally questioning her well-being, and Mary nodding in acknowledgement, their journey was made in silence. He was determined to get her to Bethlehem this day.

It was the longest day Mary had experienced. Hours seemed to have passed before the scenery finally began to change.

"The walls of Jerusalem should be coming into view soon," Joseph encouraged her. "We are about to cross over the fields where the sacrificial lambs are raised." Mary nodded to her husband, but that was all she could muster. She did not feel well at all, and though she knew her time was drawing ever closer, she felt desperate for a rest.

Mary raised her head from where her eyes had been focused for hours on the mane of the animal. She took notice of the scene around her. Beautiful fields nestled in valleys of green surrounded them. Small trees and what seemed like hundreds of tiny white lambs dotted the landscape on each side of the trodden path they were now upon. Men, shepherds like Levi back at home in Nazareth, kept a careful eye on their charges.

Joseph was explaining how these lambs were extremely special to the people of Jerusalem because of their sacrificial qualities, yet the shepherds who watched them were looked on as the lowest of the low in the people's eyes. His voice quieted as they neared one of those shepherds.

"Joseph," Mary broke the silence, "may we rest just for a moment?" she asked from her place on the donkey's back. Joseph stopped the animal and looked to his wife unsure of whether she needed a quick rest, or a quickened pace. The shepherd within earshot heard her plea and unknowingly made Joseph's decision a simple one.

"Your woman is tired. How far have you come this day?" he asked Joseph, without taking his eyes from his small fire.

"We have traveled many miles. Might we rest here for a moment?" he asked the old man.

"Suit yourself," the man answered him. He pointed to the small flame before him. "There's a scrap or two of bread left wrapped in the coals. Help yourself if you would like."

Joseph assisted Mary as she slid carefully from the donkey's back. He helped her walk to the base of a nearby knoll and settled her against it. The shepherd's eyes widened as he took in her fragile condition.

"Do not go having that baby out here," he stated with a small laugh. "I have birthed a lamb or two in my day but never a human child. She should not be traveling in her condition," he rebuked Joseph kindly.

"It is not due to any fault of our own, but by the command of Caesar that we travel," Joseph answered him with a smile. Mary accepted the bread the kind shepherd offered. Her appetite had long gone, but she nibbled appreciatively none the less.

"Oh, the mighty Caesar," the shepherd began sarcastically rubbing his beard. "His census is bringing hundreds into our town, including some who had left and others who should have never returned. Are you stopping in Jerusalem?" he asked.

Joseph shook his head around a bite of bread. "On through to Bethlehem," he replied.

"Then take the extra time to go around the city," the shepherd suggested. "I have never seen so many pouring in at once. You would not make it through before nightfall. Jerusalem does not look like the Holy City it is supposed to be," he said sadly. "People of all beliefs have come, and it is vexed with their spoils. I would avoid it all together if any way possible. You should still reach Bethlehem shortly after nightfall."

He and Joseph discussed an alternative route, and their pleasant visit continued with the shepherd asking questions and Joseph answering them. He kindly gave them advice on raising the young child once he arrived, much like Mary would have expected from her grandfather. Joseph asked a few questions of his own about the life of a shepherd, and as he answered, Mary sensed a sadness within the man that she could not quite identify. He was a gentle soul, though a weary one, and Mary prayed for Jehovah to bless him in a way which would not be forgotten.

As they prepared to leave, for a reason she could not explain other than because he reminded her so much of her grandfather, Mary bent and kissed the old man on the forehead.

"I will not forget the kindness you have bestowed upon us this day," she promised him. "We will tell our son of you and of the generosity you have shown. Thank you."

Mary was surprised when tears filled the old man's eyes. He patted her hand which rested on his shoulder to acknowledge his goodbye.

The couple had taken the alternative route which the shepherd had suggested, and had been gone from his view for less than an hour, before another figure quickly approached.

Elias questioned the old man immediately. "You, shepherd," he spoke in his hateful tone. "Have a man and woman passed this way recently on a trek to Bethlehem?"

"I have seen many pass this way as of late," he answered in a tone to match Elias', "how am I to know where everyone is headed?"

141

"The woman is great with child," Elias spat at the man. This old shepherd was quickly getting on his nerves.

"What is it to you who has and has not passed my way? Do you think I have taken notice of all the people who have come through here the past few weeks? I cannot count them all! It is sheep which I watch, not people!" The shepherd was on his feet clearly as disgusted with Elias as Elias was with him. He did not know why, but he certainly was not going to give Elias any details as to the young couple who had recently left his fire. "Get away from my sheep," he stated firmly raising his shepherds' hook in the direction of the man invading his space.

Elias was clearly unhappy but marched away at any rate. The shepherd watched as he took the trek which would lead him straight into the city of Jerusalem. Confident he had given the couple good advice, he asked Jehovah, if He was still up there, for their safety as they traveled and protection from the man who so desperately sought them.

The shepherd's directions had been simple, and Joseph had followed them exactly. The journey took them within view of the city walls but not inside them. As they walked carefully around the city of Jerusalem, Joseph silently thanked Jehovah for the guidance of the old shepherd. Smells of strong incense, drunken noise, loud music, and laughter came pouring over the walls, proving the man was correct in his account of what was taking place inside the city.

"Jerusalem is not supposed to be like this," Mary spoke sadly from the animal's back. "It is supposed to be a holy place."

142

"It is," Joseph agreed with her, "however it seems as if the people currently inside those walls are not aware of the sanctity of the city. Or perhaps they do not care. Praise be to Jehovah that He saw fit to keep us from among them."

Mary closed her eyes as another pain ripped through her side. They were past Jerusalem, so Bethlehem could not be far away. She could hold on a bit longer. No need to alarm Joseph yet. Her back was aching and her stomach continued to clench and release, more often than before. She knew this as the early signs of labor.

The sun had begun to dip low in the sky before she knew she could wait no longer to say something. Her pains were coming closer and closer with each passing mile.

"Joseph, how long before we will be in Bethlehem?" Mary asked. She tried to keep the pain from her voice, but he caught the tone and it was not a soothing one. Looking around to see his wife bent forward over the donkey's back sent alarm coursing through his body.

"We are close, Mary. Hold on!" he answered her as he began to trot with the animal. He could see the city gates ahead and knew he could waste no time in finding her shelter. However, what he saw once he reached those gates struck fear in his very soul. Like Jerusalem, Bethlehem was overflowing with travelers. Never had so many people been in the small city at once. The fact that night was upon them meant the streets were beginning to clear, but the people he saw settling in the alley ways and under tents set up along those streets was a sure sign the inns were full.

"Joseph!" Mary called to him. He could sense her alarm before he looked to her. Reaching to touch her knee from her place on the donkey to try and calm

143

her, he felt her water soaked tunic. Her water had broken. "The baby will be here soon, Joseph!" she cried softly.

Joseph loosely tethered the animal to a nearby post. "Stay here, Mary. I will find you shelter!"

She managed a small laugh despite the fear running through her body. "Where else would I go, husband?" she asked as a pain ripped through her side causing her to double over. "Joseph, please hurry!" She could not stop the tear which slid down her cheek.

Joseph ran to the nearest inn which was still in clear view of his wife. Quickly knocking on the door, he begged for shelter. The innkeeper barely cracked the seal while yelling to Joseph they were full and had no room.

"Please! I beg of you. Anything!" he called quickly running from door to door in the small town. Again and again he was met with the nodding of heads and sorrowful answers, some more kind than others. There was just no room. All of the inns were full! No longer able to see Mary, he fought to keep his composure. What were they going to do? Where else was there to go? Joseph stood desperately looking to and fro at the overflowing buildings around him. He had failed. Mary was going to give birth to the Son of God in the overcrowded streets of Bethlehem. Kneeling in the middle of the street, he turned in the only direction he knew left to go. Up.

"Please, Lord!" he begged urgently from his knees, there in the middle of the road. "Please give us shelter. Show me what to do! We need you! Your Son needs you!"

"Joseph!" a voice cheerfully hailed him from across the way. "Joseph, you have returned to us!" Joseph searched the crowd frantically to find the voice calling his name. His grin stretched from ear to ear as

144

he saw the familiar face running toward him. It was the very man he had told Mary about only a few hours ago! His prayer had been answered!

"Thank you Father!" he prayed before he had even spoken to his friend. "Avaraham, do you have shelter?" he asked immediately as he grasped the broad man's shoulders.

"Are you well Joseph?" he asked shaking his head in confusion, "Why are you on your knees in the middle of the street?"

"Do you have shelter, Avaraham?" Joseph asked again, desperation edging his voice.

"I am sorry, Joseph, my inn is full, but how is your father," he inquired joyfully, crossing his arms as though they had all night to catch up.

"Father is well, Avaraham, but I need shelter. My wife is expecting and about to give birth at any moment. Please, is there nothing you can spare?" Joseph pleaded with his friend.

Avaraham looked at the young man and finally realized the urgency in his voice. A thought occurred to him, though he was embarrassed to voice it; yet, he felt he had to offer something. "Come with me, Joseph. I have no room, and I am ashamed to offer such, but you are welcome to our stable. It is not much, but it will be warm, it is clean as far as stables go, and it will get you and your wife off the street."

"We will take it!" Joseph could not believe all he could provide for Mary was a stable, but at the moment, he could not refuse it. Running as quickly as he could back to his wife, he found she had slid from the back of the donkey and stood grasping the animal's mane to keep herself on her feet.

"Mary, I am here. I have found shelter for you," he exclaimed as he ran to her side. Without time for her to hesitate, he swept her feet from under her

145

taking her securely in his arms. She did not speak, but wrapped her arms tightly around his neck. Her breathing was labored and he knew the baby was coming.

Quickly he found Avaraham who led them to the stable. "Joseph I am sorry I have nothing better to offer you. My wife and I have given up our own room to travelers this night. This census…" his voice trailed off as Joseph gently laid his wife on mounds of hay.

"Joseph, do not leave me!" Mary begged him, clenching his tunic in her fist.

"I promise, I will not leave your side," he assured her, brushing wet hair from her face. She was covered with sweat and her pains were very close. He could not believe the strength of the woman he held in his arms.

Avaraham's face was ashen as he realized the intensity of the situation. Joseph was not exaggerating. That baby was coming. Now! He quickly hung his lantern on a post near them, then began to back his way out of the stable nervously.

"I will see if I can locate my wife to assist you," he spoke quickly as he left "she has gone to a neighboring inn to see if she could trade supplies…I am not sure in which direction she has gone…"

Mary interrupted him with a loud groan as another pain hit. Her face was pale and Joseph knew there was no time.

"Thank you, Avaraham," he said with a nod, politely dismissing the man, who continued to back away from their presence. As soon as the stable door closed, Joseph looked to Mary. Sweat continued to bead from her brow which tightly puckered as the pains racked her body. "What do I do?" he asked her absolutely. He could do this. With the strength granted from God above, he could deliver His child.

Mary gave the current pain she was enduring time to pass before speaking to him through clenched teeth. "Scraps of cloth," she managed, "and something to cut...the cord once... He has come." Another pain took the breath completely from her lungs. Joseph was not sure how the donkey had arrived in the stable. The loyal beast must have pulled himself loose and followed them there, but there he was right outside the stable door. Joseph hurriedly pulled the cloth from the animal's back and began to rip it into long pieces. He then took the knife from his satchel and wiped it clean as best he could.

"Joseph," Mary cried, even more urgently than before, "it is time!" She drew her knees close about her body as Joseph respectfully lifted her tunic.

With the only audience being their donkey, a few goats, a couple of sheep and a cow, the Son of God swiftly made His entrance into the world. The most precious cry Mary had ever heard met her ears just as Joseph cut the cord that attached the baby to His mother. Tears were streaming down his face as he dipped the scraps of cloth in water. He wiped the baby clean before gently wrapping Him ever so carefully in the veil he had presented to His mother only a few months before. Gazing at the child, the wonder of the moment rushed over him as he felt the reality of holding God the Son in his meager hands.

"He is beautiful," Joseph whispered laying the child in Mary's arms. Her own tears streamed down her face as she accepted the tiny baby and immediately offered Him nourishment from her breast. Joseph pulled Mary's tunic over her legs and covered her with the one blanket they had left intact. He then settled himself beside her, kissing her gently on the head. Neither of them spoke, each realizing the miracle which had just taken place. The stable was filled with light from the stars beaming overhead. Moments passed as they gazed on the tiny being now feeding from His mother.

Joseph was the one to break the silence. "Are you well, Mary?" he asked his wife, taking his eyes from the infant only to look into her face.

"I am well, Joseph," she smiled back at him, her eyes heavy with exhaustion yet bright with the wonder of all she had accomplished.

"You are no doubt the most amazing woman I have ever met," he grinned to her. His grin faded with his next statement. Looking around them at the dusty rafters and hay covered floor, his face flamed with embarrassment. "I am so very sorry I could not provide better for you," then looking back to the baby held in his wife's arms, "and better for Him."

"You found shelter for us, Joseph, in a town where there was none to be had."

"God provided for us," Joseph acknowledged, "as He always does." Reaching to touch the baby's tiny hand, he laughed out loud as tiny fingers encircled his larger one.

Mary ran her finger along the face of her newborn son. She looked into the tiny eyes which had beheld heaven only a few months before. She had done it. She had given birth to the Son of God, and she had not had to do it alone. Closing her eyes in peaceful prayer, she again thanked Jehovah for the man beside her.

Joseph broke the silence quoting scripture she had often recited to herself in days most recent. "*For unto us a child is born, unto us a son is given: and the government shall be upon his shoulder: and his name shall be called Wonderful, Counsellor, The mighty God, The everlasting Father, The Prince of Peace.*"

The look Mary gave her husband stopped him. "What is it?" he questioned her. "Are you in pain?" His voice held worry and fear.

"Joseph, how do we raise Him?" she replied slowly, voicing a question of her own. "Will He need us as a normal child needs his parents? How can we teach Him anything? He is **God** in human flesh," she seemed to suddenly remember looking back at the child.

"God the Father has brought us this far," her husband answered with a certainty he was not sure he possessed, "He will not leave us now. He will show us how to properly care for His son." Joseph knew part of being the husband God intended him to be included encouraging and supporting his wife. He could not let her know those same questions often radiated throughout his mind.

At that moment, a short portly woman rushed into the stable splashing a basin full of water in every direction. They could hear her before they saw her as she continued to speak upon her entry, never looking toward the couple whom she was speaking to.

"Have you seen that star?" she exclaimed still looking behind her outside the doors as she walked. "I have never seen a star so bright! And right over this very stable! What in the world do you think that could be about?" The woman continued to rattle on as she walked not careful as to where she was going. "I am so sorry we have nothing better to offer you fine folks, but I am here now and I have birthed many a baby, once even two at a time! Don't you worry about a thing! We'll have you all fixed up…ah!" she gasped as she finally looked in the direction she was headed and took in the scene before her.

She stopped dead in her tracks, her water basin almost emptying itself on her feet. She stood completely still and quiet for a moment before slowly approaching, looking first at Mary, then Joseph, and then the baby. The look on her face was quite quizzical. At first it was in surprise of missing the excitement of the birth and then in uncertainty as to what it was exactly that she was beholding. Something was very different about this small family. And the child. Something about that baby. Pulling her eyes from the scene before her, she sat the basin at her feet then turned to walk, as if on glass, to the only window which faced north from the stable. Pushing the window open, she stretched her short neck so that she could clearly view the star still beaming brilliantly above them.

Drawing back, yet leaving the window open wide, she again approached the family as gently as she had left and sank slowly to her knees. Her voice quivered when she attempted to speak. "There's something far different about this night. And there's something different about this baby," she managed, her voice thick. "Who exactly are you folks?" she asked with reverence.

"I am Joseph," he answered the woman before him quietly. "And this is my wife Mary, from Nazareth. This child," Joseph answered slowly, his eyes again on the now sleeping infant, "is the Son of God."

The old shepherd pulled his blanket tighter about his chin. The chill in the air tonight was heavy, and the old man was struggling to keep himself warm. His fire had reduced to smolders and reluctantly he rose to stoke it, hoping to bring new life to the flames once again. He found his mind wandering to the couple who had crossed his pasture earlier in the day. What about them was so different? Why could he not get them from his mind? He had seen many pass his way as of late, yet none had haunted his memory as these two continued to.

Perhaps it was the fact that she was so expectant. He hoped they had made it to their destination before the babe was born. Maybe it was that she would have been only a little younger than what his own daughter would have been had she still been with them. Yes, she would probably have had children by now had it not been for the sickness that had destroyed her body and taken her last breath.

The old man shook his head to dispel the images of his daughter in her final days. Nothing could be done about it then and nothing could be done about it now. The flames began to dance again as he looked across the pasture. The animals had quieted for the night, bedding down in their usual places. It was a beautiful, clear night. At least the weather had been pleasurable for their journey.

Then there was that stranger who tracked them. What business could he have where they were concerned? Though the shepherd knew nothing about them, he felt they were honest, God-fearing people. The young lady especially had been too kind to be anything else. Perhaps he should've sent the strange inquisitor another direction all together instead of allowing him to continue toward Jerusalem. Nonetheless, he had surely gotten himself lost in the crowd, allowing the couple to gain time and miles ahead of him.

With another quick check of the animals, and a deep breath, the old shepherd settled himself again against a knoll blocking the gentle breeze that stirred. He could see fires continuing to burn across the hills where his fellow shepherds settled to watch their flocks throughout the night. They were scattered about to be able to view the animals well, but not so far that they were unable to aid one another quickly if the need arose. It had been a while since they had been forced to defend their flocks, which meant that they must constantly be on their guard. It seemed as soon as one let his guard down, a lion or bear would find its way into their midst creating havoc among their flocks.

Leaning his back against his pillow of grass and earth, he thought again of the young woman. His mind had just began to wander when he noticed his sheep growing restless. Raising to get a better view, he noticed other shepherds stirring as well. Staff in hand, he walked closer to the crest of the hill where he sat, trying to see what exactly was disturbing the flock. He looked to his left, to the shepherd closest to him, to find him pointing his staff at something behind him in the distance. Looking first over his shoulder, and then turning his body completely, he wiped his tired eyes to get a better view at what he believed he was seeing.

It began as a shimmer in the clear night sky but slowly began to grow brighter. It took him a moment to figure out that it was indeed a star, but a star like none he had ever seen in the fifty plus years he had attended sheep.

"Have you ever seen anything like it?" one of the younger shepherds questioned as he came to the old shepherd's side.

"No. I cannot say that I have," he answered him honestly as he continued to take in the beautiful orb.

The younger shepherd slapped the old man on the shoulder. "Just proof there's still a God in heaven, I'd say," he smiled as he turned to return to his station, clearly impressed, but now over the spectacular sight.

The next instant, however, sent them both quivering to their knees. Just as the old shepherd turned to return to his knoll, the sky above them seemed to come alive in the darkness. The light was amazing at first, then dimmed ever so slightly, allowing them to remove their hands which had instinctively covered their blinded eyes. The being which stood before them high in the night sky was no man, but most definitely an angel sent by God himself. Shepherds across the hill were on their knees, heads bowed as low to the ground as possible, none of them knowing whether to flee in fear or to bow in worship.

"Fear not: for, behold, I bring you good tidings of great joy, which shall be to all people," the angel spoke to them in a voice clear and strong. *"For unto you is born this day in the city of David a Saviour, which is Christ the Lord. And this shall be a sign unto you; Ye shall find the babe wrapped in swaddling clothes, lying in a manger."*

The shepherds rose slowly to their feet as if the angel himself had instructed them to do so, watching in awe as the sky was suddenly filled with a multitude of heavenly hosts. Songs and praises filled the air as the angels began to praise God, saying *"Glory to God in the highest, and on earth, peace, good will toward men!"*

The shepherds stood in awe beholding the magnificent sight taking place before them, before they, too, began to raise their staffs in praise to Jehovah. Then as quickly as the host of angels appeared, they were gone, leaving the shepherds alone in the quiet night. Looking to one another, they almost questioned the vision they had just beheld.

"If you had not seen this along with me, I would have thought myself either crazy or dreaming," the old shepherd admitted.

"I did see it. And I believe it!" the younger man responded enthusiastically. "Were we not just speaking of that star yonder?" He pointed eagerly to the beacon continuing to brighten the sky. "I told you our Creator is still present! Right over that knoll, we shall be in His presence! Come, let us go to Bethlehem to see this thing which has come to pass which the Lord has made known to us." Though he was encouraging the old shepherd to come along with him, he had already began to depart.

"But what of our sheep?" another called as he ran toward them. "Do we just leave them unattended?"

The older man grinned as realization dawned. "You do as you wish," he smiled while turning to follow the younger shepherd, "you may watch these lambs if you choose, but I am going to see THE Lamb who has come to set us free!" As his old legs gained new life, he ran to catch up to the younger shepherd just a few feet in front of him. He knew exactly who the mother would be that he would witness attending the newborn King.

Chapter 17

Elias stumbled through the darkness. He had finally made his way through the town of Jerusalem, but night was heavy upon him and he knew there was no way he would find Mary and Joseph at this late hour. He had somehow found himself turned around, and had exited the city in the exact location as to which he had entered. He knew he would gain no sympathy from the shepherd he had encountered earlier, but perhaps another would allow him to warm himself by their fire if he could make himself appear humble enough.

Elias laughed at the situation in which he currently found himself. He was thinking of humbling himself! To a shepherd! He who had stood before King Herod's armed guards time and again, relaying information they desperately sought, was now thinking of asking a dirty, filthy, shepherd for aid. "Hilarious," he laughed aloud.

As he continued to laugh at himself, Elias paused noticing a peculiar sight in the heavens. *What is…is that a star?* he thought to himself. Quickly he rounded the corner of the city wall to better see the spectacle which appeared to be hovering over

Bethlehem. In all the palaces he had ever found himself, he had never seen anything quite so spectacular, especially in nature itself. With nothing better to do, and for reasons he could not explain, Elias decided to see where exactly the star was pointing. Pulling his cloak more tightly about his body, he set off toward Bethlehem.

The road was dusty and the night quiet, but the light from the heavens guided his path. What kept pushing him forward he did not know, but something continued to draw him toward the small town. On more than one occasion, he found himself almost racing down the road, eager to find the spot where the star rested.

As he drew near to the city, he slowed his steps and quieted his breathing. The air around him seemed thick with something he could not explain. It reminded him of the way he felt as a boy when his grandmother would allow him to accompany her to the temple. He was never allowed inside, as she was a woman and he a mere child, but the aroma of incense would spill into the courts where they were allowed to wait, carrying with it a sense of reverence and holiness.

His chest was heavy as he entered the town, the streets littered with people who could not find room in the inns surrounding them. Strangely, most of them seemed to pay the star no heed as they slept, and buildings were obstructing the view of what was anchored right above them. More than once, he started to turn back, thinking himself a fool and fearing what he was about to face, but something kept him pushing forward.

At last, finding himself almost directly under the star, he found it hard to decipher the exact spot over which it stood, yet he continued to round this corner and that attempting to follow where it shone brightest. Finally, he rounded a corner well off the beaten path. At the end of the alley was an inn and behind the inn a stable. As he approached the door way of the structure, he quietly tiptoed so as not to disturb who or what took shelter inside. The presence of God was so imminent; he had to force himself to continue. Slowly, he pulled at the latch and was surprised as the door creaked open. His heart felt as if it would burst as he peeked inside the stable doors, unsure of who or what he was about to see.

Elias was a man, but the sight he beheld humbled him to the stature of a mere boy. Before him was Mary, now holding her tiny baby in her arms. A baby which looked like all others, but was, indeed, so much more. Shepherds knelt around Him, along with others Elias assumed to be the owners of the inn, and the few who were drawn to the sight as he was. Joseph was protectively behind Mary and all were gazing at the child held tenderly in her arms.

Elias took in the animals gathered around them, unusually still and quiet. His eyes continually looked back to the child he had sought, who now lay before him, but something was different. As if suddenly realizing who was in his presence, Joseph jumped, causing the shepherds around him to leap to their feet. In but a matter of seconds, Elias found himself facing Joseph and a small army of now not-so-humble looking shepherds, whom he knew would do whatever was needed to protect the child whom they were here to worship.

"What is your purpose here, Elias? Why have you followed us?" Joseph asked, his tone smooth yet firm.

"This man was enquiring as to the direction you had gone earlier today," the older shepherd spoke up. "I gave him no information."

"Joseph. Mary," Elias pleaded straining his neck to see the woman blocked from view. "I mean you no harm. It is true I have followed you with malice in my heart. I confess I intended to take the child from you and turn Him over to Herod's soldiers. But now…now, something has changed. Something is different because I have seen Him."

"You had to see the child to believe in God, Elias?" Mary questioned him, still blocked from his view. Joseph seemed to relax somewhat in his stance but was still firmly planted in front of Elias, clearly not trusting the man. The men behind him were at full attention looking more like Roman soldiers in rags than peaceful shepherds.

"I…I, am not sure, Mary, exactly what I believe anymore," Elias stammered. "Yet I cannot deny I have found something far different than that which I expected to find." He seemed to finally find his voice. "May I see the child?" he asked Joseph, clearly fearful that he would be denied the opportunity.

Joseph looked behind him to where his wife was seated, the child held protectively in her arms.

"He has come to provide forgiveness to everyone, Joseph," she spoke gently to her husband.

Elias could tell Joseph was still unsure as to whether he should allow him what he requested, but he slowly began to step aside after a moment's consideration. At his nod of approval, the shepherds parted, and Moses and the Red Sea came to Elias' mind. Slowly, Elias stepped forward, never taking his eyes from the infant. As he approached the mother and child, he slowly sank to his knees at Mary's feet.

Realization dawned upon him as clear as the breaking of the morning sun. This child was not an illegitimate child which Mary had concocted a story about to cover her shame. He was not just a story which some would accept as true and others would not. This child was not a myth; this child was indeed the Son of God.

A sob suddenly broke in Elias' throat as he covered his face with his hands. "Can you ever forgive me for all the wrongs I had planned to commit against you?" he asked of Mary. "Will He forgive me for the wrongs I have daily committed against Him?" His response was a warm smile from the woman in front of him.

Joseph approached him, tenderly laying his hand on the broken man's shoulder. Though he was trying to accept the situation for what it was, he was still leery that perhaps this was just another of Elias' schemes to get close to Mary and the baby. Yet, he felt a peace he could not explain, and he would do his best to aid Elias in his search for true forgiveness.

"We have all done wrong in the sight of God, Elias," he spoke, "yet, God has sent His Son to save our world. You are witness to this miracle this night. You did not come here by accident. It is not too late for you to turn from your wicked ways and to accept this child for who He is. The Son of God Most High."

A moment passed before Elias was able to gather his emotions and wipe the tears from his eyes. "I do accept Him, and I vow to do Him no harm. He nor any of you."

With joyful praise, the shepherds turned and headed back into their fields. Mary and Joseph listened as they repeated the angels' songs as they walked and knew their silent night would not be very silent for long. The shepherds would tell everyone they encountered all that they had seen and heard. Just as they should.

Elias continued on his knees in front of the baby, for what seemed like ages to Mary, who allowed him to weep and worship as long as he desired. Finally, he raised his bowed head and stood to his feet, tired and broken, but for the first time in his life he was complete.

"How did you find us, Elias?" Joseph asked breaking the silence. "Did the angels speak to you as they did to the shepherds?"

Elias shook his head no before answering. "It was the star overhead which caught my attention and peaked my interest. I know not why I was so determined to find where it rested."

"It was God, Elias," Mary smiled as she tenderly laid the child in the hay filled manger. "He brought you here to witness this for a reason."

"I know not what all will become of this, what all He has planned for my life now that I serve Him in place of man, but the first thing I will do is return to Nazareth to make things right with Shira," he paused briefly before he continued, "and I know your family accepted your story Mary, but I will also tell them all I have witnessed this night. You were indeed telling the truth, word for word."

"Thank you, Elias," Mary spoke, a small smile again lighting her features, though her eyes were heavy and a yawn escaped her upturned lips. Joseph adjusted blankets the innkeeper had provided for her and she finally laid her head comfortably on her bed of straw. Joseph made sure both she and the baby were settled before leaning against a bale of hay himself, still within close proximity of Mary and the baby. Elias settled himself near the door of the stable gaining permission from Joseph to pass the night with them and had the best night's sleep he had ever been afforded.

The first traces of light were beginning to break through the darkness when Joseph stirred again. When had he fallen asleep? With a jolt he sat upright, quickly assessing his surroundings. Mary was still sleeping soundly, though her position had changed. Elias was nowhere to be seen, and Joseph was not sure if he was gone or had just excused himself. The baby...the baby! On his hands and knees Joseph crawled hastily to the manger, fear tearing his heart into pieces. Had Elias deceived them and taken the child as they slept?

Tears of relief and exhaustion filled his eyes as he peered into the manger and saw a tiny pair of eyes staring back out at him. A heavy breath escaped him as he realized the child was safe. Reaching into the manger, he took the baby in his arms and brought Him close to his chest. "How will I ever be the parent You deserve?" he whispered to the infant alone. "And how does one parent the Son of God? Whatever will I be able to teach You that You do not already know?" He did not expect an answer, though he knew if God chose, He could deliver one, even from the mouth of a newborn infant. As if the baby understood, one tiny hand stretched out from the folds of cloth surrounding him. Joseph accepted the sign and his heart lightened.

"Yes, I suppose You will teach me more than I shall teach You," he grinned. "Just a few short months ago, You walked among the angels in heaven, and now You have chosen to walk the dusty streets of Israel. Thank You for choosing me to be Your earthly guide." Joseph felt pressure on his shoulder and turned to see his wife's lovely face resting there.

"Good morning, husband," she grinned, her voice still scratchy with sleep. Elias chose that moment to appear, carrying a basin full of fresh water and feeling as if he were intruding on a very special moment. Unlike before, when he would have captured the moment to make another feel uncomfortable, he felt uncomfortable himself for interrupting the couple. He was about to back away when Joseph spotted him.

"I wondered what had become of you," the man smiled in greeting, motioning him forward with a jerk of his head. He realized Elias' discomfort at interrupting them and did not wish for him to leave because of it.

"I had gone for fresh water from the well," he began slowly as he came farther into the dwelling, "I knew you would be thirsty," he directed to Mary. "On my way back the innkeeper's wife spotted me and said she would send a morning meal very soon." Joseph nodded in thanks and handed the baby to His mother for His morning feeding.

Elias sat the basin on the windowsill of the stable and stood watching as the sun began to ease across the horizon, causing rays of light to cut through the dimness of the early morning. He still could not understand how the God Who made all of this, Who controlled the wind and the rain, the changing of the seasons, Who could turn the darkness into light would care so much about him and souls even darker than his had been. In fact, God had cared so much that He had sent His Son from the gates of Heaven to a world which would ultimately reject and despise Him all in an attempt to save these sinners from themselves.

He knew the prophecies. His grandmother had taught them to him years and years ago, and though he had rejected them, he had never forgotten them. He had tried, choosing to ignore them until now, but they had always been there, playing in the back of his mind.

Now they came flooding back as clear as if she had only spoken them yesterday.

Joseph approached him quietly, placing his hands on his shoulder. "It is all a bit overwhelming, is it not?" he spoke sincerely. Elias turned to look at the man he had despised so recently, but now whom he held a deep and passionate respect for. Never removing his hands from the windowsill, he spoke to the outside world.

"I still cannot comprehend a love like this," he admitted. "A love so deep for a man as cruel as I."

"It is not about how cruel one is or one is not, Elias. It is about accepting that we are all sinners, and that none of us are worthy to reach Heaven. You are no more of a sinner than myself, or even Mary, we all fall short. That is why He has come to redeem us all." Joseph explained.

"But at what cost, Joseph?" Elias turned to him whispering so that Mary would not hear. "You know what will become of the child! Surely you were taught the same prophecies as I. He will be rejected, and," looking to Mary, who sat feeding and cooing at her son, Elias lowered his voice yet another notch, "and killed!" he whispered with emphasis. "He was born to die," he finished sadly.

"Not today, Elias." Joseph smiled to his friend. "We all shall die, yet those who believe will be together again once this child's purpose is fulfilled. The reason for His coming, is to save His people from their sins–sins which we all commit, sins that blacken all our souls, yet souls that will be made clean with the blood of this child. He will die, Elias, but not today." Joseph turned to his wife and son, giving her a smile of assurance that the conversation was not a heated one. "I will care for Him and for His mother until my dying day, even if I must die in order to protect them. God in

163

Heaven only knows why I was chosen for this task, but I have accepted it, and I will do my best to keep them both safe for as long as I live."

"Will you return to Nazareth?" Elias asked.

Joseph looked to the infant still feeding in His mother's arms. "I believe we will stay here in Bethlehem for a yet a little while, at least until after the circumcision of the child. That will give Mary some much needed rest. The innkeeper has promised us the next available room, and he has some work he will allow me to trade for the cost of it. After that, I will pray for guidance and do my best to follow the will of God where His child is concerned."

Elias held his hand out to Joseph, expecting a hand shake before he departed. He was surprised when the man pulled him into an embrace. "Take care my new-found friend," he spoke sincerely. Elias pulled away without a word but Joseph saw the tears welling in the man's eyes. Picking up his pack, he nodded goodbye to Mary, bowed low before the baby, then turned and headed for home.

Chapter 18

The next few days passed quickly for the new family. A room opened up inside the inn, and they were quickly settled in for what the innkeeper, Avaraham, promised was theirs for an "unprecedented amount" of time. "It is yours for as long as you wish," he assured them. "I have much work which needs to be done, and your presence here is a blessing to my weary soul in more ways than one," he added with a huge smile. Avaraham's wife doted on the tiny baby and His mother and provided Mary with welcome advice on tending to a newborn, much as her mother back home would have done Mary was sure.

Eight days were soon upon them, and the time for the circumcision of the child had come. Mary assisted in the preparation of the meal which would follow the ceremony. The task was performed, and the baby called Jesus, per the angel Gabriel's clear instruction. The feast was a bountiful one shared by Joseph and Mary with the innkeeper, his wife, and the few still boarding in the small house.

Thirty more days passed quickly and the young couple had grown accustomed to their life in Bethlehem. Joseph, now comfortable holding the child, talked easily with Avaraham as the women cleared the evening meal. They were discussing preparations for their trip the following day in which the couple would travel to Jerusalem to present their child to the Lord.

"Is that really necessary?" the innkeeper's wife questioned, "I mean, the child *is* the Lord, yet, you will present Him to…Himself?" she stumbled over her own words.

Mary laughed at the quizzical expression which crossed the older lady's features. "It is written in the law that every male that openeth the womb shall be called holy to the Lord," Mary explained to her. "And I must offer a sacrifice as well."

"We will uphold the law as best we can," Joseph added to clear any confusion still lingering. "We must not give anyone cause to accuse Him of not obeying the law fully."

"We cannot thank you enough for the hospitality you have afforded us," Mary spoke genuinely. "You have gone above what anyone could have ever asked."

"It is nothing compared to the blessing which has been bestowed upon us by having you under our roof–not to mention this precious child who is indeed Lord of all," the innkeeper's wife spoke as she smiled and beckoned Joseph to hand the baby over.

"You sound as if you will be leaving us soon?" Avaraham directed his statement, which was more a question, to Joseph.

"We will return here tomorrow after the sacrifice is made, but we do not wish to overstay our welcome," he answered honestly. "With the child so small, however, we do not wish to make the four day journey back to Nazareth just yet."

"You are still welcome for as long as you desire to stay," the innkeeper reassured him. "I could not ask for a finer nor more helpful guest." He stood, clapping Joseph loudly on the shoulder. "I believe I shall turn in. Woman!" he exclaimed playfully to his wife. "Let us retire!" He spoke enthusiastically, causing her face to flame as she giggled. Reluctantly she handed the baby over to his mother, kissed him gently on the forehead, bid them goodnight, and entered the back room with her husband.

Mary began rocking her son and humming a soft lullaby. Once sleep had claimed Him, she rose and bid Joseph to accompany her to the room they called their own. Laying the baby upon a straw mat separate from the one they shared, she bundled him tightly and kissed him goodnight. She then turned to her husband who stood taking in the scene before him with love and admiration.

"Husband," she spoke softly, standing directly in front of him. Swallowing hard and visibly struggling, she continued, her eyes fixed on Joseph's broad chest instead of looking into his face. "You have been overly patient with me throughout the circumstances we have endured." Mary's face flamed as she spoke the words which weighed heavily upon her heart. Her eyes darted to his face for a moment before she continued. "The baby has been safely delivered, and the days of my purification have ended." Immediately, Joseph knew exactly to what she was referring.

Quickly he held up his hand to stop her. He knew she struggled with what she was trying to say. He also admired her concern that all her duties as a wife had yet to be fulfilled. It made him love her even more that she so regarded his well-being. Most women would have continued to use all they had been through

167

as an excuse to keep to themselves for as long as possible, but his Mary was not most women. She had recognized the fact that he had been in her presence day in and day out, that he had lain close beside her at night, he had shared in her most intimate of moments when delivering her child, yet he had not yet claimed his rights as her husband. Her days of purification were barely over, and she was willingly attempting to give herself to him, no matter how uncomfortable it was for her to do so.

"I would be lying to say I do not desire my wife," Joseph admitted honestly, his hand still in mid-air, "but I do not wish for you to be uncomfortable, Mary. I am willing to give you as much time as you need," he finished sincerely. Mary smiled and looked up at him, loving him even more for his patience and understanding.

Slowly she raised her hand to meet his hovering in the air between them, gently entwining her fingers with his. She then reached to his side, and took his other hand. Moving closer to him, she angled her face until her lips were right below his. His breathing was labored at her closeness, and looking down at her, he gently lowered his lips to touch hers for the first time. He had kissed her hand, her palm, and even her cheek, but never had he allowed himself to kiss her lips. The kiss was gentle yet passionate, and Mary's knees grew weak just as Joseph reached to lift her lovingly into his arms and carry her to the cot they shared, now completely, as man and wife.

The next morning they were up early, each eager to begin their journey to Jerusalem. Their plan was to reach the holy city early enough to offer their sacrifice and still be able to return to Bethlehem before nightfall. It would be a rushed journey but with most of the crowd from the census now dispersed to their own cities, the roads would be good for traveling. Joseph packed the few provisions he felt they would need to get them through their day and they were on their way.

The road to Jerusalem from Bethlehem was well traveled, and just as Joseph had predicted, uncrowded. Mary enjoyed walking what was left of the soreness of childbirth from her limbs. Joseph and the innkeeper had fashioned a sling where she was able to carry the baby, yet have her arms free. It felt wonderful to stretch her legs in the early morning sun. The couple laughed and talked as they walked, reflecting over all the events which had transpired since they had become husband and wife. No other couple they could think of had experienced quite the beginning as they had.

Joseph relayed stories his father had told him of their ancestors, and they discussed facts in depth, ranging from the beginning of creation, to the destruction of the world by the flood in Noah's days.

"Can you imagine looking out of a floating vessel such as the ark and finding nothing but water as far as your eye could see?" Joseph asked her with a gleam in his eye.

"You almost look as if you would like to experience it," Mary smiled to him.

Joseph slightly shook his head. "No," he answered honestly. "The sea has never been in my blood like that of a fisherman, though I am a bit curious as to what lies beyond the shoreline. However, I would not wish to be at the sea for as long as Noah was forced to."

"Do you wonder," Mary asked, her own eyes searching the vast land lying in front of them, "why God chose to destroy the world once by flood before sending His son to redeem the lost?" Out of habit she braced the baby hanging from the sling around her neck with her arms.

"I confess the thought has crossed my mind," he admitted. "I wonder what our son may have to face one day in order to carry out His plan."

The thought brought pain to Mary's heart. What would their child have to go through once the purpose for His coming had ensued?

They continued their walk in comfortable silence, each of their minds reflecting on thoughts of the recent past. Neither of them spoke again until the city gates came into view. The spire atop the temple cut through the bright blue sky, tall and proud as it reached to pay honor and tribute to the One for whom it was intended. The purpose of their journey became clear to each of them, and again their hearts were filled with gratitude and thankfulness as they approached the holy city.

Joseph used a portion of the money they had left to purchase a pair of turtledoves to offer as sacrifice, thanking God as he did so for His provision and that the innkeeper had been allowing him to work for their room and board. He would still have the five shekels required to pay the redemption price for his son. At least they still had food and shelter provided for them if they had nothing else at the moment. Mary watched her husband as he handed over what little money they had left, knowing in her heart that God had provided for them thus far, and as long as they continued to do His will, He would not let them down now.

As they approached the outer courtyard, Mary examined her husband's face, reaching up to wipe dust from their journey from his brow. She then dusted off her own garments, removed the sling from her neck, tying it securely about her waist, and once again used the veil Joseph had given her to wipe her face and that of her son.

"Are you ready, Mary?" Joseph asked her.

"I am ready," she assured him as they entered the temple, "but also a bit nervous," she laughed quietly.

They had barely gotten inside before they heard the cry. "It is He!" the voice pronounced as they began to approach the altar for their sacrifice. Looking around themselves to see who was being hailed, they were surprised to see an elderly man headed in their direction. "He is here!" the old man laughed, approaching them with his arms extended toward the baby. Mary cradled her son close, not sure if she should be afraid or delighted at the scene the old man was causing. Joseph stepped even closer to his wife and son, encircling her waist with one arm, while holding fast to the doves in the other.

"The Holy Ghost promised me that I would not see death before I had seen the Lord's Christ, and now He is before me!" he approached quickly but reverently, his arms reaching for her son. Mary felt an unexplainable peace, as she laid her infant son into the waiting arms of the old man.

His eyes were bright and alive as he looked into the face of the tiny baby he so carefully embraced. "He is Jesus. Conceived by the Holy Spirit, and sent to be the Redeemer of mankind," Joseph affirmed, staying close, but completely trusting the stranger before him.

171

"*Blessed be to Jehovah!*" he cried as he pulled the baby tight against his chest. Joseph reached to steady the man as he trembled and spoke to the child. "*Lord,*" he began, "*now lettest thou thy servant depart in peace, according to thy word: For mine eyes have seen thy salvation, which thou has prepared before the face of all people; a light to lighten the Gentiles, and the glory of thy people Israel.*"

Mary looked to her husband who was continuing to support the old man. Shaking her head and mouthing the words, so as not to interrupt his worship, she asked Joseph if he knew the stranger who knew so much about their son. At his confirmation that he did not, the couple smiled to one another, knowing it was in fact God's timing and miraculous work that had brought them all to this specific place at this specific time.

After a moment, the old man, Simeon by name, handed Jesus back into the waiting arms of His mother. Laying his withered hand upon her cheek, his eyes again filled with tears.

"Bless you, my child," his tired voice cracked through tears, "*Behold this child is set for the fall and rising again of many in Israel; and for a sign which shall be spoken against:*" he looked to the baby before looking deep into Mary's eyes. "*Yea, a sword shall pierce through thy own soul also, that the thoughts of many hearts may be revealed.*"

Mary had been leaning close to the old man, listening intently to his words, but began to draw back slowly as his meaning dawned. Fear pierced her heart. She knew the prophecies, but she had not allowed herself to think on them. Not sure what to say or do, she cleared her throat and smiled sweetly into the kind face of the old man. A simple nod was the best she could muster before Joseph took her elbow and began leading her, once again, toward the altar.

They did not get far before they were stopped once more, this time by a widow woman who fell immediately at Mary's feet. "The Lord is come!" she cried. "I have departed not from the temple, but served God with fastings and prayers night and day praying that I would see the Savior pass my way! Lo, He has come! He is here!" she cried. Mary stood still as the woman continued to thank the Lord for His coming and for the redemption which would now come to their people and their land. She did not take Jesus from His mother, but finally rose and patted the blankets surrounding him with reverence and appreciation over what she was beholding. Mary allowed her to cry over and praise her son, knowing that God had allowed Anna, also, to have her heart's desire by seeing the Savior in the flesh.

Many moments had passed before they were once again able to make an attempt and finally reach the examiners. Jesus was handed over to a priest where He would be examined closely for fault or blemish. The priest examined him carefully from the top of his smooth brow to the bottom of his tiny feet, held still as each of his toes were counted and inspected.

"I find no fault in Him," the priest exclaimed clear and loud as he held the young child high. Mary smiled to herself, knowing no fault would ever be found in her son. Her heart soared with pride as any mother's would as she witnessed the priest raise her son toward heaven and declare him acceptable. Jesus was handed back to His mother and the family made their way to the court of women where Mary's purification ceremony would be completed.

At last their visit concluded and they began their journey back to Bethlehem. Mary did not bother placing the baby in the sling just yet, preferring to cradle Him close in her arms. The silence between them was not exactly tense, but Joseph could tell Mary was not at peace. A lot had transpired this day, and he suspected words spoken by the man called Simeon were weighing heavily on his wife's mind. He did not have to wait long to find that his suspicions had been correct.

"Joseph, did you hear the proclamation the man called Simeon made?" Mary asked as they walked. Her pace had slowed, and though Joseph was eager to reach Bethlehem before nightfall, he knew it was his strength she needed at the moment. Slowing to walk beside her, he looked at his wife and saw the fear in her eyes. Finally, she completely stopped, desperately searching her husband's face for answers.

"Joseph, what will we do?" Sudden fear began to crowd into the corners of her very soul as thought after thought began to clutter in her head. "What if Elias sends word to Herod of what he has witnessed? He will come for Him! And if not Herod, others will try to defeat and destroy Him! You heard what the old man said, Joseph. Our son will die to save others. We have to protect him, we must!" Joseph took notice of the way his wife began to tremble before Him. She squeezed the baby tight about her chest and began sobbing into the cloth wrapped about Him.

Allowing her to cry for a moment, he placed his hands on each of her shoulders, then raised her face to look at his.

"Mary, God has given us the unique responsibility of caring for and raising *His* child to the best of our abilities. We will do so through prayer and supplication to God Himself. Yes, His child is in our care while on this earth, and I will love and cherish and protect Him to the best of my physical ability as though He were my own flesh and blood." Pausing for only a moment, he continued slowly, knowing that he had her full attention. "But we must never forget that Jesus is not an ordinary child, nor was He sent to us for an ordinary purpose. God chose you specifically to be the mother of His son, and He would not have entrusted you to this task had He known you would not be able to let Him have control of whatever circumstances may come."

Tears continued to slide along her face as she cradled the baby in her arms, but her stance was calming. Joseph spoke carefully, knowing that she needed to be reminded of these things although it broke his heart to have to be the one to relay them to her. Yet, as her husband, it was his responsibility to be the spiritual leader of their home and to keep Mary focused on the path God would have them tread–even when it was not pleasant.

Mary shook her head as quiet tears left their marks along her face. Burying her head again in the blanket surrounding the baby, Joseph could make out the mumbled words pouring from her mouth.

"I cannot give Him up, Joseph. How will I ever be the mother I am supposed to be, yet be willing to let Him go? To let him die? For other people? Those who do not even know Him or accept Him?"

"Mary you cannot give Him up at this time because God has not asked you to. When the time comes, IF the time comes," he continued quickly, "that you must let go of Jesus, you will be granted the strength to endure it. We may not even live to see the events come to pass that He has planned. In fact, I do not know that I want to, but even so we must never forget His purpose, Mary. We must always trust

Jehovah, regardless of the circumstances surrounding our son. We must trust Him completely to His Father's care."

Mary raised her head and looked to the wise man God had chosen for her. Nodding yes, she sniffed and calmed her frantic heart. She knew Joseph was right, but she still was not sure she could handle what she may have to one day experience. The old man's words continued to echo through her mind. "*A sword will pierce through your own heart also*," she remembered inside her mind.

"*Have faith, Mary*," another voice sounded in her heart, as audible as if Joseph had spoken, though he remained silent beside of her. "*You must trust and have faith*."

Memories of the fear she had faced when she had realized she was pregnant and alone filled her mind. The same God who sent an angel to minister to Joseph and to assure him of her faithfulness to him was the same God whom she would draw comfort from now. He had not left her then, and He would not leave her now or ever. Taking a deep breath, she secured the sling around her neck, once more placing her child inside. Reaching for her hand, Joseph kissed it softly before leading her again along the path to Bethlehem.

Chapter 19

Jesus grew as all other children His age. Mary attempted to comfort Him as teeth began breaking through His tender gums. Often she found herself voicing her thoughts aloud to her tiny son. "My poor, poor baby," she cooed during a crying episode, "could You not have saved Yourself a little of the grief other children experience?" she smiled to Him as she spoke, attempting to quiet His crying. "Was it not enough that You have left Heaven in order to save our people?" Mary continued to attempt comforting Him as he began to gum on the veil laying across her shoulder. Gathering a clean cloth, she dampened it with some water from the basin, then laid Him down, cloth in His hand, to chew on it as long as He desired.

He was a good child, not spoiled or prone to tantrums, but He did experience the same discomforts a normal child would. Mary wasn't sure if she had expected this or not. Perhaps she had subconsciously believed His childhood would be quite different from the others.

Others. Lately that thought had often crossed her mind. Would there be others? Certainly not others like Jesus, conceived by God, but would she and

Joseph ever be blessed with children on their own accord? She looked to the sweet innkeeper's wife, shaping bread dough into short loaves, who had become such a dear friend to her. She and Avaraham had never been blessed with children, and Mary could tell that weighed heavily on the dear woman's heart. Still she had not let it hinder her joyous countenance, and she constantly hummed and sang to herself.

The bread was soon baked and the last meal of the day finished. Mary carried the last of the dishes to the cupboard. It had become their evening ritual. The innkeeper's wife would prepare the meals while Mary fed her young son. Once their meal was complete, Mary would clear the meal and clean up while the older woman laughed and played with the child before finally reciting a story from her youth while rocking Him into a peaceful sleep. It was a routine Mary would surely miss once their time in Bethlehem had reached an end.

Joseph had expressed his desire to return home just that morning. "I feel our time in Bethlehem is coming to an end," he had told Mary before rising for the day. "I know you miss your family and are eager for them to meet our son," he had stated as he held her close, another routine she had come to enjoy. Mary had agreed whole-heartedly although she would certainly miss the new friends she had made. Yet, Jesus was growing quickly and was now old enough to make the journey back to Nazareth. She could not believe nearly two years had passed since they had arrived in Bethlehem. During the morning meal, Joseph had relayed to Avaraham that they would be leaving at the end of the month. Though the kindly innkeeper did not look forward to the young family's departure, both he and his wife understood and reminded them they were always welcome in their inn.

The next three weeks would be filled with preparation for their journey home.

Joseph and Avaraham now joined the women in the main room as soon as Avaraham had finished inspecting Joseph's final task. "I have never seen such fine craftsmanship, Joseph, and I am not saying that lightly," Avaraham grinned to his guest. "You take pride in your work, and you do a fine job," he finished, slapping Joseph squarely on the shoulder.

"You are an easy man to please," Joseph grinned, "and I am not just saying that because of your hospitality," he returned. Their banter was light as Mary took her son into her arms to put Him down for the night. She was just about to enter the room which was now known as theirs when a knock was heard at the outer door.

Avaraham raised to answer the call, assuming it was a poor, weary traveler in search of a room. What he saw once he opened the door, however, was far from poor. Three men dressed in the finest attire he had ever seen stood before him. The men were clearly from another country, and Avaraham bowed low and respectful, sure that he was in the presence of wise and noble men.

"We are sorry to intrude upon you at this late hour," the man dressed in gold and purple began. Sounding as if he hailed from somewhere in the Far East, his accent was deep and his skin almost as dark as the night. If not for the bit of light streaming through the doorway from the lamps shining brightly inside the house and the gold which glistened from his robes, Avaraham was sure he would not have been able to see the man standing before him. "We have been traveling for some time now, in search of the child who has been born King of the Jews."

Joseph rose from his place and went to stand with Avaraham who backed away at the younger man's approach. Joseph was eager to meet these strangers who were seeking his son. Though not unkind, his face was stern as he approached the open doorway.

"We mean Him no harm," another of the men, also elaborately dressed, but not nearly as dark skinned as the other, spoke quickly. "We have followed the star," he pointed to the heavens, "which has led us to this place. We have come to worship Him and to offer Him gifts meant only for the King of Kings." The man held up an alabaster box for Joseph to see. His accent too was heavy, though clear enough to understand, and Joseph was now certain their strange visitors hailed from the Orient.

The oldest of the men had stood quietly behind the others until Mary approached, still with some reservation, to stand behind her husband. Peeking around Joseph's broad shoulders, she held her son firmly against her chest. Upon her approach, the oldest man raised a jeweled hand to cover his mouth in awe of what he was seeing.

"This is the child?" he questioned, stepping forward, though it was more a statement coming from his thin lips. Joseph did not miss the way the man's hand trembled as he worked to contain his emotions. These men were clearly not their enemies. The peace he had come to experience at the strangest moments filled him, and he knew with certainty that God had sent these men to honor His son.

"It is," Joseph acknowledged, as he allowed the men passage into the home. Mary moved further inside and lowered herself into a nearby chair, turning her son on her lap allowing their guests the ability to see the child whom they had been seeking. Jesus stirred and opened His eyes, smiling sleepily to the company before Him. Each of the men had barely made their way inside before falling to their knees in an array of colors. Mary could not believe the fabrics before her eyes. She had never seen such rich hues, even in the palace at Jerusalem.

The men wept and cried, praising God and worshipping her son. Jesus looked from His mother to His visitors, a smile spreading across His adorable rounded face. Mary allowed them time to fulfill their desires of worship and accolade, rejoicing in the miracle that sat before them, the purpose of their journey now complete. At last they rose to their feet in joyful praise. Each of them opened their treasures slowly and in doing so presented a gift to the child. One gold, one frankincense, and the other myrrh.

The hours were stretching long into the night when they began to bid their farewells. Sleep had again claimed young Jesus, who rested His head comfortably against His mother's bosom. Mary liked to imagine that the small sighs of contentment and giggles, which often escaped Him while He was sleeping, were products of the visions of the Heaven He had left behind, returning to His thoughts as He dreamed.

"Sirs," Avaraham began, "Majesties," he spoke again humbly, "I have little to offer, but if you would like shelter this night, I offer room in our meager inn."

Joseph continued speaking once Avaraham had finished. "Allow us to care for your animals. You have traveled long and far and should rest comfortably this night."

"I do not know that I can again decline the opportunity of a bed in place of the earthen floor, and we could not be in better company," the darkest of the men spoke to the others. "What say you, brothers?" he grinned looking to his companions.

"I believe I shall rest easy here this night," the lighter man agreed, "this time under the same roof as the one, true King,"

The oldest man quietly nodded his head in affirmation. Joseph opened his mouth to speak, his curiosity peeking as to where they had previously declined rest, but the innkeeper's wife spoke before him.

"Are you hungry?" she asked quietly. "We have meat and cheese left from our evening meal." She felt somewhat strange offering leftover's to the noble men in her presence, but after all, she had been keeping company with a King for months now, and these men paled in comparison to His majesty.

"I know I speak for us all when I tell you we are still pleasantly filled from an earlier gesture of kindness this day. We shall wait until morning, my lady," the lighter colored man spoke, "but your hospitality is a balm for our weary souls." Again, the question arose in Joseph's mind as to which way the men had come, but as Avaraham began directing them to their chambers, Joseph felt it would be rude to question them this night.

Avaraham showed the three kings to rooms where they could retire and promised to care for their animals straight away. Though humbled to be in the presence of such royalty, he too felt they had nothing on the small King he had come to know and love over the past months. He would never look at mere men in the same way again, despite their rank of nobility.

Rest was peaceful that night, and the morning broke bright and clear. Joseph and Avaraham assisted the men with their animals as they bid farewell to the women and to the child they had so long sought after.

The older man seemed to have more trouble leaving than the others, and his goodbyes were prolonged as once again, he bowed his knee in worship to the Christ Child.

"What say you?" Joseph overheard the dark man whispering. He did not mean to listen in on their conversation, but the man did not seem to be attempting to hide his words, only to speak quietly enough so as not to interrupt their companion in his worship. "I thought our path was set? We will return home through Jerusalem the same way in which we came."

"Yes, that was the plan, but last night," here the other man paused as if he were still working through some event himself. He rubbed his head for a moment, then turned sharply to his companion. "Last night," he paused briefly again but then finished with surety, "last night, I was warned by God in a dream that we should depart another way."

The dark man scoffed quietly. "You were tired! We have been traveling for ages. The miles have gotten to you. 'Twas only a dream! There is no harm in our chosen path home. Besides, the food was good in the palace!" He smiled broadly while patting his round stomach in a defeated attempt to persuade his fair skinned companion to agree with him. He shook his head as he realized his friend would not be easily persuaded.

"I will not go against God," the other man stated plainly. He squared his shoulders and though his stature was small compared to his companion, his mind was made up. "I know it was not simply a dream, but a warning from God Himself. We are not to return to Herod! I know not if his plans are to worship the child as he claimed or if he has an ulterior motive for seeking Him, but I will not aid that man in finding the

183

babe. I am sure God intends for us to return to our country by a different path than which we came. I am as sure of that as I am that the child we have found is indeed the Son of God."

The darker man looked into the eyes of his friend. "I have not seen that look of determination in your eyes since you persuaded me to make this journey with you, my friend," he relented. "Indeed, we shall return home a different way."

Joseph closed his eyes as a feeling of panic swept over him. So the wise men had seen Herod. They had told him of the purpose for their journey and that they sought the child who was born King of the Jews. Herod now knew that his throne was threatened, not by a noble warrior who would obviously rise to challenge him but by a child.

Joseph knew the men had intended no harm, but he also knew that Herod would stop at nothing to protect his throne. He determined not to allow their royal visitors to know his fear. After all, he thought, as peace settled over him, God had seen fit to direct these kings home in a way that would lead them clear of Herod's temple. The Father would not be taken by surprise, though Joseph as a man, may be. Continuing to calm his heart, he reminded himself that the Almighty was in control and realized, as he so often did, that all he could do now was pray–pray for God's protection and direction for them all.

A week had not passed since the wise men's departure when Joseph was awakened abruptly from his sleep. Bolting straight up on the cot they shared, Mary rose beside her husband, alarm surging through her body.

"Joseph, what is it?" she whispered urgently as she reached to touch his arm in the darkness of the room. Sweat ran along his brow as he struggled to calm his breathing and the frantic beating of his heart. He paused for a brief moment to collect the thoughts running rampant through his head. The directions had been clear. It was not a simple dream. It was another vision, sent directly from God.

"We must leave, Mary! We must go now," he whispered urgently tossing back the blanket which covered them and standing to his feet in one fluid movement.

"But Joseph, what is it?" she questioned, though already in motion to check on her sleeping son.

"An angel, Mary. An angel has again visited me in my sleep," Joseph spoke frantically, beginning to quickly toss a few necessary belongings into a bag. "It was as clear to me as when he told me not to fear taking you for my wife. This time I have been instructed to take you and Jesus and flee to Egypt."

"To Egypt, Joseph? Why are we fleeing? Are we not returning home to Nazareth?" She was not questioning her husband, only trying to gain an understanding of what he was telling her. As she talked she was frantically assisting him in gathering the few things they could not do without.

Joseph paused and looked at his wife. He did not wish to alarm her any more than he already had, but she had to know the severity of the situation. Quickly, he placed both of his strong but gentle hands on her trembling shoulders and looked deep into her eyes. "Mary, I know not what is coming," he spoke quickly but fervently, his eyes searching hers, "but it is not safe for us to remain here. I overheard the wise men who visited us talking and I learned they had passed by Herod's palace. I know they told him of the purpose for their journey, and I know the angel who just spoke to me instructed me to get you and Jesus to safety immediately. We are to flee to Egypt and to stay there until I receive word from Heaven again. Herod is seeking for the child, Mary–our child–and will seek for Him until he has found and destroyed Him. We must leave. Quickly!"

Out of habit, Mary quickly pulled the blankets over the cot, neatly smoothing them as she did so. Then running to gather her son, she bundled Him tightly in her worn and beloved veil, silently apologizing for the rude awakening He was having to endure. Thankfully, He barely opened his tiny eyes, yawned widely, then slowly lowered them in sleep once again.

"Of course, Joseph," Mary agreed, grabbing the small pack she had assembled. "I need only a moment more." Handing Jesus over to his earthly father, Mary quickly scribbled on a small piece of parchment, a thank you to the dear innkeeper and his wife who had shown them so much love and hospitality. A single tear slid along her cheek as she penned.

My friends, It is with deep regret that we must leave you in this way, however, our urgency cannot be helped. We can never thank you enough for the friendship you have bestowed upon us. Our child will know of you and the hospitality you have shown. You were among the first to honor Him and will be the last to be forgotten. Until we meet again.

Mary stood once more in the stable where Joseph now readied the donkey. Here her son had taken His first breath on this earth. She would never forget this place. "Come Mary," Joseph interrupted her sentiment once the donkey was harnessed, "we must hurry!"

His heart raced in his chest with urgency to flee. He had to get Mary and Jesus away from here! He had not a moment to spare! "God, please," he whispered, "honor my feeble attempt to protect your Son." Quickly the lonesome trio ran into the dark of the night.

The lone bay of the donkey awoke Avaraham from an already fitful sleep. Something was not right about this night, but he could not figure out what was amiss. His sleep had been far from sound though he had remained in his place beside his wife so as not to awaken her. However, now that he had heard Joseph's donkey protesting, at what he did not know, perhaps he had a good reason to rise and see what the fuss was about.

As he expected, his rising woke his wife. "Husband?" she asked, her voice heavy with sleep.

"Tis alright, love," he assured her. "The animals seem a bit restless that is all. I just want to check and make sure all is well," he spoke calmly so as not to cause undue alarm.

"Should you take Joseph with you?" she asked hopeful.

"No need to wake him; I shall be fine," he smiled to her, pushing her gently back onto the cot. "I will be right back," he promised her.

Lighting the lantern, he noticed as soon as he opened the door of the room they shared that Mary and Joseph's room was already open and appeared empty. Slowly and quietly he made his way to the open doorway and stared down at the empty cot, neatly made, all evidence of the room recently being occupied, erased. His wife had come to stand beside him, realizing by his walk from their room that something was terribly wrong.

Her voice beside him cut the silence. "They are gone?" she questioned, her voice portraying her unbelief. "Why in the world would they have gone in the night?" she immediately asked. The same question echoed over and over in his mind as he turned from the empty room and saw the parchment lying on a small table in the main room. "And where did they go?" she continued, tears now filling her eyes.

Slowly, Avaraham took the parchment in his hand, handing it to his wife. "Perhaps this will answer our questions," he spoke quietly, still in shock himself that they had left so quickly. Reading it aloud to him, tears began to flow along her face, soaking the only connection they now had to the holy family.

He allowed her to cry, his own heart aching at the disappearance of their friends, but knowing there must be a reason for their sudden departure. Sinking into a nearby chair, he held his wife and allowed her questions and tears, wondering if somehow he could have helped them had he known…but known what? Joseph was not a man given to rash decisions. Whatever could have happened to have made them leave so abruptly during the night? Their speculation did not last long.

Avaraham leaped quickly from his chair upon hearing screams from his neighbors pour through the tiny window of their home, cutting the stillness of the night. He did not make it to the door before the thick wood was kicked from its hinges by an army of tall and fierce Roman soldiers. Blood dripped from their swords as they scoured the room with their icy glares.

188

In the street behind them, the darkness was filled with women wailing in grief, torches illuminating their silhouettes as they held the lifeless bodies of their tiny children. Husbands were held at sword point or in shackles to keep them away from the soldiers as they carried out their merciless mission.

"Where is He?" a voice thundered throughout the room, directed at Avaraham. "We were told of a child who is in residence in this inn! A boy whom men from the Orient came to worship. Is there such a child in this place?" The soldier rushed forward and grabbed Avaraham by the collar of his robes, lifting him from the floor.

"Tell me, innkeeper, or it will be death for you and your wife as well!" he spoke quietly but with no less malice. Blood was spattered across the soldier's face and smeared along his forehead. The hands which held Avaraham were covered with that same blood, the blood of children slaughtered in their beds and torn from their mother's arms. "Tell me you impotent fool!" he spat. "Herod did not take kindly to being mocked by those men from the Orient," he explained through clenched teeth. "When they did not return to him, he assumed they had found that which they were searching for in this God forsaken little village." The soldier spat in the floor beside him, relaying his disgust for the small town of Bethlehem. "Have you seen Him? Is the child here?" the soldier asked, again lifting Avaraham from his feet.

"There is no child here, sir!" Avaraham spoke sternly through clenched teeth. Though he feared for his life and that of his wife, nothing this soldier could do would cause him to reveal that the holy family had, until only a few short moments ago, occupied this very inn.

His wife had backed into a corner, discreetly tucking the parchment from Mary inside the sleeve of her tunic, as other soldiers swept through the rooms behind them looking for anyone who may be hiding from their view.

"He speaks the truth," one of them yelled. "There is no one else here. Looks as if this inn has been empty for some time besides these two." Other soldiers surveyed the rooms, clearing them as well. The burly man who held tightly to Avaraham let him go with such force that he stumbled, falling to the floor. His wife rushed to his side to make sure he had not been injured by the fall or by the rough treatment of the soldier.

Slowly turning, the small army retreated back into the street and to the next house, as women scrambled through the streets in wasted efforts to hide their small children. Never had their small town known such sorrow and despair.

With Bethlehem barely out of view, Mary faltered, looking back toward the screams she now heard cutting through the darkness in the town they had barely vacated. "Joseph!" she whispered urgently, fear causing her heart to pound in her stomach.

Joseph pulled harder on the reigns of the donkey. "Come, Mary!" he spoke firmly. "Do not look back," he instructed, "just run!"

When the dust had settled and the soldiers had departed, every child under the age of two who inhabited Bethlehem and all the coasts thereof, had been killed, under strict orders from Herod the King. Never, at this time, had such innocent blood been shed.

Avaraham looked to his wife, weeping alongside their neighbors. The men of the village had attempted to clean the blood from the streets, from the walls of their homes and from the clothes of the women who had held their dying children. The tiny bodies of all the children who had been killed were buried in quiet and solemn ceremonies. Women tried to comfort one another. Those who were barren or had children older than two years, attempted to care for and console those who had lost their babies and toddlers in the pointless massacre.

Some men who had tried to fight back in protection of their families were also buried, as well as several mothers who had thrown their bodies in front of their children as the sword fell upon them.

"Do you think they made it out?" Avaraham's wife questioned him in the stillness of their home later that night. Her voice broke at the thought of them failing.

"I feel sure they did," he answered her honestly. "God must have sent Joseph a vision or an angel, something to let him know to flee. They would not have left so hastily otherwise. I feel they were safely out of Bethlehem before the soldiers arrived to carry out their orders."

"To where, Avaraham?" she asked again, "Where will they be free from Herod's wrath? Where would they have gone?"

"We cannot tell that which we do not know," he answered her with a smile. Again she pulled the parchment from its hiding place inside her sleeve and for the first time, appreciated the vagueness in which it was written. The child lived, of this she was sure. Thank the Lord His earthly father listened for the moments when angels speak.

Chapter 20

Joseph returned to his wife and young son, a line of fish dangling from his hand. Mary noticed his brow was drawn tight, and concern for him pierced her heart. Jesus was quietly playing with a small branch he could hold and control, knocking it against the dry, dusty ground and cackling at the dust it stirred up.

Mary stoked the fire she had made. Then with a quick glance at her content son, she rose to approach her husband. Joseph was cleaning his catch on a large rock just the right height to be used as a table. Her mother's actions toward her father came to her mind. When Heli was tired and worn, there were times that no amount of words could comfort him, yet Anna would encircle his waist from behind, her head resting quietly on his back. She had heard her father say how much strength he could draw from that simple gesture of love, reminding him that whatever task he was enduring was for the betterment or survival of his family.

Mary made the quick decision to act on impulse, before she could change her mind, and gently encircled Joseph's waist from behind him. That he was startled at first did not surprise her, yet when he flinched, she softly laid her head on his back and held him close. He stood stiff for a moment, relaxed the next, then laid his knife aside and turned within her embrace to face her. He did not push her away, but drew her close once again, her face against his chest now, his chin resting upon her head. They stood that way for several moments, drawing much needed strength from one another's embrace.

It was Mary who spoke first. "Thank you, husband," she spoke without raising her head.

"For?" he questioned her.

She pulled away to look into his face. "For being attentive and sensitive to the will of God. You saved us, Joseph." It was the first time that night had been spoken of since they had fled. He was quite for a moment.

"Did I, Mary?" he asked, quiet skepticism creeping into his voice. His tone did not hold malice; Mary recognized it as fear. He broke the embrace and moved to better see Jesus who was now investigating a small stone. Mary turned where she stood to watch her husband's features. "First of all, it took a census to get me to Bethlehem. I knew the prophecies indicated God's son would be born there, but I never even thought to head that way as soon as I took you as my wife. All I could think about was finishing our home. I barely found you shelter there, and when I did, it was a stable! Then after He came, I just settled there. I should have had you safely back in Nazareth months ago, but no, I waited until danger approached, and an angel had to tell me to get out! When we fled, I did so quickly, without even thinking of the best course to take," he continued. Mary was quiet, allowing him to voice his fears. "When that angel told me to flee, I did, just as he instructed. All I could think about was getting you and Jesus to immediate safety, and heading toward Egypt per his commands, but Mary, we are now on the outskirts of the Negev desert. The past week I have dragged the two of you through the mountains of Judea, across canyons and streams, where at least then we had some shelter and water, but now," he paused, shaking his head with doubt, "now we are about to be in the open desert…and for how long?" Joseph ran his hand roughly through his tousled hair. "What if we do not reach Egypt safely? What if the path I chose leads us into more danger than what we have run from?"

"Then we will face it together. Joseph, as we ran, you heard the bone chilling screams and demanding shouts of Herod's soldiers as they tore into Bethlehem to do, heaven knows what, to those who were there. If you had faltered, but a moment, to form a plan of action, we would have been in the midst of that battle. You did exactly as you were told and not a moment too soon." She paused to let him process her words. "It is now you who is lacking in faith, husband," Mary reminded him carefully. "Jehovah has seen us safely thus far. You are forgetting," she looked to her son, waddling His way toward them, "that God is with us. He did not promise the path, any path, would be an easy one, but He did promise He would not forsake us! Even through the Negev desert! And Joseph," Mary laughed while reaching for the child who was very pleased with Himself for making His way to His mother quickly without falling, "we have an even better advantage than most. Not only spiritually, but physically and literally, we have God with us," Mary finished slowly, a smile spread across her face, her son now in her arms. At that moment, Jesus turned and looked to his earthly father, His tiny arms going out and His hands clenching. Joseph reached for the child, embracing the boy who

195

immediately laid His small head on the broad shoulder of the man who would raise Him as his own.

Mary did not miss the tear which slid from her husband's eye or the way he turned to try and hide it. Reaching to wipe it from his cheek, she tenderly kissed the trek it had left behind. "Sometimes, I still cannot believe Jehovah has chosen me for such a task," Joseph admitted as he cleared his throat. "I am so unworthy to fill this role. I just want to keep the two of you safe and to complete this task God has called me to." Joseph rubbed the boy's back.

"Then trust God to help you to do just that," hands on her hips, she comically quoted her husband. "He would not have entrusted you to this task had He known you would not be able to let Him have control of whatever circumstances may come," she smiled smugly. Joseph laughed aloud as his own words echoed in his ears. Holding his son with one arm, he embraced his wife with the other, pulling her close to him.

"You are right, Mary," he laughed. "At some point in your young life, you must have had wise counsel to speak words such as those." Mary rolled her eyes at her husband who laughed whole-heartedly at her jest. Together they prepared their evening meal, still continuing to keep their fire low just in case they were being followed, then attempted to sleep.

Five days later, they were in the middle of the Negev dessert. Mary had thought the journey to Bethlehem had been difficult when she was expecting, but she was surprised to find the difficulty had increased with a toddler in tow. Feeding times were non-negotiable, and soiled clothes were a constant struggle. The desert heat was relentless during the day and bitterly cold at night. At times, strong winds would blow the fine sand into their faces, chapping and stinging their skin. Mary would pull her veil around her son, sheltering Him from the elements.

They would walk for hours across the open plain until the sun would begin to drop low in the sky. Joseph, using his staff and a few other items he had collected during their journey along with blankets they had brought from Bethlehem, would create a shelter of sorts for them to rest under at night. Their meals were cooked over low fires created from small scraggly trees they occasionally passed and would consist of beans or meal.

Few travelers found themselves in the midst of the desert as the danger of wild animals and bandits were more prevalent here. Each night before they slept and each morning before they began their journey, Joseph would lead his family in prayer. Prayer for safety, prayer for deliverance from the man who sought them, and prayer for God's guidance and direction as they continued their journey to Egypt.

On day seven, Joseph prayed an especially fervent prayer. Though they were able to continue travel with little food, water was a valuable resource they could not go long without. That morning they had used what water they had left to prepare their morning meal. Joseph's concern was genuine, but he had peace once he had finished his petition to the Father. Before their journey ended that day, Joseph led them deep into the canyons which had loomed before them for so long. They ended their day camped by a small stream at the base of one of the larger canyons. With the walls of the canyon providing shelter and the stream supplying water as well as small fish, it was the best night's sleep any of them had been afforded in almost two weeks.

Two days later, the family stood by the Sihor River. Once they crossed the river, they would be

197

safely in Egypt and out of Herod's reach. The river was wide, but the path where they would cross did not appear too deep. Still, Joseph intended to be extremely careful with his family, as recent rains caused the water to flow quickly. He thought of delaying their crossing, but the angel had told him to flee to Egypt, and the river was the only thing separating him from completing that task. Once on the other side, Herod could not touch them.

"Mary," he instructed, "take Jesus and situate yourselves on the donkey. I will lead you across behind me." Mary did as her husband instructed, holding Jesus close to her. Though water did not normally bother her, the current was swift, and the river was much deeper and wider downstream.

Once he knew they were settled, Joseph took his first step into the river, leading the donkey slowly behind him. At the first the cold water shocked him as it gathered around his ankles, but he was prepared and showed little surprise. An uneasy chuckle escaped his lips as he carefully looked back at his wife and son.

"Do you know what this brings to mind, Mary?" he asked, as he began to wade deeper into the water.

"At the moment, I cannot imagine," Mary spoke, nervously. Joseph did not miss the way her voice wavered.

"A certain maiden dowsing me with a water jug not many years back," he laughed. The water had begun to inch up toward his knees and was now slapping at his thighs. Another glance behind him showed that Mary's feet were now in water also, even from where she sat on the donkey's back. Jesus continued to babble and coo, paying no mind to the potential danger.

Joseph used his staff, prodding it in front of him before he made each move, making sure the step he was about to take was secure. The one thing he was not thinking of, was that the animal behind him had four feet instead of only two. When the beast stepped into a hole, he lost his footing and instinctively began to swim. The current pulled against the rope in Joseph's hand, attempting to wash them all down stream. Mary gasped as she felt the donkey give way beneath her and the water suddenly surround her waist. Quickly she grabbed the animal's mane with both hands, keeping herself near him, while encircling Jesus between the donkey's neck and her own body, making sure the boy's head was safely above the water.

"Joseph!" she yelled, fearful that they would all be swept away. Jesus cried in shock of the cold water now surrounding His small body. Joseph dropped his staff, using both of his hands and all of his strength to hold onto the rope which was his only connection to everything he had in the world. The donkey bayed loudly, protesting both the river's current and the rope that was pulling him in the opposite direction. Joseph pulled with every fiber of his being, the rope digging into the flesh of his hands. He barely noticed the burns as the rope began to slip and he dug his heels into the soggy ground beneath him, grasping the rope with more force that he thought possible.

"God, please," he prayed silently with more urgency than he knew he possessed, "help us! Give me the strength to pull them to safety!" Joseph pulled with everything he had in him, the rope almost sliding from his grasp, when finally, he felt his strength take hold. The rope anchored within his palms as he strained forcefully against the current, and he began to finally gain control. The animal began inching toward him, slowly at first, and then more quickly as Joseph continued backing his way toward the bank. He didn't waste a moment of precious time once he had them back in his control, but wrapped the rope around his wrist, and turning to face the bank, quickly made his way to the water's edge.

Mary and Jesus were soaked to the bone, but unharmed. Joseph helped his wife from the donkey's back then led them all to a large rock planted firmly by the river. There he gathered some sticks and built a small fire where they could dry themselves. The day was waning, but it was still a while before nightfall. Just enough time, hopefully, for them to be warm and dry before the sunset. Once Mary and Jesus were settled and the animal was cared for, Joseph himself sank to the ground. His body continued to shake from the adrenaline coursing through his veins and he worked to control his breathing.

"I thought I had lost you both," he finally admitted from his place against the rock. Mary reached for his hand to embrace it and could not believe what she saw as he reached to allow her to take it. Blood oozed down his arm, his palm bare flesh. Looking to see why she flinched, he quickly drew his arm back and stared at the wounds. He had been so intent on saving his family, he had not realized the harm he had inflicted on himself, not that he would have cared. He would willingly give his life for his wife and son.

Mary quickly rose, taking a cloth, and ran to the river bank dipping the fabric into the cool water. Returning, she took his hands in her lap and gently washed the blood from them. The ropes had cut and burned his hands, which were already dry from the journey they had endured. He flinched at first, hoping she wouldn't notice. Now that his heart was calming from his struggle against the current, the pain was beginning to be noticeable. Once she had cleaned the burns, she wrapped both of his hands in a clean dry cloth, but she did not let them go. Jesus had settled Himself and was sound asleep by the fire just a few inches from her. Now her husband had succumbed to slumber and had fallen sound asleep as she tended to his wounds, his head against the rock. Again, before allowing herself to change her mind, she slowly pulled his head onto her lap, then removed the kippot covering his head.

"Again, Father, I come to You with thanks," she prayed quietly while looking toward the heavens. "Thank You for granting us safety from Nazareth to Bethlehem. Thank You for granting us safety on our journey from Bethlehem to Egypt. Thank You for protecting us as we crossed the river, but most of all, thank You once again for the husband You have given me to be the earthly father to Your Son. He is more than I could have ever hoped for in a husband." Joseph did not stir as she prayed, nor as she herself dozed off while softly running her fingers through the tiny curls resting so peacefully in her lap.

He was not sure what awakened him or how long he had slept. He just remembered opening his eyes and finding himself resting on a pillow which turned out to be the knees of his wife. For a moment he did not move, feeling the pressure of her arms about his back and her hand on his head. He could see Jesus from where he lay, still sleeping just inches from His mother. He thought, from the steadiness of her breathing, that Mary, too, slept.

Something behind him shuffled, bringing him to his feet in one defensive move, all traces of sleep vanishing from his features. "Easy friend," the tall man standing over them spoke, "I mean you no harm."

Joseph slowed his breathing but did not relax his stance. He was not sure where this Egyptian stood on his views of Jewish people. Mary stood quickly behind her husband, moving to place herself in front of her son. Most of her tunic was dry, except from where it had been gathered as she had settled against the rock.

"Looks like as if you have had some fun in our river," the older man laughed. "Is the child well?" he asked, beckoning toward Jesus who was still asleep behind his mother.

Mary shook her head, uncertainly at first, but then after glancing at her husband, more surely.

"Our son is fine, thank you," Joseph answered the stranger. "We had a mishap while crossing the river, but we are well now."

"Good, good," the stranger spoke. "That current is as swift as I have seen it in some years. Surprised you chose to cross with it so swift. Should slow down in a couple of days. Must have been in a hurry to make the crossing."

Joseph looked at the man who seemed so curious about them. He could not yet decipher if he was a friend or a foe. "We are where we are meant to be now, and that is all that matters," Joseph spoke matter-of-factly yet respectfully.

"I am Adio," the man continued, "and this river boarders my land. I am a friend to the Jews," he paused before continuing, "and a worshipper of God Most High." He smiled when he saw Joseph exhale and relax a bit. "I wonder if the three of you were running from Herod's most recent act of desperation in his efforts to protect his throne?"

Joseph thought he could trust the man, yet was reluctant to speak too much until he knew for certain. "We did flee from Bethlehem if that is what you are implying," he confirmed.

"So you are aware of the massacre which ensued?" he questioned them.

"Massacre?" Mary asked quietly, her hand going over her heart. "We knew something was happening but were unsure as to what."

Adio lowered his head as if what he was about to say was too painful to be said in the presence of a young woman and child. Still he continued, "We have heard news across our land that Herod demanded all children in Bethlehem two years of age and under be slaughtered." Mary closed her eyes and leaned her body against the rock they had just been resting against. The screams in the night, the thundering voices of the soldiers, they had heard it all. "Something about wise men proclaiming the King of the Jews had been born in Bethlehem within the past two years," Adio continued. "A King rising against Herod was not a chance he was willing to take, even though that King," Adio paused, suddenly wondering if he could possibly be in the presence of that very person, "was yet a child." He looked behind Mary to where Jesus had begun to stir.

Joseph was still a bit uncertain as to how honest he should be. He did not feel threatened by the Egyptian but not completely comfortable either.

"All children two years of age and under?" Joseph shifted, "Then I would say our journey was not in vain." Adio seemed to snap from the trance he had allowed himself to become caught up in. Whether or not this family included God the Son, he would show kindness to them.

"You will be interested to know that there is a settlement of Jews not far from here. I am sure you will find much hospitality there among your people."

Adio stretched his hand forth in greeting and Joseph accepted it graciously. "Welcome, to Egypt."

"Can you tell me, friend, how far we are from the temple?" Joseph knew he must keep his family on a course to uphold all the Jewish laws, including worship.

"A couple hours journey at most," Adio answered with a smile, realizing Joseph may at last be able to rest easy for at least a little while. "God is good, yes?"

Joseph returned the smile. "God is good," he agreed.

Mary allowed herself the luxury of stretching her legs as she made her way to the structure across the street from where they had made their home. Joseph had been blessed to find a job not long after they settled in Egypt at the occupation he loved, carpentry. Jesus passed many days with his papa, enjoying time with him in the carpentry shop as he sawed, nailed, and sanded. Though he was barely four years of age, He was eager to learn His earthly father's trade. His behavior and attitude was always pleasant, always perfect. Mary knew other women had noticed His obedience on occasions when their children were acting out, the way "normal" children did. Jesus could not be a more perfect child. She smiled to herself knowing the cause was simple. Her son was perfect, and he was far from "normal".

Patting her stomach, which was beginning to once again take shape, she spoke to the unborn child nestled there. "Something tells me I shall get to endure the days of a child who is not so content soon enough," she grinned sarcastically.

"Mary," Joseph hailed her upon hearing her voice. "Should you be out?" he asked coming toward her.

"With my last pregnancy I journeyed from Nazareth to Bethlehem at the end of my term, yet with this child, you do not wish me to journey across the street at the beginning!" Handing him a sack containing sandwiches and fruit, she kissed him quickly on the cheek. "How are my boys this evening? Where is Jesus?" she asked looking inside the shop.

"I am here mother!" her son called, running to embrace her legs. "You are well? My brother is well?" It was more of a statement than a question. Joseph and Mary exchanged smiles.

"Don't be surprised when it is indeed a son!" Joseph exclaimed quietly for Mary's ears alone.

"There will be no surprise," she laughed in agreement.

"Actually, I am glad you are here." Joseph took the fruit from his bag and handed it to the boy still clinging to His mother's legs. "I have word from our homeland. Adio came by a few moments ago. Word has come to Egypt that King Herod is not well. The golden eagle that he had mounted over the temple has been destroyed. His power, as well as his health, are failing."

"Joseph," Mary was afraid to hope but had to voice the question, "does that mean we can go home?"

Joseph placed his hands on each of his wife's shoulders. "We will not move until I receive word from the heavens that we may do so. Herod is not yet dead and is still ordering executions from his death bed. His next in line, his son Antipater, has been killed under orders from his father."

"Joseph, no." Mary could hardly believe what her husband was telling her.

"Yes, Mary, and though Herod's reign seems to be coming to an end, there may be other dangers we are not aware of. Until I receive word or a sign from Jehovah, we will remain in Egypt. I will not endanger the life of my family."

"And I would not ask you to," Mary agreed with him, laying her hand upon his cheek. "I will be patient, Joseph," she promised him.

Mary did not have to wait long. A week later, Joseph lay quietly, feeling his wife's steady breathing beside him. His own breathing was steady again now, but his heart continued to race with excitement from the dream which had just awakened him. Unlike before, he did not jolt upright, rousing Mary from sleep and racing against time to get to his family to safety. This time, the angel did not speak with urgency demanding Joseph flee immediately, but the soft voice came to Joseph clear and strong.

"Arise, and take the young child and his mother, and go into the land of Israel: for they are dead which sought the young child's life."

The words played over and over in Joseph's mind. Mary would be so excited to learn their time among a foreign people in a foreign land was about to be behind them. He felt peace with the decision to wait until morning but could not wait to tell his wife to pack their few belongings.

Chapter 21

Joseph's original plan when they began their journey back to Israel had been to rebuild the life they had left behind when they fled Bethlehem. He planned to return to the house of Avaraham, where he was sure they would be welcome, and he could easily find work. They would settle back into a daily routine there, and Mary could give birth to their child in safety and comfort.

Their journey was a pleasant one, and soon they were back on the soil of their ancestors. The mountains of Judea surrounded them once again as they made camp among others passing through the area. Mary spoke easily with the women, who were constantly doting over Jesus, as the men of the camp sat around the fire with full stomachs.

One by one, men retreated to their resting places with their respective families. Jesus was sound asleep beside his mother when Joseph lay carefully at his wife's back. Slipping his arm around her waist he rested his hand carefully on her stomach.

"The babe is far too small for you to feel his kicks yet, but he moves plenty, trust me," she assured her husband. Mary felt instantly that her husband was not in a humorous mood. His touch was light, but his body seemed tense behind her. Turning her head so she could see his face, she saw that his brow was knit tight in contemplation. "Is something wrong, Joseph?"

"No, nothing is wrong," he spoke quietly. "But I must confess that news which I just received has me a bit concerned about our return to Bethlehem," he admitted.

"What news?" Mary asked, shifting to see him better.

"One of the men with whom I was speaking recently journeyed from Bethlehem. Remember when I told you the golden eagle had been destroyed right before Herod's death?" Mary nodded in affirmation. "When Herod heard the news, he, of course, had those killed who had seen to the destruction of the eagle as well as his son, Antipater, because he was next in line to reign."

"Yes, Joseph, I remember." Mary answered keeping her voice as low as her husband's so as not to wake her son.

"A man named Archelaus has now been confirmed by Caesar as King."

Mary shook her head in confusion. "Alright, and this worries you, because…" Mary let her sentence hang.

"Archelaus is the son of a Samaritan mother and an Edomite father," Joseph explained. "He has been taught to hate Jews from both sides of his family, and even worse, he had three thousand people killed in the temple during the Passover simply for mourning the men Herod had ordered killed for destroying the golden eagle. Mary, that was before Caesar had officially placed him on the throne. Now that he is King, I fear he may be as power hungry as Herod or even more so. These families are here because they fled out of fear of Archelaus. They even failed to complete their sacrifice in the temple. The Passover was abandoned."

"Joseph, that is terrible!" Mary agreed. "What are we to do? We have come too far to return again to Egypt, and were instructed to leave there and return to Israel."

"We were," he agreed. "We were instructed to return to Israel, but not specifically to Bethlehem. We will pray for guidance and follow His lead." Joseph reached across his wife and rubbed the head of Jesus. "Never forget my promise to keep the two of you safe as long as there is breath in my body."

"I will not forget, Joseph. He will guide you, and we will willingly follow."

Their sleep that night was peaceful and with the morning's light, Joseph again set his family on a course toward Bethlehem. In his heart, he knew that was no longer his destination and that they would not settle there, but until he had been given clear instruction as to where to take his family, he would not change his course.

Mary could tell as the day drew to a close and the sun began to set that the decision was weighing heavily on her husband's mind. She stole a few moments that night to find a peaceful spot where she could pray and petition with her Heavenly Father.

"Dear God," she prayed as she knelt, "guide my husband as he strives to complete the journey You have laid before us. Show him where You would have us to go. Joseph has always sought Your guidance in every aspect of his life, and he is not failing to do so now. I pray, Father, that You will ease his burden by showing him what he needs to know. Lord, we do not know where to go, and the path we are on is taking us closer to those who may attempt to destroy Jesus. I pray You will give us strength to bear what we must endure, wisdom in the decisions we must make, and open hearts and minds willing to be led by You."

Mary did not realize that Joseph had overheard her prayer and lifted his own, including his thanks for the woman God had given him.

Mary opened her eyes the next morning to Joseph's face above her own. As soon as she blinked the sleep from her heavy lids, Joseph planted a kiss on the tip of her nose. The smile on his face was broad and filled with excitement.

"You know where we are going," she smiled back to him with surety.

"I know where we are going," Joseph answered. "We are to turn aside from our current path and return to Nazareth."

Mary sat straight up, almost knocking her husband from his position. "Nazareth, Joseph! Are you certain?" She was afraid to get her hopes too high. Nazareth. Home. To Mother and Father.

Joseph chuckled at his wife's response to his news, though he had expected as much. "Yes, Mary. Very certain. The angel has appeared to me again, this time instructing me to take you and Jesus to Galilee. We shall journey there at once and live again among our families in Nazareth."

Mary threw her arms around her husband's neck. "Oh Joseph, I never allowed myself to dream of seeing Mother and Father again anytime soon!"

"You shall see them, my sweet wife," he returned her embrace, "and sooner rather than later."

Mary was suddenly on her feet causing Joseph to stumble and end up on his backside. He laughed as she quickly began clearing their camp while Jesus rubbed sleepy eyes, grinning at His mother.

Within a week, Joseph, Mary, and Jesus were approaching the town of Nazareth. They would be home before the sun had set this day. They had no way to send news of their coming, and as they drew closer, Joseph noticed Mary had grown a bit apprehensive of their return. Doubt and questions began to fill her mind as they approached the city gates. Doubts she chose to share with her husband.

"Joseph," she began at one point, and for a solid mile the questions came in spurts. "Do you think things are well between Shira and Elias now? Do you think Jesus will be safe around him? Do you think Mother and Father are well? And what of Grandfather? He was so feeble before we left for Bethlehem five years ago now. I wonder if Myah and Nathan have found each other? Or perhaps they have each found another. What do you think has become of our house? Do you think your father returned after the census to care for it? What do you suspect? Do you think we will be accepted by our friends and others in the village again? Things were still rather tense when we left."

Joseph stopped and placed his hands on his wife's shoulders. "Mary," he began. "We are following the guidance of God Most High. Though I know not the answers to your questions, He does. His plan has already formed, and His instructions were clear. It will be alright." He kissed her softly on the forehead then resumed his pace. Mary took his statement for what it was. Joseph had no idea what they were going back to either, but he completely trusted the One who was guiding them there, and that One knew exactly what they were facing. She would accept the guidance offered by her husband and trust as well.

Their reception was a warm and welcome one just before sunset that evening, as Mary called tidings to her family upon entering their gate. Anna stopped hugging Mary only long enough to bow before, then embrace Jesus, then Joseph, and then back to Mary once again. Tears of happiness flooded her face as she held her daughter as tightly as she dared in Mary's present condition. They would rest here this night with Mary's family, then Joseph and Heli would head into town first thing the next morning to the house Joseph had built for his wife years before. Repairs, if any, would be made before they again settled in their home.

Once Jesus slept peacefully in what had been Grandfather's room, the adults gathered in the main room to catch up on all that had transpired in Joseph and Mary's absence. Grandfather had passed shortly after they had left, but not before he had seen a brilliant star he was sure marked the birth of His Lord, Mary's child.

Joseph and Mary confirmed that his suspicions had been correct and told of the shepherd's visit, the angel's heralds, the visit by the wise men, and their discovery by Elias. Heli confirmed that Elias had indeed returned to Nazareth a changed man and had kept his promise to the Holy Family, telling those in Nazareth of all he had seen and heard in Bethlehem that night. He and Shira now shared a happy marriage and were expecting their third child at any time. Nathan and Myah had indeed married and had taken over Debra's home and business in the marketplace. They did well in their living and were expecting their first child in the spring.

Mary and her mother stole a few moments alone as Heli and Joseph made plans for the following day. "He is a perfect child in every way," Mary told her mother of her son. "He went through everything a normal baby does: teething, learning to walk, and learning to talk. But never has He lashed out in anger or been disobedient or disrespectful. If it were not for those things and for all that transpired the night of His birth, I would almost think I had dreamed it all. He is a normal child, yet He is not."

"I have never seen a sweeter face," Anna admitted to her daughter. "Though I confess, I almost expected Him to glow like an angel," she laughed, at her admission to the truth. She noticed Mary's troubled smile. "Is something wrong, daughter?"

"I confess I am still troubled at the old man's words in the temple. He said, '*A sword shall pierce through thy own soul also, that the thoughts of many hearts may be revealed.*' What does that mean, Mother? He is my Lord, and I know there will be sacrifices which must be made, but He is also my child."

Anna laid her hands on Mary's which rested in her own lap. "We know not what tomorrow holds, Mary, but we do know Who holds our tomorrow. God will give you strength for whatever you may have to endure."

"You sound like Joseph," Mary chuckled.

"Then he is a wise man in more ways than one," her mother acknowledged, placing her hand on her daughters cheek. "Listen to the godly man Jehovah has given you! He will not fail you." Anna stood, "Now, this night is not a time for sadness," she exclaimed, "but a time for rejoicing. My daughter has come home! And in time to welcome her second child!" she beamed. "Tomorrow we shall go into the village along with the men. We will visit Nathan and Myah and select cloth for garments for your new baby

213

as well as any the rest of you may need. You are home now, Mary. Perhaps your traveling days are over!"

Joseph and Heli appeared in the opening of the room. "Planning on spending what is left of the treasures from the wise men, Mary?" he grinned.

"Not all of it, husband. But we all could use some new garments. We have traveled much with little." Rising, she lifted the sleeve of the tunic he wore, which was frayed and worn.

"Agreed," he spoke. "Get what we need to make ourselves presentable to society," he laughed pulling her close. "It is good to be home."

Chapter 22

Time passed quickly once they were settled back in Nazareth. James joined their family soon after, followed by Joses, Elizabeth, Simon, Judas and recently, little Anna. Mary was thankful for the size of their home, though it seemed to grow smaller as her children multiplied and grew. She was also thankful for the companions and friends her children kept, including Myah and Nathan's children, as well as Shira and Elias'. Many days her door seemed to continually open and close as children would come and go, asking for sips of water or a handful of pomegranate arils, and often times they came seeking her eldest son, begging Him for a story or to play a game they had imagined. To Mary's delight, Jesus was wonderful with the children, and if He was not assisting His mother, father, or an elder of their village, He was always eager to accommodate the children who sought Him.

Joseph worked hard at his carpentry trade, and more often than not, Jesus could be found by His earthly father's side. Many times Joseph would have to hunt for one of their older sons, James or Joses, when there was work he needed aid with, but never did he have to search far for Jesus. Mary felt the tension this sometimes caused among her children. Her oldest son was often mocked by His younger brothers, and Mary found herself and Joseph chastening them more and more as they grew. Jesus never gave them cause to taunt or tease Him, but it was hard having siblings, especially one who was absolutely perfect.

Jesus was ever obedient, never going against anything He was asked to do by either of his parents. He studied His lessons intently, especially the Scriptures, and was the first of them prepared and always eager to go to the synagogue each Sabbath. It was not unusual, once His daily chores were accomplished, to find Him throughout the village, assisting the widows and the elderly with their tasks of the day. He had grown strong for His age, Mary noticed, both physically and spiritually.

His spiritual growth was brought to strong realization as the family prepared to return home from celebrating the Passover in Jerusalem during Jesus' twelfth year. They had been to Jerusalem many times during His life, and the journey was one they were all familiar with. Though the trip was a pleasant one, in the company of friends and relatives, the fleeting journeys Mary and Joseph had taken in their early years together had given them both a fondness for home in Nazareth that far exceeded the others. They were glad to begin their journey home. The children, all but little Anna still being carried on her father's shoulders, were running about with other children. At the end of the day they would make their camp and regroup to dine with their respective families.

Elias had become somewhat of an unspoken leader in their village, and his family led the caravan. They had completed a full day's journey in record time, and Elias decided that to push them further may

216

not be beneficial to the older patrons in their group. They had come to the banks of the Jordan River and he gave the suggestion to make camp early, providing a good night's rest tonight and a full day's journey on the morrow. The children began to reassemble with their families to help begin preparations for the evening meal.

James, Joses, and Simon each came racing toward their father, younger Judas not far behind, each anxious to test their skills at fishing in the river.

"I shall catch the biggest fish!" Simon exclaimed. "One big enough that Father shall devour himself and need not another!"

"Sure you will," Joses chided him, "but I shall catch many! Enough to feed our entire family and have many left for the elders!"

"I know not who you think you are," James threw in, "but I shall catch many large fish so that the ones you provide will seem tiny and trivial in number!"

"Come my sons!" Joseph announced. "Put your skills to the test and let us see who can indeed prove what has been declared by each of you!"

Mary took Anna from her father's shoulders and handed her to Elizabeth. "Care for your sister while Judas and I gather sticks for a fire," she instructed her oldest daughter. Mary took her youngest son by the hand, and together they began picking up branches and twigs.

They had not been at their task for long when a thought occurred to Mary. Where was Jesus? She was able to see her other family members along the river bank, but could not spot her oldest son anywhere. Elizabeth was at their campsite with Anna, playing a game to keep her young sibling entertained. Mary worked her way to the riverbank, curious but not overly concerned as to the whereabouts of Jesus. When she was within speaking distance of her husband, she voiced her question to Joseph.

"Joseph, have you seen Jesus?" she asked.

"I have not," he confirmed, just realizing the fact. James had just pulled in his first catch and the boys were too excited by the size of his fish to be concerned with their parent's discussion. "Is He not with some of the older boys throughout the camp?"

"It is unlike Him not to seek out our camp when He knows it is time." Mary paused and then voiced a surprising thought. "Joseph, I have not seen Him since we left Jerusalem."

"It is a bit unusual," Joseph agreed. "Boys!" he spoke, his voice loud enough to be heard by his sons over their excitement. "Have you seen your brother? Where is Jesus?"

"I do not know," James answered first, shrugging his shoulders. "I assumed He was lagging behind helping out the elders or widows." James turned his attention back to his fishing.

"Have you seen Him, Joses?" Joseph inquired.

"I have not, Father," he too admitted. "I, like James, assumed He traveled with you and mother or with some of the older boys in our group. I have not seen Him all day."

Joseph turned and walked further up the bank to where Elias had made camp. Mary followed, concern now replacing her curiosity. Joseph and Elias had become very close since their return to Nazareth, and he could easily be considered Joseph's closest friend.

"Elias, have you seen Jesus?"

"I have not," Elias spoke quickly, noticing the urgency in his friend's voice. Elias called to his oldest son and to Shira, both of whom also stated they had not seen Jesus at any time during the day.

"Oh, Joseph, what have we done?" Mary began, clearly about to panic. "What has become of Him?"

"We will find Him," Joseph spoke surely, turning to his wife.

"I will help you," Elias promised them.

They split up, each of them going in a different direction until they had inquired of every family in their caravan. No one could remember seeing Jesus at any point during the day.

"My family and I shall return to Jerusalem, Elias, to see if we can locate our son there."

"I too shall help you search for Him," Elias began, but Joseph stopped him with a raised hand.

"These people need you to lead them, my friend," he spoke, motioning to some of the older families in their group who had instinctively made their camp close to Elias'. "I thank you, but we shall be fine. Once we find Jesus, we shall return to Nazareth."

"At least allow us to take your children with us," Shira spoke coming up beside her husband who instantly wrapped his arm about her waist. Though Mary's thoughts were consumed with the whereabouts of her son, she never tired of seeing the small displays of affection Elias constantly bestowed upon his wife. He really was a changed man in so many ways.

"That is an excellent idea," Elias agreed. He noticed the look of hesitancy cross Joseph's face. He had many children and did not wish to be an imposition upon his friend. "You will be able to move much faster without worrying over them, and we would be honored to have them," he gently persuaded

Joseph. "Allow us the satisfaction of helping in this way."

Joseph looked to Mary to gain her prospective. The slight nod of her head was the only affirmation he needed.

"Thank you," he stated as his way of acceptance to their proposal. "We will turn back toward Jerusalem and retrace our steps, searching the city and inquiring as to others who may have seen Him. We will return home as quickly as possible."

"Find your son," Elias stated, placing his hand on Joseph's broad shoulder. "Take all the time you need."

Mary settled her other children with Shira, and quickly she and Joseph began their return journey to Jerusalem.

The couple took the exact path on their return to the Holy City, traveling through the night. There was no sign of Jesus anywhere, and by the time they reached the city in the breaking morning light, Mary's emotions were at the breaking point.

"Where is He, Joseph?" she cried when they had stopped for a brief rest. "How can we have lost Him?"

"We will find Him, Mary," he tried, attempting to soothe his exhausted and worried wife.

"But there are so many in the city, we will never be able to seek Him out," Mary cried.

"Have faith, Mary," Joseph pleaded with her. "He must be here," he paused, "somewhere." Mary did not miss the worried tone that had crept into her husband's voice with his final words. As he spoke, Joseph continued to look past the city gate where he would not rest until he had found their son.

Three days passed, yet there was still no sign of Jesus. Mary had cried until her eyes were swollen and she had no tears left. Joseph had become quiet, which Mary had learned, was a sign that her husband was also bothered. Making their way past the temple for the second time that day, searching the crowds coming and going for any sign of Jesus, Mary heard the voice. To whom it belonged she did not know, but the words were clear.

"How can He know so much? He is but a child," a man was saying as he passed by her. Mary grabbed Joseph by the sleeve of his tunic, pulling him the same direction as the man was walking.

"This is true," another spoke, "but His realization of the Scriptures is remarkable. He asks the questions which hold amazing depth, then answers them Himself! His understanding is parallel to no other His age."

"Sir!" Joseph exclaimed, loud enough to gain the attention of all around him. The men stopped looking to him in surprise.

"Where is the boy? The child of whom you are speaking," Joseph asked, his own excitement sounding in his voice.

"In the temple," the man answered, looking at Joseph as if he were mad. Immediately Joseph and Mary turned and fled to the steps of the temple. Quickly ascending the steps, they paused at their entry, remembering just in time, exactly where they were. Forcing themselves to proceed with reverence, Mary could not slow the beating of her heart or the shaking of her limbs as she looked urgently in every direction for her son.

Joseph finally took her arm, leading her to where a crowd of the most noble of teachers had gathered, and in the midst of them sat Jesus. Mary burst into tears upon seeing her son and could not contain herself as she burst through the crowd, falling to her knees, her arms immediately going around the neck of her child. *"Son,"* she spoke as she cried, *"why has thou thus dealt with us? Behold, thy father and I have sought thee sorrowing."*

Joseph took in the scene before him. "Jesus, we have feared for Your life. How could You have tarried behind when You knew we were returning home?" Though he was rejoicing in the realization that his son was safe and unharmed, anger slightly crept into his voice at the thought that he had been disobeyed by one of his children. And by Jesus, his child who had never disobeyed him.

"How is it that ye sought me?" Jesus asked innocently, causing his mother to release Him and look as if He had taken leave of His senses. *"Wist ye not that I must be about my Father's business?"*

Mary looked to Joseph trying to comprehend what their son was telling them. Then it hit her. He had not disobeyed them; they had forgotten their place with Him. Noticing the disappointed look that crossed Joseph's features, it was then she realized the Father of whom Jesus was speaking of was not her husband. Was Joseph's look of disappointment in himself for not thinking clearly enough to have found Jesus three days ago, or was it in the reminder that no matter how much he loved her son, Jesus did not completely belong to them?

Mary rose to her feet wiping her face and quieting herself. Joseph cleared his throat, feeling as if he had, though respectively so, been put back into his place. "Let us go home now," he stated simply, though it was almost more of a question than a statement.

Immediately Jesus stood in obedience to his earthly father.

"Yes, sir," He spoke.

222

The trio was quiet as they began their journey back to Nazareth. Jesus had done nothing wrong, and both Joseph and Mary realized as much. They also realized, with sharp clarity, that their son, who was in fact God the Son, was growing up. The reason for His coming would be brought to the surface at some point, and neither of His earthly parents wanted to think about what that would possibly entail.

Chapter 23

The years continued to pass, and Mary had to say goodbye first to her father, and then only two years later, her mother. Their deaths had been hard for Mary, but not nearly as hard as what she would experience in the latter years of her life.

Her children had grown. Little Anna was now eighteen years old and had recently been betrothed to Jonas, the son of the town blacksmith. Two of her sons had left home, efficiently running homes of their own, with wonderful wives by their side. Elizabeth was expecting her first child, happily married to Elias and Shira's oldest son, Benjamin, and they had made their home where Mary's parents had lived.

Jesus, now twenty-eight years of age, continued to stay close to His parents, daily helping Joseph with his carpentry work and taking care of any jobs that would take His earthly father outside the village. Mary had noticed many young ladies in town attempting to catch His eye, but she knew her son's thoughts were far beyond that of this world.

Life seemed somewhat normal, but Mary reminded herself constantly that their family, especially where her oldest son was concerned, was far from ordinary. She would never allow herself to forget that again, reflecting on Jesus' reminder to her and Joseph when He was but twelve years of age. Though completely respectful of His parents on earth, He was here to be about His Father's business, and Mary always reminded herself that eventually, Jesus, like her other children, would leave them to complete His life's purpose. Perhaps it was fear of the unknown that nagged at her, but for a reason she could not explain, a feeling of despair seemed to have anchored itself within her heart today.

"Mary!" Joseph hailed as he came through the open door. "Where is my lovely wife?"

"I am here, Joseph," she acknowledged pulling herself from her wandering thoughts and pounding a large lump of dough with her fist. Her husband always brightened her mood. She was up to her elbows in bread dough when he found her, preparing enough for her family, as well as extra to share if needed, just as her mother had always done.

"Jesus is outside the city gates," he explained taking a bite out of an apple he snatched from his wife's table, "completing a task for me at Nathan and Myah's stables. Apparently a ram burst through the gate during the night."

"Poor Nathan!" Mary exclaimed, "He has had the worst time of it with this last flock of rams!"

"Hmm," Joseph agreed, his mouth too full to respond before swallowing. "Elias has sent word that he needs me," he stated around another bite, "Come with me and visit with Shira while I repair a broken beam in their barn."

Mary looked up for the first time since he had entered the kitchen. Joseph could not stop the chuckle which escaped his lips at the sight of flour smeared across her cheek. He slowly walked to her side, kissing the upturned cheek she offered him, and wiping the flour smudge from off it.

"Can you not wait for Jesus to return?" she asked him, "He would be of much more help than I. Besides, I am tending to this dough at the moment." Mary laughed at Joseph's feigned look of disappointment. She worried that he tended to forget his age at times. Though still young at heart, neither of them were as young as they use to be.

"I am here mother!" Anna sang as she entered their home, an empty basket swinging from her arm. "I have just returned from sharing yesterday's bread with the widow across the street. I shall finish this chore for you so you can accompany Father."

"There, you see," Joseph exclaimed cheerfully, his arms open wide as if he had won a major victory. "My precious daughter shall finish household chores, so you, my dear wife, may spend some time with a dear friend and enjoy a walk by your 'old' husband's side! Come!" he teased her as Mary began to pull dough from her fingers, realizing her defeat. "If we hurry we shall be home before nightfall!"

Anna plunged into the dough before her as Joseph escorted his wife into the afternoon sun. On the way to Elias' they laughed and talked of their early days together, recounting their first days as a family and pondering over the life Jehovah had given them. Life in Nazareth had been good to them, and God had given them good children and good friends. They spoke of how far they had come in their relationship toward one another, since Gabriel had visited them both before they were wed. Their conversation was sincere, but happy as they recounted their years together. So what then was causing this nagging feeling of dread that Mary could not seem to shake?

227

Once they reached the home of Elias, Mary first accompanied Joseph into the barn to see what task lay before him. The main beam of the loft, heavy with hay for Elias' livestock, threatened to collapse at any moment. Mary listened as the two men discussed options for repair. If not repaired, the loft would surely collapse and possibly pull the rest of the barn down with it.

Mary did not wish to question her husband's decisions, but their relationship was a strong one, based on mutual respect and understanding. She knew he would not be offended if she were respectfully open with him.

"Joseph," she spoke quietly, when he and Elias had finished their discussion, "could this not wait until tomorrow, when Jesus could assist you? I am just afraid this might be a bit much for you to handle on your own."

Joseph pretended to be appalled at his wife's admission. His fake look of shock brought laughter from his friend. Mary was not laughing. Quickly Joseph pulled his wife into an embrace, kissing the top of her head.

"Do not worry, dear wife, Elias is here to assist me. Go visit with Shira and I shall have this mended in no time. At least patched enough to hold through the night. Then Jesus and I shall return tomorrow to repair it properly."

Elias shook his head in agreement. He would not have called Joseph out on such short notice so late in the afternoon, but he could not afford to lose his barn. He was thankful to have such a close friend who was also such an experienced carpenter.

Mary agreed, though still a bit un-nerved, and made her way into the house to visit with her friend. The visit was a good one, each of them talking

228

excitedly about the upcoming grandchild they would share and catching up as women do. It had been some time since the two of them had been able to visit so freely. Mary enjoyed her visit very much and was finally able to breathe deeply feeling as if this visit was exactly what she needed.

Their conversation had just begun to lull when Mary heard the sound coming from outside. There was a large snap, a creak and then a crash seeming to shake the earth right outside the window behind her. Both women were on their feet immediately, almost colliding as they raced out the door into clouds of dust and debris. Mary felt the scream catch in her throat as the dust settled and she saw the barn, where her husband and Elias had been working, lying in a mass of rubble.

Mary looked around her, seeing everything in slow motion. She felt the pressure beside her, almost dragging her down as Shira grabbed her arm for support. Men came from all directions racing toward the mound of splintered wood, shouting commands that Mary could not make out. All she could hear was a roaring in her head and Shira crying out for "Elias" from her place beside her. Suddenly she heard another sound shattering her ears and only then did she realize it was her own, piercing scream, as the terror which had been captured in her chest finally burst forth.

"Joseph!" she cried, now on her knees with Shira as they clung to one another. "My husband!" she cried to anyone who would listen. Other women from the village approached her and Shira, falling around them to offer their support then finally attempting to get them back on their feet and into the house while the men worked to pull the heavy beams away from the men hidden somewhere underneath them.

Finally, as the light gave way to darkness, Elias was helped into the house. Mary sat staring into space as Shira rushed to her husband's side. Mary watched as his bloody arm reached up to encircle his wife's neck. His body was bruised and it looked as if his other arm may be broken, but he would live.

Moments later, Benjamin arrived, having heard about the accident. He had left Elizabeth with Anna, encouraging her to stay and wait for news there, afraid for her to be on the scene in her expectant condition. After seeing to the welfare of his father, he too joined in the search for Joseph.

Mary continued to wait, her patience beginning to wear thin when Jesus arrived, immediately going to His mother's side and holding her as she released tears she had been holding in. He had only been there for a few moments, when she heard the shout that Joseph had been found. Walking to the open door, she watched as her husband's body was pulled from the rubble.

Surprisingly, his injuries looked minor, save for the large gash across his forehead. Yet, for reason's she could not explain, her first and immediate response was not to rush to Joseph's side, but to turn and look at her son. She did not know exactly what she expected to see in His face, perhaps the answer to the question she dared not voice to those now carrying her husband's body toward the house, and though she felt a peace she could not explain, she also saw sorrow in Jesus' eyes. Mary closed her eyes and leaned against the door frame for support. Sinking to her knees, Jesus' arms going around her, she met the realization that Joseph was gone.

Chapter 24

Life had changed drastically for Mary. Her precious Anna had been reluctant to leave when her betrothal period had passed, sorrow still weighing heavily on them all, yet Mary had encouraged her to keep her promise and begin her life. As with all her children, apart from Jesus, their lives continued on, separate from her, just as they should have been.

At first, she often sat in silence, her heart heavy, allowing her tears to fall. Jesus had continued His earthly father's carpentry trade, accepting only jobs that kept Him close to home. Mary felt this may have been for her benefit, but she could sense a restlessness beginning to settle over her oldest child. He was thirty years of age, and Mary felt as though His purpose for coming to this world was about to become clear to all. Although she had always known this day would come, she was not yet ready to let Him go, fearful for the loss she would again experience. The old man Simeon's words often passed through her mind from the temple so many years ago. *"Yea, a sword shall pierce through thy own soul also, that the thoughts of many hearts may be revealed."* Prayer for grace and wisdom in time to come was a constant prayer as she wondered what part, if any, she would play in her son's great commission.

Often she and Jesus would sit after their evening meal, discussing the things of God. No one understood them like her son, seeing as how He was God in human form, and Mary enjoyed this part of her day more than any other. Thankful for their extended time together, she also loved the way the light would dance in His eyes as He spoke to her of the Scriptures. He provided joy to her weary soul and reminded her that she, too, had a purpose here. She had been chosen to be the mother of the Son of God, and she would fulfill that role to her best potential, regardless of what that may entail.

Their conversation this night was not tense, but it was serious. Mary pulled her worn shawl about her shoulders, relishing the warmth it still provided. Not so much physical warmth anymore, it was tattered in places beyond repair, but the warmth it gave to her weary soul; the memories it held of providing her own warmth, those of swaddling her children, and most of all, the cherished memories of Joseph.

"John is baptizing believers in the Jordan River," Jesus spoke in a light but solemn tone.

"I have heard such," Mary answered. "Elizabeth and Zacharias would be pleased at the job their son has done in telling others of You. He is fulfilling his purpose in preparing their hearts for what is to come."

"And how is your heart, Mother?" Jesus asked respectfully. "Are you prepared to accept the things which are to come?" Jesus looked directly in her eyes from across the room.

Breaking His gaze, Mary swallowed hard, realizing as she so often did, that His question was for her benefit. He already knew the answer, but respected her enough to allow her time to search her heart and answer as she chose.

"I have been praying for grace and mercy to accept that which I cannot control," she answered honestly. "I pray I will have the wisdom needed and the strength to endure whatever lies in our future. And though it pains me, I remember that you are much more than just my son. You were sent to this world for a far greater purpose."

"The time has come, Mother, for me to begin my ministry." He spoke forthright but his eyes were gentle, and Mary knew He did not wish to cause her pain, though He did want her to prepare herself. "I will begin by traveling to the Jordan River to be baptized by John. It would honor me if you were to accompany me." His statement was not a command, but a request.

"I would not dream of staying behind," she answered Him whole-heartedly. "When do we leave?" She attempted to muster a grin but failed. She knew by beginning His public ministry, Jesus was casting Himself into the open, and though she wasn't sure why that bothered her so, it caused a heaviness in her heart that she could feel deep into her soul.

"With the morning's light," He spoke as He rose. Holding out His hand to her, she took it and squeezed it firmly, bringing it to her lips before she let go. He paused as He passed and bent to gently kiss the top of her head before continuing to His room for the night. Once He had gone, she allowed one tear to streak her face before gathering herself and rising to begin preparations for their journey in the morning. God the Father was not finished with her just yet, and she would wallow in pity no longer.

Mary was surprised at the size of the crowd gathered as they approached the river. Over the murmurs of the people, John's words still rang loud and clear to all who listened well before they could see him standing in the midst of the large body of water.

"*There cometh one mightier than I after me*," he preached, "*the latchet of whose shoes I am not worthy to stoop down and unloose. I indeed have baptized you with water: but He shall baptize you with the Holy Ghost.*" Close enough now to see them, John paused and held his hands high toward the heavens. The crowd parted as Jesus and Mary moved toward the river. "Behold!" he cried, "*Behold the Lamb of God, which taketh away the sin of the world. This is He of whom I said, After me cometh a man which is preferred before me: for he was before me.*"

Mary paused on the bank as her son continued to make His way into the water. Approaching John, Jesus spoke to him in low tones, but Mary could easily understand John's response to being asked to baptize Him.

"*I have need to be baptized of thee, and comest thou to me*?" John asked, clearly confused and humbled that he was being asked to baptize the very man of whom he preached.

"*Suffer it to be so now: for thus it becometh us to fulfill all righteousness*," Jesus commanded him, reminding John of the importance that they uphold the law.

With a simple nod of his head, John placed his arm behind Jesus' back and his hand over the mouth and nose of his Lord. A moment later, Mary witnessed her son being submerged into the water and then rising out of it again. *A symbol of the death, burial and resurrection of the Lord,* a small voice spoke to her heart.

234

Mary bowed her head in reverence as the sky above her seemed to open, and one, lone dove descended. Jesus exited the water just as the dove lit upon his shoulder.

"*THIS IS MY BELOVED SON, IN WHOM I AM WELL PLEASED*," a voice sounded from above. Mary looked to the crowd around her, uncertain as to whether everyone else had heard the voice and witnessed the dove. Her eyes fell only on her son, who nodded in her direction from across the river, then turned and walked away.

Many days had passed since Jesus had been baptized. Mary still had no idea as to where her son had gone or what He was doing, but she had accepted the fact that much was bound to happen of which she was unsure. All she could do was trust and have faith. God the Father had never failed to give her an ample supply of grace to bring her through each trial she endured, and He would not fail to do so now. Many had spoken of Jesus' baptism, and shortly after, news had come that John had been thrown into prison as he preached. Mary prayed for God's will to be done and reminded herself, as Joseph had often, that nothing took the Father by surprise.

She had just set out her evening meal, including a place for Jesus should He return, for the forty-second time since He had left. She looked for Him every day and knew at some point, He would come into her home again. Asking for blessing over the bread before she broke it, she startled when her door opened and her son stood before her.

"Mother," He spoke simply.

235

"My son! You are home!" Quickly rising from her place she placed her palms upon the beautiful face of her beloved son, taking in His frail countenance and quickly ushering Him inside. "Are you well, Jesus? Do you thirst?"

"I am well," He spoke with surety. "I have passed many days in the wilderness, but have since been ministered to and cared for by angels sent from My Father."

They spent the next hour talking as Jesus explained the temptations He had endured in the wilderness and the purpose of them. He then told His mother of His future plans to go throughout Galilee, preaching the Kingdom of God to the people, encouraging them to believe and repent before it was too late.

"You will see me again, Mother, at the wedding feast of Nathan and Myah's son in Cana. Until that time, I shall dwell here and there preaching and teaching as the Spirit moves me."

"Then tonight, you shall rest once more under my roof and begin Your day on the morrow after You have eaten." Jesus smiled at the "mothering" tone His mother had resumed. Taking His elbow and encouraging Him to rise, she removed the mantle from His shoulders. "Go my son," she kissed His cheek and motioned to the wash basin, "clean yourself and get a good night's rest. I shall see You on the morrow."

True to His word, after the next morning, Mary did not see Jesus again until the wedding feast in Cana, though talk of His preaching and teaching was all about their land. She learned from the village that men had joined Him as He traveled, becoming more than just His followers but His disciples. She was honored to be His mother and proud of the work He was doing though the same nagging fear continued to weigh heavily on her heart.

Her other children were present also at the wedding feast, and Mary was thrilled to have the majority of her family together again. She felt sadness, however, as she witnessed the way Jesus' younger siblings regarded their oldest brother. James was especially cold toward Him, and Mary did not hesitate to call her son out when she could discreetly do so.

"James," she spoke sharply but respectfully to her adult son, "why do you treat your brother so? Have you not witnessed how different He is, how different He always has been?"

"If you are implying His perfection, Mother, we have all witnessed such, yet that does not make Him the Son of God! Because He has always been respectful and well behaved, you now expect us to believe He was sent from Heaven? Were not we all?" he scoffed. Mary stared wide-eyed at the man before her. Never had she imagined her own children would see and not believe.

"I mean no disrespect, Mother. I just do not believe Jesus to be any more 'special' than Joses, Simon or Judas, or even myself. We are all sons of Joseph, mother! You have always had a soft heart toward Jesus, and I understand your beginnings with father were different than most, but He is just a common man, as are we all. He is no more special just because He was born in a stable on a starlit night."

Mary stood in shock as James walked away from her. Anna had come up behind her and placed her hands on her mother's shoulders. "He is just jealous, Mother, of all the attention Jesus has gained lately."

Mary looked to her youngest, "You believe, Anna, do you not?" Mary's eyes searched her daughter's, begging to see acceptance there. She was disappointed.

"Mother," Anna paused. "Right now, I am not sure what I believe." Mary lowered her head, staring at the floor in front of her. Her thoughts were quickly interrupted, however, as the mother of the groom came rushing past her in a clear panic.

"Myah, what is it?" Mary asked.

"The wine is gone!" Myah spoke in hushed tones. "It is gone! We have no more! What will the people think? What are we to do? We will be laughed at. Ridiculed! Our family will be ruined!" she cried wringing her hands together until they were red.

Mary led Myah to a corner where they could have a bit of solitude and worked to calm her briefly before passing her off to Anna to console. Seeking out Jesus, Mary approached Him quietly. Sensing her approach, Jesus turned from His disciples to see His mother standing anxiously behind Him.

"Son," she began quietly, "they have no wine. It is all gone," she spoke quickly.

Jesus understood the graveness of the situation. The family would be tarnished forever due to poor planning by the hosts of the wedding party. This couple, who should be beginning a life of happiness together, would forever be marked as slothful and ignorant. Still, He made no sudden movement, but looked carefully at the woman before Him.

"*Woman, what have I to do with thee? Mine hour is not yet come,*" He spoke tenderly.

Mary smiled into the face of her son. She knew that this was not His problem to fix, and that His words were a gentle reminder to her that His gifts were to be used for the greater good. She also recognized that He had not refused His help.

Turning to the servants standing nearby, she gave them a very simple task, "*Whatsoever He saith unto you, do it.*"

"Yes, ma'am," they agreed. "Master, what shall we do?" they questioned, looking to Jesus.

Pointing to six water pots of stone standing by the wall, Jesus spoke his instructions clearly. "*Fill the water pots with water.*" Quickly the servants ran about filling each water pot to the brim. "*Draw out now, and bear unto the governor of the feast,*" He stated simply.

The servants looked to Mary, clearly expecting something more from this man she was so sure would help them. Mary smiled and nodded her head. "Do exactly as He says," she quietly reminded them.

Though slightly nervous, but knowing not what else to do, the head servant drew from the water pot and approached the governor. Holding his breath and silently praying, he waited as the governor raised the cup to his lips. The look which crossed his features caused alarm to course through the servant's body before a wide grin broke across the governor's face as he called to the bridegroom.

"*Every man at the beginning doth set forth good wine, but thou has kept the good until now!*" he applauded him. Mary looked proudly to her son who would never cease to amaze her.

As the months passed, news of Jesus' preachings, teachings, and miracles continued to spread throughout the land. More and more followed Him seeking not only knowledge, but also redemption and healing of their diseases. The more miracles He administered unto those who believed in Him, the more news spread.

Mary had been among His most faithful followers, accompanying Him and His disciples everywhere she could. Though she was not favored any more than the other women who followed Him, the disciples recognized her as the woman she was, the mother to the man they considered their Lord and Master. She was respected as such and became a kindred spirit with them all, except for one.

The man called Judas Iscariot appeared to all who knew him to be among the most trusted and honorable of Jesus' disciples. He was ever present and mindful of his Master, and was always the first to comply when Jesus made known a request. Always eager to please his Lord, Judas was kind without fault and trusted by the others enough to carry the moneybag which held what little they earned. Judas was considered one of their brothers, and any one of them would defend him to the end.

Mary had never voiced her concern to her son, for she did not herself know what it was that bothered her about Judas Iscariot. Yet, as was often the case, she could not stop the nagging notion that something about him was amiss. She had no good reason not to trust the man; he had done her no wrong. Because of this, she would often pass her concerns off as a silly notion and would force any corrupt thoughts from her mind, reminding herself that her purpose was not to judge others but to follow wherever her son led. Besides, there were matters on her heart of a far more urgent nature.

Shortly after she, Jesus, and His disciples had settled in Capernaum, news had come that John had been killed. He had been thrown in prison simply because he had preached against an act which had been performed by the king. Unwilling to back down from his beliefs and preaching, his life had been taken by beheading. Mary shuddered at the thought; the man

Simeon's words playing in her mind as they had done a hundred times before.

When John's disciples had come to Jesus with news of his murder, her son had looked to His disciples instructing them to *"Come ye yourselves apart into a desert place, and rest awhile."* She had respected their need for solitude and realized her own, returning to Nazareth for some much needed rest herself. That was over two years ago.

She had seen Jesus on several occasions since, though getting close to Him was impossible more than once. She knew He felt her presence when she was near, whether or not He would come close enough to feel her touch. More often than seeing Him, she heard others speak of their encounters with "the Man who claims to have come to seek and to save the lost."

The most popular stories were those of His miracles. Whether healing blinded eyes, making the lame to walk, or even raising the dead from their sleep, it seemed the miracles Jesus preformed were on the lips of everyone she encountered. Elias had even spoken that Herod had been heard voicing his fears to one in his company that John the Baptist had risen from the dead.

A sudden knock at her door startled her. "Mary," a voice called to her. A sigh of relief escaped her as she recognized the voice.

"Shira!" she exclaimed opening the door and embracing her friend. "You always know when I need a visit!"

"Are you well?" Shira questioned as she was ushered inside.

"Just old and tired," Mary remarked with a smirk. "I fear I forget how aged I have become until I allow myself a rest. Where is Elias?" Mary stretched

241

her back, unaware of how long she had been lost in thought until she was interrupted.

"He is finishing duties required of him before night falls. And Jesus? He is well?" Shira answered, her voice marked with concern for her friend.

"He is," Mary answered a bit hesitantly, "at least I believe so," she finished honestly. "I confess I worry about my son, Shira," she continued. "He is becoming too well known."

"I do not understand, Mary," Shira admitted. "He had to make Himself known in order to win others to Himself. Is that not His purpose?"

Mary returned to the chair where she had been lost in thought only a few moments ago. "His purpose is to save His people from their sins," Mary agreed. "But at what cost, Shira? John was murdered for simply preaching what is right. There are as many who do not believe, as there are those who do. I am not sure the world will remain a friend to my son. I just cannot shake this feeling of dread."

"Nonsense, Mary," Shira gently rebuked her friend. "You are only tired and being cynical. Once you have rested, you will feel more at peace. Elias and I have been discussing the Passover, and we want you to accompany us to Jerusalem. We plan to leave in plenty of time to avoid the crowds and so that the journey will not be a rushed one. Elias has already secured lodging for our time there, just outside the city, and we plan to stay for an extended period of time. You will see Jesus there and will at last put your fears to rest."

Mary looked to the woman who was her dearest friend in the world. Though she agreed to journey with them to Jerusalem for the Passover, she felt her fears would never truly be at rest.

Chapter 25

Mary sat alone on a small terrace outside their dwelling. The night was dark and again an uneasy tension had settled in her heart. They had been in Jerusalem for days, and though she had heard news of her son, including accounts of miracles He had recently performed and of His grand entry into Jerusalem, she herself still had not seen Him. What troubled her most however, was news she had received of a confrontation which had taken place in the temple between Jesus and the religious leaders. She knew that to confront them meant to challenge them, and that would not bode well with the chief priests, scribes, and elders who considered themselves so perfectly sound and accurate in their beliefs.

She almost chuckled at the thought of Jesus running the dove sellers and the money changers from the temple with a whip as she had heard it told. "A den of thieves He called it," the lady had told her who had witnessed the event first hand. "He flipped over their tables and ordered them from His house!" she had told enthusiastically. "He reminded everyone quite clearly that the temple was a place of prayer not a place to be used for extortion." Mary allowed herself a smile.

Everyone knew how corrupt those who were selling sacrifices had become, and though Jesus was perfectly meek and usually very serene, He was not to be trifled with, especially where the temple was concerned. Years of hard carpentry work had turned His human body into one quite capable of overturning the heavy wooden tables the moneychangers used. The thought made her ache to hold Him in her arms.

There was also the issue regarding the number of followers Jesus had gained. At one point, the crowd was massive and news spread quickly of Jesus feeding at least five thousand from a basket consisting of only enough food to satisfy a young boy. If anything unnerved the palace officials, it was the fear of someone becoming more admired and more revered than they.

Jesus was God's son, and Mary was wise enough to realize that fact was not something which would remain quiet, only realized by family members and those few close enough to call Him a friend. Yet deep in her heart, she had always hoped her body would be cold in the grave before His purpose for coming to this world revealed itself. If she could just get word that He was well, perhaps she could rest. Mary did as she had always done when she was troubled, she began to pray.

Only moments after she had bowed her head, the simple word came softly to her ears. "Mother." It was so soft in fact that she thought she had fallen asleep while praying and had begun to dream. Still, she looked around, and at last her eyes caught sight of Jesus in the shadows.

Rising quickly to her feet, He raised His hand to stop her from approaching. Tears filled her eyes then rolled along her face, as her hand went swiftly to her mouth in an attempt to quiet her cry at finally seeing Him. He was in the shadows, which meant He did not wish to be seen. Her heart ached with fear, yet of what she was not sure. Seeing Him so close, yet still out of reach, was almost more than she could bear.

"Mother, you must trust more than ever in the hours to come," He spoke quietly. *"Behold the hour cometh that I will be betrayed by a friend and delivered into the hands of those who wish to destroy me."*

"Betrayed by a friend?" she questioned softly. Before the question had left her lips, she knew exactly of whom her son was speaking. "Judas Iscariot," she whispered quietly, sinking back onto the bench for support, her hand going to her racing heart. So her mother's intuition had been correct. "Why, Jesus? For what cause? What profit would he gain from such treachery?" Her heartbeat increased, and her mind ran wild in an attempt to make sense of what He was telling her.

"The Son has come to seek and to save those which are lost. Remember not the scriptures?" He softly rebuked her, *"So they weighed for my price thirty pieces of silver."*

As He spoke the words, other prophecies began flooding her mind. Everything she had been taught as a young child, things she had forced herself not to think upon since she had been told she would bear the Son of God, prophecies too painful to allow occupancy in her thoughts…the man Simeon's words which had haunted her since that day in the temple.

"Then flee my son!" she spoke with certainty. "Do not allow yourself to be taken!" she pleaded quietly, yet fervently, with His figure still in the shadows. Her sobs broke in her throat as she worked to quiet herself yet again.

"This that is written must yet be accomplished in me, And He was reckoned among the transgressors: for the things concerning me have an end."

"No, Jesus. Please, my son, flee," she begged, now falling to her knees, her heart feeling as if it were being wrenched from her chest. "You can hide in the mountains, call upon Your angels, You are the Son of God, Jesus, please do not allow this to pass. You have done no wrong! There must be another way for the sins of man to be forgiven! I cannot bear to watch You suffer!"

"Ye now therefore have sorrow:" he began, *"but I will see you again, and your heart shall rejoice, and your joy no man taketh from you."* His eyes were tender as He spoke to her from His place in the shadows, His voice falling upon her ears as if a gentle breeze. *"For the Father himself loveth you, because ye have loved me, and have believed that I came out from God. I came forth from the Father, and am come into the world: again, I leave the world, and go to the Father."*

Mary allowed her head to fall onto her arms as she sobbed, her heart broken in two. Though she knew what her son was telling her must come to pass in order to fulfill His purpose for coming to the world, the mother in her could not bear to let Him go. Not like this. Sobbing quietly, she felt His presence come near as He approached her from behind, placing His hands on each of her arms. He gently assisted her back into a sitting position on the bench before continuing to speak. His last words were still hushed, but as always, they were rich with wisdom and instruction, *"And when ye stand praying, forgive, if ye have ought against any: that your Father also which is in heaven may forgive your trespasses."*

"How can I ever forgive those who bring this destruction upon my son?" she spoke through clenched teeth. She did not turn and look at Him, for she did not wish the anger in her eyes to be seen by the boy she had carried, the boy she had raised, the boy she had loved, who had now become a man willing to give His life for the sins of a world which rejected Him, at the hands of those who would betray Him.

"The man who was born, is, and will always be, The Son of God," He reminded her gently, finishing the thought she had neglected to. Mary continued to stare at the ground before her, stunned at how easily He read her thoughts and the gentleness of how He reminded her that it was not she to whom He belonged.

"I go now to pray," He whispered, and Mary was certain she heard His voice break. *"The effectual fervent prayer of a righteous man availeth much.* I covet your prayers, Mother. *The spirit indeed is willing, but the flesh is weak.* Never forget, I love you. "*

She felt the pressure of His kiss as He gently bent to touch the top of her head, followed by an emptiness swiftly filling her heart at the loss of His touch. Rising quickly from her place, she longed for one final embrace, but saw only the dark of night where her son had been.

"Shira, have you seen Mary?" Elias asked of his wife.

"She went out onto the terrace several hours ago. I felt her need for solitude, Elias. Her heart seems so heavy. I have checked on her several times but have not disturbed her. She was praying, Elias, pleading with the Father. I did not linger to hear her words. I felt to do so would be disrespectful, but her prayer appeared agonizing."

Elias too had noticed Mary's solemn countenance during the last few days. He knew their friend missed her husband and worried over her son. Thoughts of Joseph took him back to a night far different from this one just over thirty-three years before. Then Elias had stood looking out a stable window as the sun crept over the horizon to begin the day, after a night which had been filled with elation and excitement over the birth of their King. This night was dark with heaviness in the air that seemed to add weights to his shoulders. That night, Mary's face had been flushed with joy over giving birth to the Son of God. This night, her face was laden with worry and despair.

It was then that the conversation he and Joseph had shared that early morning, so many years ago, came flooding back to his mind. The conversation over the prophecies they had been taught as children. The prophecies of the coming King, whom they now beheld, and those concerning the death of the Son of God.

Elias bolted upright from the chair in which he was sitting, shocking Shira so that she dropped the garment which she was mending. At the same moment, Mary came through the back door of the dwelling, her eyes swollen from crying, her breath labored from intensive praying. "Elias," she spoke, but her voice, heavy with emotion, was interrupted by a pounding at the front door before she could say more.

Shira rushed to Mary's side as Elias opened the front door and John, one of their Lord's disciples, burst through, falling to his knees before he stopped. He stood, barely allowing himself to catch his breath before making eye contact with the mother of his Lord.

"They have taken Him, my lady," he spoke through an exhausted and trembling voice. "They have taken Jesus."

Chapter 26

Mary stared blankly at the man before her. She could not speak or think, she could only stare, his words echoing over and over in her head, "They have taken Him," John had said.

"Taken Him?" Elias broke the silence. "Who has taken Him?"

"The soldiers!" he almost yelled. "They came into the garden where Jesus had been praying and took Him! As if He were a criminal!" John explained with rasping breath. He attempted to calm himself in order to be understood. "As we were leaving the garden, Judas came upon us with a band of men and soldiers," he recounted. "They looked as if they were anticipating a battle, yet Judas approached the Master, and simply kissed His cheek as in greeting. Then the soldiers moved to arrest Him. Peter drew his sword in an attempt to stop them, even cutting off a soldier's ear, but Jesus rebuked him! We all tried to defend Him, but He instructed us to put up our swords so that the Scriptures may be fulfilled. He even healed the soldier by replacing the ear Peter had cut off. He put it back into place as if it had never been severed."

"And still they arrested Him?" Shira asked in surprise from her place at Mary's side.

John paused and lowered his head as if suddenly he himself had trouble believing all that had transpired. "They did. They bound Him with ropes and chains and led Him out of the garden," he said, his voice breaking at the realization of it all.

"Where, John? Where were they taking Him?" Elias questioned.

"I do not know," he admitted, looking to the man before him as a single tear escaped his eyes. Dropping his head, his eyes filled with shame and guilt, he finished, "for I, as well as the others, fled." He pinched the corners of his eyes in an attempt to stop more tears which threatened to fall over the admission that he had fled from his beloved master's side.

Mary left her place from the shelter of Shira's arm and approached John. Raising his head to look into his eyes, she gently took his face in her hands. Reaching up, she wiped the tear that rested on his cheek and softly kissed the place where it had been.

"You have been a loyal friend to my son," she spoke softly. "Do not condemn yourself. It is Judas who has betrayed Him. Think John," she spoke calmly, "did you hear anything that might give you an idea where they have led Him?" she asked. There was strength in her voice that betrayed the fear in her heart.

"It all happened so fast. I had to get to you as quickly as I could; I do not even know which way they went once outside the garden." He was quiet for a moment while he attempted to pull something, anything, from his memory. "I would assume...I believe I overhead one of the soldiers utter something about Annas and Caiaphas would be expecting them."

"They plan to put Him on trial," Elias spoke up. "They would not take Him to Annas or Caiaphas otherwise."

"On trial?" Shira questioned. "For what cause?"

"I do not know, but I expect the Sanhedrin will be involved." Elias looked to Mary. Their eyes met and held.

"I must go to Him," she spoke confidently, though her eyes were filled with fear and unshed tears.

Elias thought upon the prophecies and shook his head. "Mary, I do not know that you wish to be present at a Sanhedrin trial," he began. "Already they have taken Him in the night which is beyond the normal laws. There is evil about, and I am not sure…" He stopped as he saw the determination on her face.

Mary remembered the prophecies as well. "I may not be able to save Him, Elias, but I will not abandon my son," she spoke plainly.

With a nod of his head, John led the way as the solemn few made their way quickly into the night.

Because their lodging was right outside the city gates, it did not take long for them to reach the place where crowds were beginning to gather. Fires burned in large barrels as people warmed themselves, torches held high to illuminate the darkness. Hundreds, it seemed, had found themselves outside the palace of the high priest Caiaphas. Though they could not get close, they were close enough to see Jesus standing before the assembly, Caiaphas before Him. The high priest raised his hands to his followers, the crowd quieting quickly as he raised his voice to be heard.

"Is there one who has an accusation against this man?" Caiaphas asked, a smirk playing on his lips. Quiet murmurs began to circulate throughout the crowd, but no one spoke up against Jesus.

"Surely this man has been brought to me at this hour for some wrongdoing," he continued. "Surely someone has found wrong in Him," he continued, his eyes searching the crowd for any sign that he would gain the accusation which he sought.

A burley man finally spoke from the crowd. "I heard Him say He could destroy the temple of God and build it back in three days," he yelled, seemingly proud of himself for finding something that might interest Caiaphas.

"Destroy the temple of God and build it back in three days?" Caiaphas emphasized to the assembly before him. Clearly he expected Jesus to begin pleading His innocence behind him but was puzzled when no sound came forth from his prisoner. "*Answerest though nothing*?" he asked turning to look at Him. "What have You to say to the charge which has been made of You?" Stepping directly in front of Jesus, he spit his next words into His face. "Did You claim that You could destroy the temple of God and rebuild it within three days?"

All eyes turned to the Son of God, who continued to stand silently in the face of contempt. Not a word was spoken; no movement was made. Caiaphas moved closer, anger kindling in his eyes at not being answered immediately. He raised his hand as if to strike in an attempt to create fear in the man before him but did not quite have the courage to carry through on his threat. Instead, he lowered his hand and straightened his robes, yet his anger still obviously raged.

"*I adjure thee by the living God, that thou tell us whether thou be the Christ, the Son of God*," he yelled into Jesus' face. "Have You not made that claim?"

Mary knew Caiaphas would not have been so forceful had her son's hands not been bound. Straining her neck to see over the crowd, she searched the face of her son, not sure if He would audibly answer or not. Even from her place she could see the swelling on His jaw and brow from earlier mistreatment by the soldiers. She knew Him well enough to know that He would not have struggled as they bound Him.

"Thou hast said," Jesus answered simply.

Caiaphas screamed out in frustration, ripping frantically at the robe he wore. "*He has spoken blasphemy;*" he yelled to the crowd. "*What further need have we of witnesses? Behold, now ye have heard this blasphemy*! What think ye?" he asked turning to the people, a huge smile spread across his rounded face.

"He is guilty of death," a man from the crowd yelled, and immediate cheers went up throughout the crowd.

"NO!" Mary shouted, though her words were muted by the multitude. She looked around herself frantically as she realized that she and the three others with her seemed to be the only ones present who were in protest of the outrageous verdict. "NO!" she screamed out again. "Please, God, let there be another way!" She pleaded, lifting her voice yet still not being heard.

John attempted to keep her on her feet as Elias supported her from the other side. The crowd was wild around them, cheering on the verdict that Jesus be condemned to death. "He claims to be GOD!" they yelled.

255

"He is blasphemous!" another screamed. Mary covered her ears with her hands in an attempt to muffle the cheers continuing around her, all while begging the Father to have mercy on her son, on HIS Son.

At that moment, the world seemed to pause around her, save for the single sound of a cock crowing loudly in the distance. Mary looked to her son seeing His eyes land upon another of His disciples, Peter, who immediately turned and ran, almost knocking Elias over in his attempt to flee. The trio looked to John who seemed shocked as he explained to them what had taken place. "Jesus told Peter, despite his objections, that he would deny knowing Him three times before the cock would crow this day. Peter will be devastated by his own actions, though it is proof of yet another prophecy being fulfilled this night."

"There is still hope, Mary," Elias spoke beside her, loud enough for her to hear above the crowd who continued to roar. "They must take Him before Pilate and the Roman government for the death penalty to be carried out. Perhaps they will find no fault with Him there."

It was not the answer Mary was hoping for, but it was enough to give her the strength to carry on and to allow her heart, which seemed to have stood still in her chest at the mention of His death, to beat once again. Mary watched as the soldiers jerked the chain which bound Jesus' hands, forcing Him back into the temple and out of the crowd's view. She saw the soldiers as they struck His face even though He went with them willingly without struggle. Though she longed to go to Him, she knew such an attempt would be useless. With John's arm still supporting her, they made their way from the midst of the crowd to a small alcove between two large buildings.

"I am sorry, but I do not understand," Shira cried from Elias' shoulder. "Why are they putting Jesus through this? What has He done? I do not understand the charges."

Elias looked first to the mother of his Lord then to his wife before speaking. "The Roman government is afraid of Him, Shira. His followers have increased; His fame is becoming wide spread. He questions their every claim of religious understanding."

"They fear a political upheaval," John went on to explain. "He is becoming more powerful in the eyes of the people than they."

"They are afraid He is who He claims to be," Mary spoke slowly, breaking her silence. Her breathing was still labored, but she was somewhat calmer now, calmness she could only attribute to grace from the Father above. "He is the Son of God, and that threatens them."

"But He has done no wrong," Shira spoke sincerely.

Mary's next words stunned them all. *"He was oppressed, and He was afflicted, yet He opened not His mouth,"* she spoke plainly, quoting word for word the prophecy from Isaiah. *"He is brought as a lamb to the slaughter, and as a sheep before her shearers is dumb, so He openeth not His mouth."* Again, Elias was in awe of the strength the woman before Him possessed. John pulled her to himself once more, allowing the tears which now fell to soak his robe.

Little time passed before the crowd began to shuffle and the outer courtyard of the temple began to fill once again. The sun was just beginning to rise over

257

the courtyard as the governor, Pilate, stepped before the assembly. Cheers went up all around them as Mary, John, Elias, and Shira made their way back into the crowd. Jesus was pulled onto the balcony behind Him, and Mary noticed the blood which ran along His face. He continued to stand tall and strong despite the injuries He had sustained at the hands of the soldiers, and Mary feared what more He would have to endure.

"Governor," a man Mary did not recognize began, "we found this fellow perverting the nation and forbidding to give tribute to Caesar."

"He claims that He Himself is Christ the King," another shouted.

"That is treason!" yet another called out causing the crowd to once again call for His punishment.

Pilate raised his hands to quiet the assembly before turning to look at the prisoner behind him. "What have you to say to these accusations? *Art thou the King of the Jews?*"

"*Thou sayest it,*" Jesus responded clearly.

Turning back to the people, Pilate held out his hands in question. "*I find no fault in this man.*" Mary immediately released the breath she did not realize she had been holding, yet fear still nagged at her chest. Something was still not right.

"*He stirreth up the people, teaching throughout all Jewry, beginning from Galilee to this place*" a man beside of him argued.

"He goes about questioning the religious leaders and professing to have come directly from the Father!" another yelled. The crowd began to murmur and argue, clearly unhappy with Pilate's decision.

Pilate again turned to Jesus, "*Answerest thou nothing? Behold how many things they witness against thee,*" he spoke as if Jesus were deaf and could not hear His accusers. Jesus uttered not a word but allowed Pilate to continue with his ponderings.

"Galilee?" Pilate began again with only a moment's hesitation as he straightened the hem on the sleeve of his garment, "did you say he began his teachings in Galilee? So this man is a Galilean?" Pilate asked. "That is Herod's jurisdiction," he continued. "He should have a say in what is to become of Him. Take Him to Herod," he announced waving them away.

Mary watched as again her son was led away, this time to a fate far worse than she had hoped.

Chapter 27

John had disappeared right after Jesus had been sent to Herod. Mary took little notice until he appeared again with canteens of water and some bread for herself, Elias, and Shira. Though she could not eat, she accepted the water and was appreciative of it.

"News has come that Judas was found swinging from a tree shortly after sunrise," John whispered to Elias. "Children witnessed the 'crazy' man as he ran to and fro before he took his own life." Elias had no response that he felt he could utter in the presence of the women before him.

Surprisingly, little time passed between the time Jesus was taken to Herod and when He was returned to Pilate. Yet, each time Jesus was removed and then presented again to the crowd, Mary noticed new cuts and bruises appearing on the face, arms, and neck of her son. She knew that He was aware of her presence, even if she could not be near enough to tend to Him. She saw His eyes cross her face more than once and hoped that her presence might be a balm to His pain.

Mary took in the scene before her realizing that another prisoner had been brought onto the

261

balcony. He leered at her son, spitting toward his feet and calling out false accusations. Jesus did not so much as glance his way, but kept His face forward.

Again Pilate appeared before them, ordering them quiet as their cheers ascended. "Herod and I are in accord that there is no direct fault in this man," he began pointing to Jesus. "Therefore, it being feast day, one of these two prisoners shall be released again unto you. *Whom will ye that I release unto you? Barabbas,"* he asked pointing toward the burly man on his left, *"or Jesus, which is called Christ?* I will find your answer when I return."

Pilate moved to the judgment seat which was at the corner of the balcony. Mary observed others around her already convinced that Barabbas should be the one to be freed. She was one of the few who also observed Pilate's wife approach her husband, which was something unheard of. The discussion appeared to be fairly heated before the lovely woman turned and ran back into the palace seemingly in distress. Pilate appeared to be in thought before shaking his head and rising to again address his people.

"*Whether of the twain will ye that I release unto you?"* he asked of them.

"*Barabbas*!" the multitude yelled.

"*What shall I do then with Jesus which is called Christ*?"

"*Let Him be crucified*!" the crowd yelled.

Crucified! Mary's knees buckled beneath her, but she was held up by John's strong arms. Not crucifixion! She knew her son would be brought as a lamb to the slaughter, she knew the prophecies, but to hear that word come from the mouths of the very people He would give His life for. Please, God, not by crucifixion.

"NO!" Mary yelled out. "Elias, you must stop them!" she cried out. "John, please! He does not deserve this!" Mary knew her pleas were useless, but she could not stand by helplessly as He was condemned to such a death.

"What evil hath He done to you that you would ask for such a death?" Pilate asked of the people.

"Crucify Him, crucify Him, crucify Him," the crowd began to chant.

"Please, God!" Mary cried out, though she could only be heard by those around her. "Do not ask this of Him," she cried aloud.

Pilate dipped his hands into a bowl of water which had been presented to him. Twice he dowsed his hands into the water, making a huge display of washing them before the multitude. "*I am innocent of the blood of this just person: but see you to it,*" he proclaimed. "Release Barabbas," he continued. "Do as ye will with Jesus," he finished before turning and walking away.

"John," Mary spoke, and he quickly ushered her out of the crowd to where a bench rested against the wall. Mary sank onto it right before her knees would have given completely away. Shira noticed how pail and fragile her friend seemed.

"Mary, perhaps we should return," she began.

"No. I will not abandon Him," Mary spoke with surety. "I will see Him through to the end. I only need a moment..." she began, her voice breaking. Mary took several deep breaths, attempting to calm the world spinning around her. Finally, she took a normal breath and stood again to her feet.

"Mary this will in no way be comforting to you," Elias began, but stopped abruptly as she raised her eyes to look into his.

"I have had very little comfort since I entered into womanhood, Elias. I was granted the miracle of giving Him this life–this life which He is now willing to give for me. I gave Him nourishment and protection as a child. I watched Him take His first steps, and I will watch Him take His last. I may not be able to protect Him from harm or from hurt or from death, but as long as there is breath in my body, I will not abandon Him. I can do nothing else for Him, but if He searches me out, He will find me," Mary finished trying to choke back more tears.

"I will not leave your side," John promised her. Mary saw his jaw set in determination not to flee from fear again.

"Nor will we," Elias agreed for himself and Shira, who moved to wrap her arms around her friend and hold her as she cried.

Mary was only allowed a moment's grief before the crowd shifted to the inner court. There she noticed a beam which rose from the stone floor, standing at what she expected to be about four feet tall. Other Roman officers stood around it, men Mary had not seen before in the city, each of them holding large rods with long strips of leather tied to the end. It looked like each of the rods contained at least three additional whips, each of those about three feet long. Mary did not have to be close to see the shards of metal glistening from entwined leather and the pieces of bone so intricately woven within the pieces designed simply for the torture of their victims.

At last a cheer arose and Mary saw her son being led by the chains which bound Him into the center of the court. Though her mother's heart could sense His fear, He made no move to escape, voiced no plea of innocence, but simply approached the beam to which they led Him. A smaller soldier, though he was small by no means, performed the task of removing the clothing from Jesus' back. Mary noticed the bruises already forming across the broad back of her son.

"*I gave my back to the smiters*," Elias quoted quietly from the book of Isaiah.

Slightly bent, so to expose his back perfectly, Jesus was bound to the beam. *So that is why it only stands so tall* Mary thought to herself, *to ensure a perfect target.* She had heard stories of criminals being scourged in the past, but only those so wicked and vile that the evidence presented against them was clear and there was no question as to their guilt and wrongdoings. Never had she witnessed the likes of what she was about to see. Though she wanted to cry out, she held her peace. If her son was willing to accept this torture, she would not make things harder on Him by having Him hear her pointless cries. Yet in her heart, oh how she prayed.

The first lash came, and Mary closed her eyes immediately as blood poured from the back of her son. He winced, but no sound came from His lips. Another and another thrash followed, each seemingly more targeted and harder than the first. At last she allowed herself to close her eyes again but not until she had witnessed flesh being ripped from bone as one of the whips wrapped around His side. There it embedded and had to be pulled with force, bringing with it flesh and muscle, in order to return to the soldier who had issued it.

Finally, He had taken all He could where He stood and fell to His knees. "They will stop now," she thought, but she was mistaken. Again and again they continued to deliver their punishment, the whips now going about His face, neck, and anywhere else they chose to fall. Mary heard her son groan in agony, but

265

still, no outraged cries or pleas to stop, and she wondered if He had breath left to do so.

Able to witness no more, Mary bowed her head, her eyes cast to the ground before her when the soldiers finally stopped their thrashing. With His hands still bound near the top of the post, Jesus lay on His stomach in a pool of blood and pieces of His own flesh.

"He can tolerate no more and continue to breathe, if in fact He continues to now!" Elias yelled, anger tearing at his own heart.

"Would you care to take his place at the thrashing post?" a stocky soldier yelled in his direction. A small scream escaped Shira's lips at the thought of her husband being beaten.

"The man is right," another soldier spoke up. "Remove Him so that this mess can be cleaned up," he ordered. "And do away with these flagellum; they have served their purpose and will be of no more use to us. They are worn out," he smirked throwing his whip to the ground. The soldiers around him burst into laughter as they followed his lead and threw their whips to the ground.

Mary watched as Jesus was released from the post, yet failed to move. Only when two of the soldiers approached, one grabbing Him by the wrist, and another by the hair of His head and began dragging Him away did Mary see one of His eyes open. She knew He saw her standing in complete shock as they dragged Him away.

Mary stared at the scene before her, blood covering every inch of the marble floor. Tears streaked her face as she continued to stare though images of Jesus as a little boy falling and scraping His knee came to her mind. Then she could hold Him, comfort Him, and cleanse His wounds. Now she could do nothing, for these wounds were meant to cleanse and comfort her, along with the rest of mankind.

"Come, Mary," John spoke from his place beside her, "you have endured enough."

"No," she simply stated, "I will not leave Him." Her voice was tired and weak and her eyes were swollen from the tears which had fallen, but her answer was strong.

In little less than an hour, Pilate again appeared on the balcony.

"Behold!" he began, *"I bring Him forth to you, that ye may know that I find no fault in Him! Behold the man!"*

At that time, Jesus was led out, stumbling, yet surprisingly on His feet. A purple robe had been draped around his broken body and a cruel crown of thorns had been pushed into the top of His head. Mary saw it for the mockery it was. The beard Jesus had always kept so precise and neatly trimmed was now filled with gaping holes where the hair had been ripped from His face.

"A*nd my cheeks to them that plucked off the hair: I hid not my face from shame and spitting."* Mary quoted aloud again from the scriptures. John was concerned that almost no emotion showed on her face. She wore the look of someone utterly defeated. Placing his arm around her shoulders, he prayed for her strength as well as his own. He knew she would not leave her place, nor would he.

"Crucify Him!" the chief priests and officers yelled, "Crucify Him!"

Pilate looked to the men before him, clearly surprised by their determination. *"Take ye Him, and crucify Him:"* He challenged them, *"for I find no fault in Him.* He has suffered enough for whatever shame He has brought upon you," Pilate admitted.

"*We have a law!*" the Jewish leaders protested, "*and by our law he ought to die because he made Himself the Son of God!*"

"The Son of God?" Pilate repeated. He looked as if the man before him had slapped him. Clearly he was taken aback by this proclamation. He knew Jesus had claimed to be called Christ, and he knew He had professed He was indeed King of the Jews, but the Son of God? Mary noticed his hesitancy and allowed only a small spear of hope to pierce her heart.

Turning to Jesus, Pilate asked him simply, "*Whence art thou?*"

Jesus stood silently before him, and for a moment, Pilate wondered if He was still coherent enough to be able to speak. "*Speakest thou not unto me? Knowest thou not that I have power to crucify thee, and have power to release thee?*"

Mary looked at her son, her eyes pleading for Him to make His own power known. Would He call upon His angels? Would the Father above allow this to continue? Finally, with a clear, yet exhausted and pain filled voice He spoke.

"*Thou couldest have no power at all against me, except it were given thee from above: therefore he that delivered me unto thee hath the greater sin.*"

Pilate felt a fear rise within his chest that he was unfamiliar with. His fear showed from the look which crossed his face to the way he stood in front of the man before him. That he wanted to allow Jesus His freedom was evident to all who stood about witnessing the events taking place.

"*If thou let this man go,*" a Jewish priest shouted, "*thou art not Caesar's friend! Whosoever maketh himself a king speaketh against Caesar!*"

"*Away with Him, away with Him, crucify Him!*" the crowd shouted.

Pilate seemed to shake himself in order to focus his attention again on the crowd and not so much on the prisoner. *"Shall I crucify your King?"* he questioned them once again.

"We have no king but Caesar!" the chief priest answered him plainly.

Pilate shook his head again in confusion at their determination, and for yet another brief moment, Mary thought he may trust his instinct and let her son go free. However, tribute to Caesar was not something he took lightly.

"Very well," he acquiesced. "Prepare the cross and do with Him as you will," he waved to them as he turned and went back into the temple.

Cheers went up throughout the crowd as Mary felt her knees buckle and the world close in around her.

Chapter 28

Mary stood in a small alley between two of the buildings she knew Jesus would pass by on His route to Golgotha. Along with her immediate company, a small family stood with them, seeking refuge from the crowd. The older of the two boys peered from the corners into the street, fear of the current events feeding his curiosity, while his father stood close by, a firm hand on his son's shoulder. The woman, appearing close to Mary's own age, attempted to comfort the younger of the two, whose face was currently buried in the older woman's side. Mary assumed from the looks on their faces that they had simply come to Jerusalem for the Passover and had been completely taken off guard by all that was transpiring. She hoped the children especially had not been witness to the cruel beating her son had endured only moments ago.

Two criminals were also to be crucified alongside Jesus. It seemed like hours passed as they waited. Mary noticed the woman continuing to stare at her. Did she know that her son was among those condemned to die? Was one of the others dying along

271

with Jesus a relative of the stranger before her? Finally the woman broke her silence.

"Excuse me," she began speaking to Mary, "I beg your forgiveness, but I must ask if we have met before?" Mary looked at the woman carefully, searching her face for a sign of familiarity. Finally, she thought she may recognize her from many years ago. Was it possible?

Directing her attention to the husky man accompanying the woman, Mary attempted to speak to him, the raspy and broken sound of her own voice surprising her. She did not sound like herself, and she cleared her throat in order to continue.

"Does your name happen to be Simon? And do you hail from Cyrene?" she asked the tall, muscular man before her.

"Yes, it is, and yes, we do," he spoke politely. Immediately Mary turned and embraced the woman before her who began to tremble at the realization.

Elias could not believe part of the caravan he had stalked in years past had been reunited on such a day as this. He remembered seeing Mary talk with a fellow traveler, who was expectant as well, when they were on the road to Bethlehem so many years ago. When the couples had parted ways, he had almost become confused and if he had not known with surety that Mary and Joseph were journeying to Bethlehem, he would have followed the wrong couple and missed the event which had changed his entire life. The birth of his Lord.

"The son you carried those years ago?" the woman spoke through her tears, "The son we spoke of as we journeyed, this son is Jesus of Nazareth? The man condemned to be crucified this day?" she asked.

"It is He," Mary admitted though her heart broke anew to do so, "And this is your Simon?" she

272

asked indicating the man who had now come alongside his mother.

"It is," she spoke proudly. "And my grandsons, Alexander and Rufus." She paused only a moment before continuing. "Is it true, Mary?" she asked sincerely. "Is your son indeed the Son of God as is proclaimed? I have heard of His miracles and His teachings, but I admit I have always been skeptical. Can you confirm for me, my friend, that He is indeed who He claims to be?"

"There are scores of angels just waiting for my son to summon them," Mary spoke with surety. "I imagine Heaven is grieving at this moment as they watch their Prince being tortured, for yes, He is very much the Son of God, sent to fulfill the prophecies."

"He approaches!" John announced though his heart broke at the sight he beheld.

At that moment, one of the thieves condemned as well to die this day, came staggering by, his cross heavy upon his back. His beating had been nothing compared to what Jesus had endured, and though the load he bore was great, he had little trouble managing the wooden beams throughout the street.

Jesus was close behind him, the robe he wore now covered with the blood that continued to seep from His many lacerations. John noticed the thorns from the crown which had been driven into his Lord's scalp oozed drops of blood as well. Jesus took step after step, slowly, each one visibly harder for Him than the one before. Determination and love were the forces driving Him to Calvary, and anyone witnessing His suffering knew that.

As He drew close to the alley where Mary was waiting, he stumbled, sending the cross crashing to the earth, His body underneath it. Mary could hold herself back no longer. She was at His side before the soldiers could be, before the men in her own company could react. Though she was unable to push the cross from His back, she eagerly attempted to wipe the blood from His face, kissing His cheek and forehead. Soaking His face with her tears, she poured every ounce of strength she had left out to her son, speaking to Him of her love and sorrow for all He was enduring.

Almost instantly the soldiers were upon her, jerking her from His side and slinging her back into the alley from where she had appeared. Elias caught her, holding her tightly as she attempted to break free and reach Jesus again. John aided him in holding her, refusing to allow her freedom though her pleading was almost more than he could bear. Were it not that the soldiers would kill her instantly if she interfered again, John would have stepped aside, but he realized to do so would mean another innocent life lost on this dreadful day.

"YOU!" a cruel and menacing soldier directed toward Simon. "Carry His cross!" Simon heard the man but did not move from his place, protectively planted in front of his family. His lip curled as he stood firm in defiance of the soldiers command. "I said, carry His cross!" the soldier demanded once more louder this time and drawing his sword. Simon did not wish to bring violence upon his family, nor for his sons to witness his death due to pride. Looking first to his mother and his sons he approached Jesus reverently.

He looked at the broken man lying on the ground before him. He had never seen this man but could not have recognized Him if he been in His presence every day of his life. Suddenly, something pressed upon Simon's heart and he knew the stories his mother had been telling him were true. His convictions told him that no man would go through what this man had endured were He not sent to be the Savior of the world.

"My Lord," he spoke bowing down to Jesus. Jesus looked up at the man before Him, struggling even to stand. Simon helped Him to His feet before taking up the cross. Balancing the cross on one shoulder and aiding his Lord's steps with the other, the two continued up the street to the path that would lead them to Golgotha.

Mary's strength for the moment was gone. Elias and John released their firm grip on her, but she noticed John did not completely let her go. She watched as Simeon of Cyrene and Jesus continued to make their way up the hill before them. She looked at the veil she continued to cling in her hands. The veil that brought her such joy on her wedding day, had held Jesus as a newborn, had kept Him warm on their journey to Egypt and back to Nazareth, the veil she had wept into when Joseph had died, the veil which had been a comfort to her when she felt she had no other, this veil was now stained with the blood of not just her son, but of her Savior. Burying her face in the fabric, again she wept. She allowed herself only a moment before carefully folding the treasured article and placing it inside her cloak.

"Mary," Shira began gently touching her arm. "Let us go. This torture of Jesus will only continue. You have endured so much already and there is nothing more that can be done. Witnessing the events bound to transpire will only make things more difficult for you."

"No," she repeated once more. "I will not forsake my son," she spoke slowly as she turned to follow the crowd to Golgotha, then turning again to look at her friends, she finished, "or my Lord."

"Neither shall I," John announced, taking his place beside Mary.

Elias looked to his wife and held out his hand. Reluctantly she accepted it, and together they all started the long walk up the hill, followed by Simon's mother and his children.

Shira was thankful by the time they had gotten to the place called Calvary, the tortuous task of nailing the accused to the crosses had already been carried out. They knew this because they had heard the pounding of the hammer before they approached as huge nails were being driven into the hands and feet of those being crucified. She did not think she could witness more blatant torture this day. The soldiers were lifting the third cross as they approached, dropping it with force into a hole at the top of the mountain.

Mary saw her son lifted high between the two thieves being crucified with Him. At the top of His cross was the superscription, "THIS IS THE KING OF THE JEWS", written in Hebrew, Greek, and Latin.

She stood along with the other believers watching as Jesus closed His eyes; the pain and agony of all He had endured, and that which He continued to, weighing on His human flesh. Then He would open His eyes again, and Mary knew He could see her standing by Him. Her heart broke over and over as she watched Him hang there, until she felt she could endure no more. Making her way to the cross, she knelt before Him and closed her eyes in prayer. "Father, please," she whispered, "take my life now so that I may not have to witness my son's final breath!" she cried quietly at the foot of His cross. She was not allowed to stay in her position long before she was driven back by soldiers who had been sent to guard the cross.

"Get back, get back!" he commanded her. "Just let one of His followers make an attempt to free Him," he scoffed to the officer beside him. "We shall see how powerful they are!"

"He does not need His followers to save Him, for He is God's Son!" the other laughed. "He can save Himself! Where are all your angels, oh Son of God?" the soldier barked, spitting at the foot of the cross where Mary had just been kneeling.

"*Father forgive them,*" Jesus spoke clearly from His place on the cross, "*for they know not what they do.*"

The soldiers below Him burst into laughter, Mary's tears coming anew.

"*If thou be Christ,*" the thief to Jesus' left spoke, "*save thyself and us!*" he demanded.

Before Jesus answered, the thief to His right lifted his voice, "*Dost not thou fear God, seeing thou art in the same condemnation?*" he directed to the thief on the left. "*And we indeed justly; for we receive the due reward of our deeds: but this man hath done nothing amiss. Lord,*" he continued now directing his comments to Jesus, "*remember me when thou comest into thy kingdom.*"

"*Verily I say unto thee,*" Jesus spoke to the thief on His right, "*today shalt thou be with me in paradise.*"

Hours passed and Mary stood with John, Elias, and Shira watching the Son of God as He struggled to breathe. The soldiers had tired of making sport of Him. They had torn His clothes to shreds but kept his coat intact and cast lots for it, fulfilling yet another prophecy.

"*They part my garments among them, and cast lots upon my vesture,*" Elias had quoted from the Psalms.

"Is there another prophecy yet to be fulfilled?" Shira had asked, realizing Jesus would not breathe His last breath until He had fulfilled every prophecy which had been spoken.

Before anyone could answer, a heavy darkness began to cover the land. Soldiers began looking around in wonder for it was only the noon of the day. Mary could sense restlessness in those around her, knowing that this darkness should be the least of their worries.

The darkness lingered, and slowly she approached the cross once again.

Jesus moved slightly, and Mary noticed the muscles in His legs now tense and hard from dehydration and from His attempts to raise Himself enough for air to enter into His lungs. If only she could ease some of His pain.

"It will not be long now," John spoke quietly, coming up beside her.

At John's voice, Jesus again opened His eyes.

"*Woman*," He spoke with ragged breath to His Mother, "*behold thy son!*" Then, His eyes shifting to John, "*Behold thy mother!*" He spoke with clear direction.

"It would honor me, my Lord, to care for Your mother as if she were my own." John assured Him, tears streaking down his face as His Lord and Master issued the command to him.

"*My God, My God*!" Jesus yelled with strength no one knew He had left, "*Why has thou forsaken me?*"

Mary could just reach where the nails pierced the feet she had once coddled and played with. The feet she watched take their first steps. The feet she cleaned while He was yet a child. Tenderly she kissed those same feet one more time, now nailed to a cross, meant to cleanse her own weary soul.

John approached her and took her shoulders pulling her gently away from the cross. "Come Mother," he spoke immediately following the instructions he had just been given by His Lord. As he pulled her back, a soldier ran forward, a long reed in hand with a sponge attached to it filled with vinegar and stale wine.

"Drink," he commanded of Jesus pressing the sponge to His mouth. Jesus turned His head away and cast one look more in the direction of His mother. Finally the words she had been waiting for were heard.

"*It is finished*," Jesus called out to all who could hear Him. "*Father, into thy hands I commend my spirit*," He spoke loudly, and with those final words, Jesus died.

Chapter 29

The earth began to shake as soon as Jesus had drawn His final breath. The veil of the temple was rent in two, no longer needed to separate man from God as the columns rocked back and forth, shaking with the force of the earthquake. Mary and John stood in their places, clinging to one another until the earth stood still once again. Mary looked around and above her.

"God's very own heart is broken by what has happened here," she acknowledged to John who nodded his agreement.

Quickly, soldiers rushed forward to break the legs of the crucified. This would force suffocation on them and ensure their death before the Holy Day that was rapidly approaching. John began to usher Mary away, but she stopped as the soldiers approached her son. She did not utter a word, but felt sure what would happen next.

"*He keepeth all His bones: not one of them is broken*," she quoted to herself from the Psalms.

"This man is already dead!" the centurion shouted to those in his presence, then ran quickly to break the legs of the thief on His other side, leaving Jesus' legs completely intact.

Another centurion approached Jesus and lifting his spear, thrust it quickly into His side. Reflexively, Mary buried her head in John's arm. Yet, surprisingly, as what blood and water was left inside Jesus' body trickled to the ground, the centurion cast aside his spear and removed the helmet from his head. Falling to his knees before the Lord, he relayed one statement to those around him.

"Truly this man was the Son of God," he said to those around him. Reverently he bowed his head, before standing and backing away.

"*And they shall look upon me whom they have pierced*," Mary spoke aloud quoting the prophet Zechariah, "*and they shall mourn for Him.*" She barely finished before sinking to her knees wailing in grief and agony as she never had before.

John allowed Mary to mourn until exhaustion weighed heavily about her. Elias and Shira had remained near, Elias holding his own wife as she grieved. When Mary had collected herself, she realized as she raised her head and stood that they were not alone. Other followers of Jesus had approached them, each waiting in reverence for the mother of their Lord to rise. One of the men stepped forth to speak with her, and John recognized him as a wealthy member of the Sanhedrin. Protectively, he stepped closer to Mary.

"Though I am of the Sanhedrin, I was a believer and follower of your son," he assured Mary. "You see, I hail from Arimathaea and I too have waited for the kingdom of God. I have gone to Pilate who has agreed to my request," the man called Joseph continued to explain to her, "My greatest desire would be fulfilled if you would allow me to care for and bury the body of my Lord."

Mary stared at the man in front of her. "Where will you take Him?" she asked simply, her voice relaying her exhaustion.

"I have a tomb prepared. I had intended it for my own use, hence no man has yet been laid inside. Nicodemus," he continued indicating the man to his right, "has brought fine linens as well as the mixture intended for a proper burial. You all are welcome to accompany us to the place."

Mary looked to John before nodding her head in approval.

The small assembly included both men and women, all who had become followers of Jesus during the time He had spent on the earth. Nicodemus cleaned and then gently wrapped Jesus in the fine linen he had provided, assisted by both Elias and John. Once His body had been properly prepared, Jesus was carried inside the tomb and then gently laid on a raised bed of solid stone. A large boulder was then rolled in front of the sepulcher, so heavy that each man in their company had to assist in the placing of it.

"He will not be bothered," Joseph of Arimethaea assured them. Mary had not the energy to thank him more than uttering the simple words. Once the tomb was sealed, she turned with John and walked away.

Though she longed for solitude, several of the assembly accompanied them to John's home, which was now considered her own as well. One of the women in particular paid close attention to Mary. Mary of Bethany, who explained to her Lord's mother, that she, her sister Martha, and her brother Lazarus were personal friends of Jesus. John assured her of Mary of Bethany's sincerity and relayed the account of Jesus raising Lazarus from the dead and of her selfless act of anointing Jesus' feet with her precious ointment before cleansing them with her hair.

Mary felt closer to her son in the presence of His dear friends. John was encouraged that, though grief still weighed heavily on her heart and she remained extremely quiet, she seemed at peace hearing others exchange stories of her son.

John had learned that the chief priests and Pharisees had petitioned Pilate for guards to be placed at Jesus' tomb at all hours for the next three days in order to prevent His body from being taken by His followers. He hoped the guards would not cause problems for those who wished to visit His grave after the Sabbath.

The Sabbath came and passed. Three days after the burial of their Lord, Mary Magdalene, another devoted follower out of whom Jesus had cast seven devils, prepared the necessary spices to once again anoint the body of Jesus. Though asking His mother to accompany her to the tomb had crossed her mind, she felt to ask her to view His broken and empty body again would be cruel. She would see to the task herself. It was the least she could do for her Lord.

Mary Magdalene began her journey to the sepulcher early, just as the sun was beginning to light the darkness. A friend accompanied her, their paces slowing as they came nearer to the sepulcher, suddenly contemplating how they would move the stone covering the entrance in order to access the body of their Lord. Continuing to press forward Mary Magdalene decided to address that problem once they arrived.

As soon as the sepulcher came into view, however, Mary Magdalene stopped short, her basket of spices almost spilling out. Two Roman soldiers were lying upon the ground as if they had been struck, but that vision was the least to amaze her. Sitting atop the stone, which had been rolled away from the tomb, was a man whose countenance was like lightning. His raiment was as white as snow. She first thought her grief had driven her to madness, but then realized she was beholding no ordinary human being. An angel was before her, which had descended directly from Heaven above.

Mary Magdalene and her companion turned to run, but were stopped at the angels words.

"Fear not ye: for I know that ye seek Jesus which was crucified," he spoke with surety. *"He is not here: for He is risen, as He said. Come, see the place where the Lord lay,"* he instructed motioning for them to enter the tomb.

Mary Magdalene slowly approached the entrance to the tomb not sure what she expected to find there. Her heart raced as she peered inside. The solid stone, on which she had witnessed their Lord's body being laid, was empty save for the grave clothes He had worn. The napkin which had covered His face was neatly folded and laid separately from the rest of the garments. Mary Magdalene quickly covered her mouth with her hands as a gasp escaped her lips.

On the right side of the stone, which was intended to have been His final resting place, sat another glorious being. This angel, too, was dressed in a long white garment, his countenance equal to his companion atop the stone. Mary Magdalene and her companion immediately bowed their heads to the earth

"*Why seek ye the living among the dead? He is not here, but is risen:*" the second angel began. Mary Magdalene realized the confusion she was feeling must show on her face. "*Remember how he spake unto you when He was yet in Galilee, saying The Son of Man must be delivered into the hands of sinful men, and be crucified, and the third day rise again*?" Suddenly, the words Jesus had spoken came flooding back to her memory as if He were whispering them to her very soul.

"I remember," she spoke truthfully.

The angel smiled into her face. "*Go quickly,*" he instructed her. "*And tell His disciples that He is risen from the dead; and, behold, He goeth before you into Galilee; there shall ye see Him: lo, I have told you,*" he finished.

Mary Magdalene dropped her basket of spices in haste, almost knocking over her companion still frozen in fear, as she ran from the tomb. "*Ye shall see Him,*" the angel had said. She would again see her Lord along with His disciples, and she knew exactly who she must tell.

Mary Magdalene did not stop running until she again reached the house of John where the other disciples had gathered, still mourning the loss of their Master. Almost bursting through the door, she had to allow herself a moment to catch her breath before she could continue.

"Mary Magdalene, what is it? What has happened," John asked, bracing her shoulders.

"Our Lord," she explained through rasping breath, "His tomb is empty. He has risen!"

Immediately, Peter sprang to his feet. "What is this?" he spoke in clear confusion.

John led Mary Magdalene to the chair he had vacated. "Slow down, and tell us what has happened."

Mary Magdalene took a deep breath to calm herself before she began. "I went to the sepulcher this morning to anoint our Lord's body once more, and when I approached, I witnessed an angel sitting on top of the stone that had been placed in front of the tomb. The stone had been rolled away!" Mary Magdalene continued back on her feet with excitement. "I looked inside and saw only His grave clothes! His body is gone, but another angel was there who instructed me to come and tell you that we will see Him again!"

"Quiet this woman!" Peter demanded of John. "Grief has caused her to believe her fanciful stories! What if His mother hears?" he asked indicating the closed door where Jesus' mother still rested.

"I do not speak fanciful stories, Peter!" Mary Magdalene defended herself, keeping her voice low. "Go and see for yourself! His tomb is empty!"

She spoke her final statement to his fleeing back. John rushed past her as well, and she quickly followed. How she longed to see the Lord once more! The other disciples stared at one another, contemplating what they had just heard.

John reached the sepulcher first and stopped abruptly as he saw the stone rolled away just as Mary Magdalene had said. Looking inside, he too witnessed only the linen clothes lying upon the stone surface. Peter was right behind him, but made his way quickly into the tomb, not stopping until he reached the linen clothes. As she had told them, the napkin was neatly folded and was positioned in a place by itself.

"He has risen, Peter!" John exclaimed, slapping his friend squarely on the shoulder! "Praise God, He lives! And see how the napkin is laid!" John continued excitement filling his voice, "He will be back Peter! He will come again"

287

Peter continued to stare at the linens before him, unsure of what had transpired before turning and following John. The disciples made their way back to the home of John to discuss what had just transpired.

Mary Magdalene continued to stand outside the sepulcher. Now that she had calmed herself, she began to wonder over her own proclamation. John was convinced that death had not been able to hold their Lord and that He had indeed risen. Peter wanted to believe, but the look of uncertainty Mary Magdalene had seen on his face as he exited the tomb proved he was still unsure of what had happened.

Had she imagined the whole event? What if Jesus' body had been stolen? Had the angels she was so sure she had witnessed, been figments of her imagination formed by her grief as Peter had said? Mary Magdalene could not control her weeping. Here alone in the garden where her Lord had been buried, she allowed herself to weep freely. The man who had freed her from the seven demons inhabiting her body, whom she had witnessed being tortured and killed for all mankind, was laid still in this grave only three days hence, and was now missing from His final resting place. Sliding along the outer stone wall, she sank to the earth beneath her, burying her head against her knees, and weeping bitterly.

"*Woman, why weepest thou*?" a voice spoke. Mary Magdalene quickly clamored to her feet, wiping her eyes as she stood, embarrassed at being caught so broken. "*Whom seekest thou*?" the man before her asked.

Mary Magdalene turned her face from the man before her ashamed of her present state.

"*Sir*," she spoke through sobs while continuing to wipe her face with her veil, "*if thou have borne Him hence, tell me where thou hast laid Him, and I will take Him away,"* she pleaded.

"Mary," the voice sounded again and immediately Mary Magdalene recognized the voice which spoke her name.

"Master?" she questioned dropping quickly to bow at His feet, though she knew the answer.

"Touch me not; for I am not yet ascended to my Father;" Jesus instructed, *"but go to my brethren, and say unto them, I ascend unto my Father, and your Father; and to my God, and your God."*

"Yes, my Lord!" Mary Magdalene spoke rising. "I will tell them immediately!" she promised as she began to back away. She had seen Him! Mary Magdalene had beheld Him once more. Her Lord was alive and this time, no one, including herself, would convince her otherwise.

Chapter 30

John watched his Lord's mother as she walked leisurely through the garden that bordered his property. He understood her continued need for solitude, and though Jesus had overcome death, their sorrow of all He had endured was still great. He knew Mary would remain safe as long as she was within the borders of his home, and some time for reflection would do her well. He could afford her this freedom, he thought as he turned to continue his chores.

The sun was just beginning to set, and the day had been long. Mary thought of all that had transpired throughout her life as she deeply inhaled the fresh air. Most people had never been granted the miracle of seeing an angel, yet angels had been present throughout the duration of her life.

First, when the angel Gabriel had announced to her that she would give birth to the Son of God. Then, when the same had assured Joseph of her innocence and instructed him to take her as his wife. Elizabeth had told her of the angel who had told Zacharias he would be a father. The night Jesus was born, the air above them was filled with heavenly beings directing the shepherds to them and praising

291

their Prince of Peace. Joseph had told her of the conversation he had overheard the wise men relaying to one another about an angel who had appeared to them in a dream instructing them not to return to Herod, then through Joseph's dreams again as he was instructed to flee to Egypt to escape the hand of the evil King. Again, Joseph had beheld an angel in separate dreams as he was instructed to return to Israel and then to Nazareth. Jesus had told her how angels had ministered to Him after His days of temptation in the wilderness, and she was sure He had dealings with them which He had never even spoken of.

Now angels had appeared once more, this time relaying the news to Mary Magdalene that Jesus had indeed risen from the dead as He had promised. Mary smiled to herself. No, most people had never had the privilege of seeing angels, and though she had been granted that privilege, both directly and indirectly, that was not the privilege which she held most dear. She had been given the opportunity and privilege of being the mother to the Son of God. She had witnessed His birth, His life, and His death and though she had not physically seen Him, she knew He lived still today! Others had seen Him since He had overcome death on the cross. Yes, He lived, of this she was sure.

Writing to her other children, she had told them of all that had transpired in Jerusalem, about their half-brother's terrible scourging and His death on the cross–the death He had died so that they may have life. She had told them that He had instructed her to remain with His disciple, John, and that she would do so, spending her last days here in Jerusalem. She then told them of His resurrection and that Jesus lived today!

She had sent the letters with Shira and Elias, who had promised to deliver them on their own route home. She prayed that her children would believe on their half-brother and repent of their earlier rejection of Him. In her heart, she knew they would.

Mary stopped and looked across the small stream she had come to. The events of the past month had aged her. She had hoped to see Jesus herself before He ascended into Heaven to be on the right hand of the Father, but if that was not to be, she had accepted it. Yet, how her heart continued to ache with the tragic events leading to the crucifixion of her son.

She sank on the bank of the stream, resting her head on her knees. She had no tears left, but could not escape the sigh which came forth from her lips. Mary closed her eyes. As had happened before, she thought she had fallen asleep when the word came softly to her ears.

"Mother." Before she opened her eyes she knew what she was about to behold. On the other side of the stream from her stood her son. She had heard His disciples explain His countenance when He appeared to them, but He was different than she expected. He looked perfect. The lashes across his head and body were gone. The wounds where the crown of thorns had been lodged into His scalp had healed, but in His hands and feet, were the distinct nail prints where the nails had been driven holding Him to the cross He chose to bore. As she looked at those prints, however, Mary knew it was not the nails which had held Him to the cross. It was love.

"My Lord," Mary spoke never taking her eyes from the man who was both her son and her Father.

"*Peace I leave with you,*" he began, and Mary knew this would be the last time she saw her son on this earth, "*my peace I give unto you: not as the world giveth, give I unto you. Let not your heart be troubled, neither let it be afraid. Ye have heard how I said unto you, I go away, and come again unto you. But of that day and that hour knoweth no man, no, not the angels which are in heaven, neither the Son, but the Father. Take ye heed, watch and pray: for ye know not when the time is.*"

She knew He was not awaiting her approval, but the mother in her could not help but grant it. "Go my son," she spoke quietly though she knew He heard the words. Mary watched Jesus raise His hand, and she, kissing her palm first, returned the farewell greeting. They stood facing each other for only a moment, then Mary blinked, and He was gone.

John had proven himself a worthy son, caring for Mary in her old age as if she were his flesh and blood. She had been a picture of health until the past few months, but now Mary was tired. The years which had passed since she had come to live with John had been good ones, and it broke his heart to watch her move slowly about in her old age.

Her disposition, however, had always been full of joy regardless of her aches and pains, and people came from all around to hear her stories. Stories always of Jesus, the child He had been, the life He had lived, and the price He had paid to save His people from their sins. It never bothered John that she spoke so highly of Jesus, for He, too, praised Him and rejoiced in His resurrection. He used the opportunities she presented through her accounts of His life to tell others of the time He spent with the Savior during His life on earth, and how they could have eternal life by accepting Him as their Lord.

Tonight, Mary was extremely tired, and in her heart she longed to see her son and husband again. John had helped her settle onto her cot, moving to his own room for the night, reminding her to call for him if she had need of anything or before she attempted to rise.

"I promise," she had assured him as she motioned him out of her room. What she really wanted was solitude. How good her cot felt as she closed her eyes. Her breathing was steady and even as sleep began to overtake her. She thought of Shira and Elias, who visited often for a while, but as their age increased, their visits decreased. She thought of her other children and the joy she felt as their letters returned to her years ago, telling her of their acceptance of their half-brother. James could not speak of Him enough, the son who Mary felt would be the hardest to reach, was now telling everyone he could about his Lord and Savior, who was also his half-brother. She thought of the friends she had made once she settled here after the death of Jesus and how precious John had been to her as a son.

As she often did, she began dreaming of her younger days when she and Joseph first came together and the life they shared. Joseph. Oh how she missed him.

Mary opened her eyes, but it took a moment for her to realize where she was. This was not the room she had fallen asleep in. She was sure John had assisted her to her own room. Blinking her eyes to better focus on her surroundings, she took in the sights around her, still a little unsure of where she was. Was she dreaming? This did not feel like a dream. This felt different.

Then she saw it. The familiar hand reaching out to her. There was no mistaking the nail print in the precious hand of her son. Her Savior. Without hesitancy, she reached to accept the nail scared hand as Jesus pulled her close to Him, surrounding her in His arms. She had longed for years to feel His touch, now He held her close against Him. He held her only for a moment before releasing her.

"Welcome home, Mother," he spoke with the most glorious smile she had ever seen lighting His face. Then, He turned her slightly. As if seeing the face of her son and Lord were not enough, standing beside Him was her Joseph, waiting most patiently to embrace her as well. Mary sank into his embrace and released the breath she had been holding. She knew exactly where she was. Home.

Closing Thoughts

When Angels Speak is an historical fiction account of the life of Mary, the mother of Jesus, but is based upon actual events. This story was written from a mother's perspective of what life may have been like for her as she witnessed the life and death of her son. The unedited version of the life of Mary, in regard to the life of Christ, can be best accounted for in the four gospels of Matthew, Mark, Luke, and John in the King James Version of the Holy Bible. Many of the other events which transpired in this book can be found there as well.

Though some of the events and characters in my book are fictional, one fact remains absolutely true. Jesus Christ, the Son of God and God the Son, walked upon this earth in human form. He was born of a virgin, lived a perfectly sinless life, and then gave that life willingly on Calvary so that we, through acceptance of Him, may be free.

I tried not to embellish actual events by making them more dramatic than what would have actually transpired. Yet, I wanted to convey the true sense of the way things happened. Hours of study went into Jewish law, the true concept of scourging and crucifixion and research of the prophecies that were fulfilled during the life and times of Christ. Some chapters I wrote, then erased and wrote again, in an attempt to make sure anything I put to paper could and in many cases, did, actually take place during the time period in which it was written.

Mary is not someone who should be worshiped, but she is someone who should be respected for the life she lived and the task she was chosen by God the Father to perform. Little is said about her in the Bible, other than the fact that she bore Christ and followed Him to Calvary, and I hope to have conveyed a story worthy of the woman she was.

I strongly encourage you to study the life of Mary and in doing so, to study the life of Jesus and the price He paid so that we may live eternally with Him. If you have never accepted Christ as your Savior, I encourage you to do so. It is the most important decision you will ever make.

Most of the words Jesus speaks in "When Angels Speak" were actually taken from scripture. I had a hard time "speaking for" my Lord and chose, on most occasions, to use words from scripture which He was recorded speaking.

I could not record an account of all the miracles He performed because Mary was not a part of many of the things He did, but I tried to at least relay some of the events that would have shaped her story and helped to create her world.

One of my favorite verses in the Bible is taken from my "favorite disciple," John. In John 21:25 he writes, "*And there are also many other things which Jesus did, the which, if they should be written every one, I suppose that even the world itself could not contain the books that should be written. Amen.*" How forward I look to one day hearing of all those things not recorded!

If you have questions or comments about this book or my previous book, *The Prudent Queen*, I would love to hear from you! You may contact me through email at: greatisthygoodness@gmail.com.

www.ingramcontent.com/pod-product-compliance
Lightning Source LLC
Chambersburg PA
CBHW060534180626
46817CB00002B/566